Four To Go

James O. Feltham
Ret. Air Force

Noble House
Baltimore, Maryland

Four To Go

Library of Congress
Cataloging in Publication Data
ISBN 1-56167-325-0

Library of Congress Card Catalog Number:
96-069975

Published by

Noble House

8019 Belair Road, Suite 10
Baltimore, Maryland 21236

Manufactured in the United States of America

This book is dedicated to my family and friends, the places I have visited during my military career, and the special places I have enjoyed following my retirement.

—JAMES O. FELTHAM
Master Sergeant
U.S.A.F. Retired

INTRODUCTION

This story takes place during a time in history when the world was introduced to a completely new and devastating way to wage war. Faster, more deadly and powerful aircraft were the new weapons in the arsenals of all the countries involved in the global conflict that was World War II.

A B-17 Bomber called the Flying Fortress is stationed somewhere in England with the United States 8th Air Force. It is shot down over Germany on its final mission. There are nine crew members on board, only four of them will live. This story will show the differences and growth in each individual man as he faces the desperate situations that they must somehow survive. These four men were forced into war time happenings that might have actually happened. Only history could have created these sets of most unusual circumstances.

Four To Go is a fictional story and is not meant to represent any persons, living or deceased. These four men will find that post war America was well worth the sacrifices that they lived through.

ONE

Twenty-five thousand feet above Western Germany, the old B-17, 42001 was part of a two hundred plane formation that was now on its way to the heartland of Nazi Germany.

Aircraft 001 and its crew of nine American airmen had earlier been briefed about this combat Bomber mission. The only difference between this sortie and the twelve other objectives flown by this crew was the greater distance and time it would take to complete. The plane itself had done a total of forty-five missions prior to Captain McCrea's crew taking over the well used 001.

McCrea had insisted on renaming his plane because it had now become his responsibility. He had ignored the advice of others, that it would be bad luck to change the name of any aircraft. "My crew and I don't believe in luck, good or bad! Today's success is based on science and disciplined training."

Louise E. Ann was the name chosen, agreed upon by her crew, in honor of Mrs. McCrea. Louise had showered attention on every one of the men, with little surprises given to all of them, things like individual flight scarves, homemade candy and cookies had made her their special girl.

At this morning's briefing, the subject of a greater volume of faster German Fighter Aircraft had been discussed. There had also been an increase in enemy antiaircraft guns. The weapons were more accurate and had a higher range of altitude.

The increased danger from these new arms had been talked about as well as the propaganda broadcast every night by Axis Sally's program. Her new harangue was, "You can't get away, we can destroy you at any altitude now!"

This was one more thing to fear and the psycho cases started to increase amongst the already over stressed crew members. The youngest member was copilot second Lieutenant Freestone, now just twenty-one years of age, who had already become a chain smoker. The Navigator First Lieutenant Farnsworth had called him a basket case.

Of the nearly two thousand men on this mission of destruction, most had already silently prayed for or fantasized for a lucky and victorious ending or at least a safe return flight.

Technical Sergeant Sacket had beamed with pleasure when the subject of "increasing danger" was mentioned. "Maybe today is the day that I get me a couple of those damn German son's of bitches. This time I've got a good chance to make my gun speak loud and clear." He had already told a friend that he wrote to that his "Ol Geronimo [referring to his 50 caliber waist gun] was ready for any German fighter dumb enough to attack his airplane, plus we are flying tail end Charley today, that's the target they all like to go after."

Suddenly the thoughts of survival and no danger vanished as the big guns below started their systematic firing at their targets above. The puffs of smoke were all around the tail end of the formation and all five gunner's of the Louise E. Ann were cursing the flack bursts around them because there was nothing for them to shoot at.

There was a tremendous jolt, the red fire warning light for number three engine had never seemed so bright during preflight check. McCrea started his emergency shut down procedure with his well known "Shit Fire To Hell!" Lieutenant Fuzz, nickname for the copilot, shouted out the check list in a frightened, screaming voice.

The interphone began to sound with some of the voices of the nine crew members of the war weary, B-17.

Mac shouted into the interphone, "Stay off the intercom until I call you. What's number three look like, top turret?"

"Number three is feathered but still burning on top of the wing. My turret is stuck and I'm hit in the arm and my new friggin' watch is smashed all to hell!"

Mac grinned as he called for a head count of each crew member. He had just loaned Reber the money the day before to buy that watch to replace the GI issue Reber had lost in a crap game.

"Tail gun to A.C.!"

"Go ahead, tail guns!" Shorty was brief, "My guns and I are OK!"

"Waist guns right and left?" McCrea called.

"We are freezing our ass, but the guns are OK. Flack holes are overhead, some of them are really massive. Sacket's got a piece of hot flack inside his flight suit. How come we're so far out of formation?" Barney's question went unanswered, "What about my date tonight, huh!"

"Shut up, Barney," said Mac, "and see if Reber is OK! Navigator!"

"Lieutenant Farnsworth and equipment are in good shape sir."

"OK Magelan, keep me in touch and take the shortest route home," replied McCrea.

"Lieutenant, Co-Pilot Freestone reports engine shutdown is completed and fire conditions still exist, all crew members put on parachutes and recall your emergency check lists ASAP!"

Things could be worse, the burning number three engine could have a broken fuel line and as long as it did not effect the wing structure, McCrea would wait for a coded message from the Formation Commander.

The Navigator had contacted Red Leader Fox Trot Tango for directions. Within seconds the reply came in, "Return to the base and drop bomb load on an opportune target. If bailout is required, crew members should follow escape and evasion plans as they were briefed."

Bombardier Young sounded really shook up when he answered, "Thanks a lot, that really sounds like a bummer!"

Mac had just started a long slow turn to the left and would make a lengthy enroute decent towards the coast. Their altitude was still 25,000 feet and a three engine return should not be any big problem.

Suddenly, Reber, who was in the top turret, broke the silence by shouting, "There are three Faulk Wolf 190's coming at us from two o'clock high. My guns are stuck and the starboard waist can't see or hear me! Nobody can cover them! I'm getting out of this friggin' turret and I'll go back and help the waist."

Immediately, Mac stopped his left turn and shifted to the right in a shallow climb so that the nose guns could get a view of the incoming enemy.

The attack came from above and the starboard side as the shattering and pounding of the twenty millimeter shells tore great chunks of metal out of the starboard wing and waist section. Mac saw the three fighters out of his side window as they fanned out for another attack.

Lt. Fuzz borrowed Mac's personal expression, "Shit fire, Captain, they got our other starboard engine."

"Screw the check list", shouted Mac, "and help me hold the rudder!"

The top waist section of the fuselage was gone. Sacket was sprawled on the waist deck and was now screaming into Moody's once used mike. "Those dirty bastards got Moody. I hope his chute will open!"

That was the last transmission from the Louise E. Ann.

Reber had just reached the waist gun position when the German fighters struck. Moody had been blown out of the aircraft with his flexible 50 caliber in his hands. Sacket was lying on his back, blood was streaming from his face. Mickey grabbed Sacket's parachute harness and dragged him through the gapping hole in the dying aircraft. His last act before he went out was to pull Sacket's rip cord.

With the sudden end of noise and his own out of control actions, his sight, hearing, and feeling were suspended into nothingness. He looked above him and watched his once proud warrior, B-17, #42001 in an uncontrolled, rotating dying fall.

Reber's brain had restored sight and sound, he knew that he was falling faster than the doomed aircraft. Two objects or bodies appeared at the front hatch of the plane and started their fall below the ill fated giant, then above and behind him he saw what had to be Sacket's open parachute, out loud he said, "That's three of us, maybe four!" His soundless decent was being controlled by his unintentional movement of his hands and feet. He was no longer tumbling through the air and he was falling on his back. With a few small adjustments of his hands he could turn himself in any direction he chose. Off to his right he could see the trail of smoke behind the cart-wheeling aircraft that he had recently departed.

Sacket's parachute was far above him and drifting away. The last object to leave the stricken giant was above and beyond Sacket, who was it? It appeared that no others had struggled out or had been ejected. Had the others been frozen in their seats by the forces of gravity or had they been killed in place by the fighter attack?

Suddenly, he realized that he was not just floating in space, he was falling toward the beautiful green earth that was coming up at him in greater detail with every passing second. By free-falling as he was there was less chance of being strafed by the fighters or being shot at from the ground.

Now the roads and a small village were becoming visible in greater detail. If no changes were made in his decent, he would probably land in the hamlet. His right hand reached for the handle of his rip cord and without hesitation he gave it a hard yank, his chute opened with a sudden, big "whoosh pop" sound that made his frightened mind produce the smile caused by the canopy that billowed overhead. He had read about guiding a parachute by pulling on the cords connecting him to the canopy above him. Slight, cautious tugs caused him to move parallel to the ground. In a matter of seconds he was moving away from the village and out into the country that appeared to be dairy farms. This was a valley bordered on two sides by green forest and covered hills and was probably on the German, French border.

Slipping his parachute, he glided into a pasture of brown and white milk cows that was bordered at the far end by a barbed wire fence with a small barn just beyond. Before he touched down he noticed a group of people running down the road toward him.

"If I can get over that fence ahead I will run for those hills and the forest."

He could not float over the fence so he ejected his chute from the harness to keep from being dragged into the barbed wire.

The people were behind him and were still some distance off, he thought he could run to the forest to hide and escape. As he ran past the small barn, two young females with pitch forks stepped out and in front of him. Instantly, he reached for and drew his 45 caliber automatic, as he aimed the weapon at the young women he found that he could not shoot at either of them. Without further thought he threw the pistol to the ground and raised his hands over his head.

He was full of fear and anger. Why had he not been able to fire his weapon at his enemy?

One of the women pointed to the ground, yelling ,"Plots!"

He understood a little German and obeyed her command. As he sat down, both women kept up their guard while jabbing the air with their pitch forks.

Reber began to hear the excited voices of the local people from the road, the loudest was the deep voice of a man, who by his authoritative words was probably in charge of this group. The man approached him with a shot gun that was pointed directly at him. He repeated another command in German over and over in rapid succession. Reber could not understand and again fear shot through him.

A child's voice said in English, "Lay down and turn over!"

Reber obeyed and rolled over on his stomach, with his arms stretched out in front of him. He tried to look around, but a boot was pressing against the back of his head, forcing his face into the damp barn yard soil.

The smell of the fresh cow manure made his eyes sting and he shouted, "Damn it, cut it out!"

His remark brought laughter from the growing group of captors. Turning his head he noticed his still bleeding arm and his new shattered wrist watch, he felt totally intimidated and defeated.

"Oh shit." He knew that only minutes had passed since that first deadly burst of flack had started the destruction of the Louise E. Ann and the end had come for some of his buddies.

He had joined the military to help end this friggin' war. Now what?

The Faulk Wolf attack on the starboard high side of the Louise E. Ann had instantly killed Bombardier Lieutenant Young.

The explosive 20 millimeter shells had torn through the plexiglass nose section, destroying Young and the bombsight that had been his joy and responsibility. He had named it "Norton," after the manufacturer. He had taken such pride in his ability to operate this ingenious instrument and his aircraft's missions were always on target.

Young had applied for a Commission in the Army Air Corps while in his second year at the University of Kansas in Wichita. His family back home, in Liberal, Kansas, had plotted with an uncle who was a Commander in the Military to get Young into the Air Force as a Bombardier. It seemed the whole Air Corp combat effort was to drop bombs on the enemy, so the Bombardier had the job that all of the other crew members were there to support. He was good and his dad had referred to him as "Number One" when he graduated and received his Commission.

TWO

Captain McCrea, on this his 22nd mission, had decided that he must stay with his dying bird as long as possible. He must give the rest of his crew a chance to get out of this alive. To release what control he still had in order to leave the aircraft would cause the plane to go into a spinning action, freezing all of the men in place, they would have no chance to escape.

At first it seemed like he could navigate this plane all the way to the ground if it were possible. His first action after he realized that both engines on the starboard side were gone and the aircraft was steadily becoming unmanageable, even with Co-Pilot, 2nd Lieutenant Freestone trying to hold the rudder peddles straight, other damage to the B-17 would cause it to crash.

Because the nose section had been torn away, and the high wind velocity coming from the Bombardier's nose section, he knew that 1st Lieutenant Young was probably dead.

His radio interphone was inoperative, his only means of communication was to shout. He looked over at his copilot, 2nd Lieutenant Freestone, the crew had nicknamed him Lt. Fuzz. He saw the strain and fear on the very young man's face, "Get out of here, bail out!" Mac yelled. "Right now, damn it, move, that's an order!"

Fuzz raised up and was out of his seat, he had an unbelieving look on his face, he reached out and took hold of his Commander's shoulder.

"Get the hell out of here now!"

Fuzz moved with difficulty toward the hatch and was gone.

In the next second a roaring explosion shook the aircraft and the starboard wing folded up and over the fuselage. What was left of the Louise E. Ann started its long twirling fall toward German soil.

Captain McCrea tried with all his strength to get up and out of his seat, it was impossible, his fate was now sealed. He took his hands off the controls and called out to his wife, "Louise, honey, I love you. Kiss the kids and family for me." Thoughts of his mother and father flashed through his mind and then he relaxed and closed his eyes.

In less than the two minutes it would take to get to the ground at one hundred and sixty miles an hour scenes of his wife and parents waving good-bye on that last sunny warm day in California came to him. From the cockpit he had saluted his family and had taxied out to the runway where he made a long, safe take off headed for a war that would bring adventure and the promise of a promotion for his future as a career pilot.

A few hours later, the fire and smoke were hardly noticeable to the farmers in the valley where the dairy cows grazed and life seemed at peace.

Lieutenant Farnsworth had immediately plotted his return course to England after the Louise E. Ann had received its first direct hits from flack. His Commander had issued the order to head home and for the moment he had felt greatly relieved. Everything had happened so fast that he had not put the usual gum in his mouth that always went along with any changes that might effect his job. Magelan, as Farnsworth was known to the rest of his crew, was a very self confident and precise officer.

He liked and got along with all of the crew members of the Louise E. Ann, but he let the enlisted people know that he was an officer and he demanded their respect.

After Staff Sergeant Mickey Reber had said that his turret

guns were inoperable and had jumped down from his upper turret and Sergeant Barn's lower ball turret had received a direct hit that killed him instantly, Farnsworth had thought, "This is really bad and we are going in!"

Still in control of his actions he had started to put away his navigational gear, it was then that the explosive 20 millimeter rounds had begun to tear up his airplane around him. The interphone contact was lost and he had decided, "It's all over, I have got to get out of here now!"

At the same time Farnsworth got to the forward escape hatch, he found 2nd Lieutenant Freestone reaching for his ejection handle. There was no hesitation, they both went out of the hatch on top of each other. They were free falling for ten or fifteen seconds and somehow managed to open their chutes very near the same time. Later Farnsworth had said he had wanted to stay with somebody on the way down.

It was nearly four minutes later that they landed within one hundred yards of each other on a hillside. The area was covered with a crop of white grapes. The vines gave them the perfect hiding place for their chutes; they gathered them up and pushed their ejection buttons, releasing the chutes from their harnesses, and took time to push the obvious paraphernalia in under some of the lush grape vines. This should give us some extra time to escape.

They looked around and saw no one. What a contrast— Farnsworth had an expression of achievement on his face and Fuzz had the look of absolute fear in his blue eyes and his face was white with the shock of the last minutes' happenings.

"So far so good," said Farnsworth.

Staff Sergeant Woods had felt the impact of the flack bursts on the aircraft, he had heard the Commander give the emergency call to his crew members to stay off the interphone unless called. He was in the tail of the plane and could not see the horrendous damage and the injuries that had been inflicted further up the inside of the aircraft. He could see the smoke from the burning number three engine. He had searched the sky for the enemy fighter aircraft, but his rear facing gun would not be of any help. He was panic stricken because the aircraft was starting to shudder and stall.

He turned and looked forward to the waist section, there was no one in sight. Moody was gone. He did not know at that time that his crew mate had been blown out of the waist section without his parachute on. Sacket and Reber were no where to be seen and he did not know of their fates either.

Staff Sergeant Woods had been called "Shorty" by the others on the crew; his position was a tight cramped space and required a small person to fit in the tail gunner's seat, he fit that description perfectly.

Woods reached for his chest parachute that was behind him. He had to get out and now! As he backed out of his gun position the handle for the chute ejection became snagged in the frame work of the aircraft fuselage. He tried to pull it loose, but this caused the chute to eject into the narrow crawl way. A blast of outside air billowed the chute into a tangled canopy over him. Shorty was trapped. He fought all the way to the ground and became the last victim of the Louise E. Ann's destruction.

Reber and Sacket had pushed through the right waist gun hatch, Sacket's chute had opened and had separated them. Reber had waited for some minutes of free falling time before opening his chute. He was now several thousand feet below Sacket and the cross winds aloft had taken Sacket several miles west of Reber's position. Sacket could only wonder when he would see Reber again, and said, "Hope you make it OK, buddy."

Sacket drifted towards the forest covered hills, several miles west. He was barely conscious and settled slowly into the pines on top of the hills above the valley. His chute had tangled in the upper branches of an ancient tree, keeping him fifteen or more feet above the ground. He was lucky as he would have surly received serious injuries if he had hit the ground in a falling stop.

When his head cleared and he was more aware of his surroundings, he realized where he was and what his condition had become. The wounds on the side of his face and neck had dried but were very painful. His flying suit was torn and another cut on his leg still oozed blood.

"I am too far above the ground to release my harness from this entangled chute. I have got to try and figure a safe way down, but how? If I fall I'll probably break my ankle or leg and then what?"

Suddenly the sound of a dog barking was all that Sacket could hear. "Sounds mean to me. He is going to give my position away, I've got to do something about him."

He reached under his chute harness and got his 45 automatic from its holster and aimed it at the moving dog. It was difficult to get him into the weapon's sight, and he knew that the sound of the gun would call attention to him, but he had to try something. He aimed. Just as his finger started pressure on the trigger a shot rang out and a bullet whizzed past his head. He dropped his weapon and it hit the ground. "What in the hell was that?" he said.

From no where came this gunman. Sacket had not paid any attention to anything but the annoying dog. The man must have been in the woods. He held a Luger in his right hand, and he was the one that had fired at Sacket. The man looked up at his target in the tree and said, "Wie gehtes ihen?"

Sacket tried to recall some of the German words he had been taught and replied, "Ich bin Amerikaner."

The gunman picked up Sacket's 45 automatic, and he examined it like he had found a real treasure then looked up at his captive with a cunning knowing smile and motioned for Sacket to let himself fall down to the ground.

The German still held his Luger and now had Sacket's 45 automatic. He was in charge, there was no use doing anything but what he was being ordered to do, so without delay Sacket reached up and released himself from the entangled parachute. Maybe this man knew that he would fall on the ground covered with layers of thick pine needles, because when he landed he found his fall to be relatively easy with no additional injuries. The dog was right in front of him with his teeth bared in a hostile manner.

At this moment Reber knew he was a prisoner and he could only wait for his captors to take some course of action. He could only see the shoes and the boots of about twenty people. He was sure most were adults, but he distinctly heard the voices of young girls. There was one voice that was male, older sounding somehow. The man's voice took over the conversation with what sounded like firm, strict orders to the others.

Everyone stopped their loud chatter and the man gave instructions to one of the older females. He called her Fräulein Reider. The man had placed his gun barrel against Reber's neck and had removed his boot. The soft voice of the woman, Fräulein Reider, spoke in English to tell him that she would tie his hands behind his back and let him sit up so that he could answer her questions.

Cautiously and with some pain, Reber rolled over on his back and sat up. He was very awkward at first; his injured arm really bothered him when he moved. Looking around he saw that he had been right, there were mostly women and teenage girls. The elderly man with gray hair stood directly in front of him.

Fräulein Reider knelt beside him, she looked directly at Mickey for a long minute, when she spoke it was again in English with a slight German accent and a nonthreatening smile on her pretty lips.

"You are our prisoner and we will treat you well if you cooperate with us. If you cause trouble, Herr Graef will take you to a prison where your very life could be taken from you. We are giving you this choice because of your restraint when you first landed here. You had a gun and you could have shot and maybe killed Frau Miller or myself. Herr Graef saw your self control and has judged you to be a good person.

"You will remain our prisoner and will be held under guard; it will be your duty to help us with our labors of farming. Most of our young men are fighting the war and it has taken them away to the battlefields throughout our lands. Herr Graef and I are teachers and wish only for an end to this fighting and bloodshed.

"I noticed that your arm and the cut on your leg will need some medical attention. We will give you a chance to think about your requested position here with us and then we will talk about your future. If you can, will you please get to your feet and I will take you to the building where you will be held."

Herr Graef called all the others to attention and after a brief discussion they were marched by Frau Miller back to the fields where they had been working.

Mickey was on his feet now with his hands tied behind his back. Fräulein Reider and Herr Graef led him, walking, the mile or so to a very small village.

There were about ten buildings settled amongst a small orchard of apple and pear trees. In the center of some buildings constructed of wood stood one stone and cement structure. This appeared to be an office. He asked Fräulein Reider what the buildings housed and she replied that one was for the mayor, the other a post office, and one was a medical clinic. "The mayor is Herr Graef, I am the Post Lady, and Frau Miller is the medical supervisor."

They entered the larger building. The largest room was partitioned off. There were two smaller offices that took up the whole interior. Reber was led to one of the smaller rooms and told to sit on a cot. Fräulein Reider explained that it would also be his sleeping quarters and the cot his bed.

Herr Graef sat at the only desk in the room while Fräulein Reider put a chair directly in front of Mickey and sat down and looked him directly in the eyes. "Now it is your turn to talk. We don't know the sound of your voice yet."

Reber lifted his injured arm and looked at his wrist watch with the broken crystal and softly said, "I am Staff Sergeant Mickey Reber, serial number 19178855. That's all I can tell you!"

The attractive women said understandingly, "I know that this is your country's policy for soldiers captured by the enemy, but we don't want any of your country's secrets. You must realize that you have a choice and can help yourself by growing the food that we need here for human consumption. When I speak of humans I include the sick and injured and the children that you have already seen who are housed here.

"Your freedom and survival depend on how well you help us feed these people. This room will be your quarters. Your lavatory and bathing facilities will be through that door," she pointed to the other room.

"Now, if you will let me, I will look at your injured arm and leg and clean and dress your wounds."

Reber smiled for the first time since his capture and showed visible signs of relaxing, he said, "I thank you for your kindness and understanding."

Fräulein Reider took scissors and cut through his sleeve and pants leg so that she could dress his injuries.

Herr Graef walked over to Mickey and put his hand on Reber's shoulder and said gently, "Gut soldat."

The woman gently took the broken watch off Reber's injured arm and handed it to Herr Graef, saying, "He will fix it for you." She smiled and said, "You are young and handsome and I believe that the young people will like and trust you. If you like you can take your meals with all of us at the other end of this building."

She washed his injuries and put bandages on his arm and leg, then said, "It has been a long and complicated day for all of us. I will be back soon and show you to our dining room." She looked directly at Reber and said, "Please help us and don't disappoint me."

Dinner was a real relief; for the moment he felt that he was no longer in any real danger. The food was mostly vegetables with a small amount of sausage and it had been prepared in as tasteful a manner as possible.

The young girls stayed at the table long after all the food was consumed, they laughed and giggled and used the few words of English they had been taught.

There was one young boy in the group; he was crippled. Apparently he had been born with a club foot and he knew that he was there only because of his affliction. The boy sat next to Reber and seemed very happy to have another male in this group of women and girls.

After dinner Reber was led back to his room by Fräulein Reider. He was told that everyone went to bed early and got up at first sunlight to go to work in the fields; the same would be expected of him.

He was in his room with the door locked. The only light was from the big room outside his door. The faint glow from the lamp on the mayor's desk in the big room shown through a very small window in his door.

His thoughts of that day's events kept him awake while he lay in his new bed, a canvas cot. What had happened to the others? What were his friends back at his home base in England saying? Surely they knew what had happened to the Louise E. Ann and its crew.

He was exhausted and wondered what life would hold for him now. Too tired to care, he finally fell asleep in this different world of the unknown. His Mom and Dad came to him in his dreams and somehow seemed to comfort him and let him know that things in the future would be all right for him.

It seemed to him that someone brushed the hair from his forehead and smoothed the blanket over him. Was he dreaming?

THREE

Sacket took a deep breath as he recovered from his fall. The dog was moving now; he was still protective and had a menacing manner about him. He was circling and barking in the excitement of his find. The gunman was there too. He stood tall, looking down at him with his pistol in his right hand and Sacket's 45 stuck in his belt. He picked up a heavy stick and began to prod Sacket in his back with it. Movements made in an upward direction made Sacket think that he was being told to stand up. He cautiously stood, balanced himself for a moment, and turned carefully toward the German. He had been taken prisoner and could make no threatening moves with that Luger pointed at him.

His captor used his stick to push Sacket between the shoulders and pointed him in the direction of a path that was to his right. They walked for five minutes along an ascending route. All the while the man was speaking to him in German as though he were giving Sacket instructions. The dog was still barking and jumped up on his master several times. The man pushed the animal down, pointed his finger down the path, and yelled "gehen.". The dog took off running and disappeared.

The dirt path ended and they came to a flat stretch of gravel road that continued on around the side of this mountain. Sacket looked up at the fading sun and knew that they were heading west and were now moving in a downhill direction.

Sacket looked ahead to an opening in the trees and a small village came into view. They walked through a gate into a fenced area. There were older men dressed in dark green work uniforms and many guards. A structure with a long porch across the front was in the distance.

Each man in uniform had a saw or an ax and carried a pistol in a holster on his belt. It would seem that this was a wood cutter's camp.

Sacket's captor led him across the yard to the building and he started talking loudly to a guard that he had singled out to take charge of his captive. He pulled Sacket's 45 from his belt and handed it to the guard, saying in German, "It's loaded and ready to fire."

The soldier came down off the porch toward Sacket with his own 45 pointed at him in a menacing way, what a feeling of power that had to be, to threaten the prisoner with his own weapon. He directed Sacket to a bench and motioned for him to sit down. No one spoke any English and under the circumstances he was doing his best to follow hand directions given by his captors.

The German guard gave some orders and two of the woodsman, with their pistols drawn, took control of Sacket while the guard in charge entered the building. The door was open and Sacket could hear a discussion going on between the soldier and someone on the other end of the telephone. A few minutes passed and the soldier returned to where he was sitting and tried to tell him something in German, he could only say, "I don't understand." His German captor strutted around flaunting his 45 that was stuck into the front of his uniform.

Sacket pulled up his flying suit sleeve to look at his watch; it was late afternoon. His guard saw the watch and brandishing his gun, demanded that it be given to him. Sacket handed it over to the soldier. He thought of all that had happened this day and in such a short span of time. It had been less than four hours since they had first been hit. He wondered how many of the crew were still alive.

Sacket looked up hoping to get his watch back, the German looked at him and sarcastically said, "Danke," and put the watch in his chest pocket. Sacket knew that this was only the beginning of the cruel and sadistic acts that were sure to follow in the days ahead. He hoped that he could get through the rest of this day without being shot by his own gun.

Soon a German truck drove in the narrow driveway and stopped in front of the building where Sacket was being held. At the orders of the guard, the woodsmen fell into formation and stood at attention.

The driver of the truck got out and went around to open the door for the officer riding with him. The Sergeant in charge raised his hand and shouted, "Heil Hitler," all the others repeated the salute. Sacket did not, and looked down at the ground.

The officer strolled over to where Sacket was still seated and, in English, shouted at him, "Stand up and repeat the verbal salute!"

Sacket remained seated and shook his head. The officer strode up the steps, pulled Sacket to his feet, and repeated his command.

"No sir."

The officer roughly pushed Sacket off the two steps, causing him to sprawl on the ground. Again the officer picked him up by his arm and demanded the verbal salute and again came a "No sir" from Sacket. This time the Officer struck a hard blow with the swagger stick he carried, hitting Sacket across the face. The deep wounds and cuts he had suffered in the explosion of his aircraft opened up and bled profusely.

The officer looked at the prisoner for a moment and suddenly called the vehicle driver over and told him to tie Sacket hand and foot and then throw him into the back of the truck. The Sergeant drew Sacket's own pistol and ordered him to spread eagle himself on the ground. The German language is difficult to understand and Sacket could only guess what was being said to him.

The German Sergeant kicked Sacket in the upper leg, as he pointed his hand to the ground. Sacket got the idea and fell to the ground and placed his arms and legs apart. The Captain chose two wood cutters to tie Sacket's hands and feet. When they were done they roughly threw him into the rear of the truck. He was helpless. He was sore, felt sick and defeated.

The officer asked the group, "Who captured this American pig and where did you find him?"

The elder woodsman that had seen Sacket hanging in the tree came forward. "I found him. He landed in a tree and I forced him to drop to the ground. My dog was with me when I captured him. He was going to shoot my dog and I fired my Luger at him. His weapon dropped to the ground and I gave it to that guard over there."

"You have done well," said the officer. "Keep a sharp watch as there should be more of them. We know that their bomber was shot down by our brave pilots. Five of them died in the crash that was not far from here. Four American airmen were seen parachuting to earth and we have this one, there are three others out there."

He approached the guard with Sacket's gun, "I'll take that, it will be a good war souvenir."

As the truck drove away, Sacket lay bouncing on the hard floor of the truck bed. Every bone in his body hurt and there was fear in his gut. He was sure things would get worse long before they got any better. If he was going to get through this he had to fight.

"Those god damned bastards! I'll never say Heil Hitler, but see Hitler in hell I will!"

FOUR

Lieutenants Farnsworth and Freestone had traveled several miles from the place they had first landed and had hidden their parachutes. They both wore shoulder holsters with 45s; this was standard equipment for crew members.

Farnsworth cautioned, "Under no circumstances do we use these weapons. It would give us away. We have got to get into the high ground ahead. We will be safer and there will be far less chance that we will be captured. Come on, let's get a move on!"

They kept up their hiking pace for another hour or so. It had been a grueling time for them. Escaping from their lost aircraft had been a terrifying experience, staying away from German capture would be something else. They were both in good physical condition, but they were beginning to tire from the uphill exertion.

Farnsworth slowed their climb and said, "Let's find a good hiding place and rest for a while."

Farnsworth outranked his companion and had lots of survival training. "We can stay together; it might be better if I took charge, besides I have more experience. Have you ever had any prior survival instruction?"

Freestone shook his head, saying, "No, I sure wish that I'd had. I'll follow your orders and do my best to get out of this damn mess we're in." He hesitated for a moment and asked, "Do you think the others made it down OK?"

Farnsworth said, "I sure as hell hope so, but remember Freestone, we are free. Others have escaped from this God forsaken country and so can we! If you have rested enough we have got to make it to the mountain top. It will be safer up there and we can have a good look down this valley."

They walked and sometimes crawled through the uphill thick forest and brush, they stopped to listen to make sure they had not been seen or were not being followed. They rested every twenty minutes. Farnsworth went out at least fifty feet from their position and circled it to be sure they were not walking into a trap.

On one of these down times they heard rustling in the brush behind them. Freestone panicked and started to run.

Farnsworth caught him and said, "It's OK, just a couple of deer, nothing to worry about yet!" He had spoken quietly, "From now on not a word above a whisper and we have to be careful how we walk. Don't step on broken branches or stones that could make a noise that could give us away to a German. There does not appear to be a road or a path here, so just a little farther and we can find a place to settle down and make plans for tomorrow."

Freestone said, "Hey wait a minute." He unzipped his flight suit's upper pocket and pulled out a pack of cigarettes and his zippo lighter, but before he could shake one of the cigarettes out of its pack Farnsworth whispered, "You're going to have to wise up, Lieutenant. We will never make it out of this mess if you don't start using your head! Just the sound of your lighter and the smell of cigarette smoke could give us away to any smart Kraut-head that might be out here looking for a survivor of a plane crash."

Freestone stepped back and with an apologetic look on his face said, "I'm sorry, I just wasn't thinking."

"You better had next time or we will be prisoners or dead! If we survive this gaggle and make our escape it will be because we did not make any stupid blunders, from now on don't do anything without checking with me. I know I am being rough on you, but I'm older and I'll use my survival training. Let me take the responsibility for us for now, OK? Stay right here for ten minutes. I'll be back. Look at your watch and check the time."

Farnsworth again left their position and walked the distance of one hundred feet out, again circling their intended location to be sure it was safe.

He returned in the specified time and said, "This looks like a safe place to spend the night. We are going to need all the rest we can get. It's four o'clock and the sun is getting lower in the west. Tomorrow we can see further up and down this valley and decide what our next move will be. I checked the area, take a leak, you will feel better."

When Freestone returned, Farnsworth said, "We will take four-hour guard shifts, you get some sleep, I'll take the first watch. I think I have something here that will help us," he pulled a broken candy bar out of his zippered pant leg and broke it in half to share with Freestone. "That will have to do for tonight. I'm going to check my automatic and ammo clip. You do the same, OK?"

Reber awoke. He was startled, for the sounds around him were not familiar. The one window high up on the wall let the beginnings of the morning sun shine into the room. Just seconds after his awakening he heard the sound of a key being turned in the lock and the door to his room opened.

Mickey saw Fräulein Reider. She stood just inside the door and Herr Graef was there too.

"You must rise. Take care of your personal needs and get dressed. You have twenty minutes to do this and then you will join us for your breakfast. Here is some soap. Use it sparingly, for it is scarce now days."

Mickey had gone to bed fully clothed and he still had his boots on. He decided to just wash his face and hands. The soap was not what he had been used to and it reminded him of what they had used at boot camp to scrub the floors with. He had been given a thread bare piece of cloth that looked like a worn out dress to use as a towel. Things must be really tough here, he thought. He rushed and cleaned up the best he could, knowing that what he had been through yesterday would not make him feel very clean at all. He hurriedly used the latrine.

"Hope I have some time tonight to get this crud off of me. This torn flight suit is a mess!"

He looked out of the doorway and there was Fräulein Reider smiling at him. "You look some cleaner and a little more rested. Come with me and we will eat breakfast with the others."

There was hot porridge—it was a lot soupier than the oatmeal he really enjoyed—a piece of hard dark bread with what smelled like bacon grease on it. One of the young girls who sat across the table passed him a tin cup of what appeared to be coffee; it tasted like bitter medicine.

Fräulein Reider laughed and said, "This is what we have every morning. I am sure you will get used to it. Sometimes we have an egg and a bit of fruit. We must eat now and join the others outside."

Mickey finished the tasteless meal and drank the hot liquid. The Fräulein had advised him that it was something that would keep him healthy. Hope she knows what she is talking about, she sure seems fit, Mickey thought.

When they were outside Mickey looked at the Fräulein and said, "You folks have lost a lot, haven't you?"

She ignored his question, and said, "Come with me. We must join the group ahead."

He noticed all the others were forming into three lines, with the taller ones toward the front. This put him at the very head of one of the lines.

His mind raced back to yesterday morning at what must have been just about this time. He had just climbed into the Louise E. Ann and was preparing to preflight his top turret gunners' position for the coming mission of the day. The rest of the crew was talking in loud voices to each other and settling into their own places aboard the B-17 Bomber, lovingly called Balls One, the last three tail numbers on the aircraft.

The name "Louise E. Ann" and a painted picture on the left side of the nose below the pilot's side window were never referred to during the preflight or any official business. The beautiful shapely girl with the red flowing hair was there only to be looked at.

Mickey was shocked, and caught off guard by the loud command to "March!" After a stumbling start he managed to get into step with the woman on his right. Herr Graef was in front and while he led he counted in a loud voice, "ein, zwei, drei, vier." All the laborers wore heavy high shoes and they made a sound on the pavement like he had seen the German Soldiers do in the newsreels.

From start to finish there was a strict discipline about this march. After a mile the command to "Halt!" sounded and a "Recht Gesicht" followed, then the command "Auf Lindern" given by Herr Graef who began issuing orders in German.

Mickey did not understand a word he said.

All the others, except Herr Graef and Fräulein Reider, broke up into small groups of four or five and walked down a path to a nearby shed. Graef called Fräulein Reider aside and spoke to her for several minutes. She listened and seemed to make comments back to him. Herr Graef spoke very forcefully to her and pointed in Mickey's direction and he seemed to have the last word as he turned and walked off toward the fields.

Fräulein Reider approached Mickey and spoke to him in a commanding way. "You and I are going to fix our outdated irrigation system! The well must be repaired and made to produce the water we need for the crops. Have you had any experience with farming, in particular with water wells?"

"Some," Mickey replied, "during the summer I spent a few weeks at my Grandfather's farm in Pennsylvania. He grew corn and most of its water came from the rain that seemed to come at the right time. He did raise a few acres of vegetables that were taken to the markets in the nearby towns.

"The water for those crops came from a nearby well and was pumped into a small reservoir and distributed by ditch to the crops. Sometimes he had wind and too much rain, but during dry times he rarely had any trouble getting the water that was needed. The well had an electric pump that seldom if ever gave him any cause for concern."

Mickey's response pleased Fräulein Reider and she

explained, "Our problem here is a shortage of electrical power to run our pumps. Farther up the valley are several defense factories that require all of the available electricity."

"Do you have a reservoir in the area?" asked Mickey.

Reider replied, "No."

Mickey said, "If you could get a portable generator from the German Army we could use it to power the pump and then store the water in a reservoir to irrigate the crops.

"I don't know why I am helping you! You are the enemy of my country, "said Mickey defensively.

Fräulein Reider walked up to Mickey and placed her hand on the pistol she had on her belt and said, "You are the prisoner of the enemy that you speak of. We have chosen to keep you here on this farm to help feed and save these many children. It is your choice, stay and cooperate or be sent to a Prisoner of War Camp. There you may not survive. Herr Graef and I thought we could take a chance and ask you for your help. Your being here would give us all an opportunity to survive this senseless war. If you are what you appear to be, a decent man that believes in what your country stands for, you too can get through this experience with the knowledge that you have turned a losing situation into something honorable. If it were known how many others, including myself, how we really felt about this war and our Furor, we would all be put to death."

She continued, "Herr Graef and I are teachers and we have lived with the negative effect that the fascist style of government has inflicted upon us. Please stay and help us. Our leader here is a much respected and admired man. He realizes that you are a young but also a loyal man that has grown up in a democracy, that you have taken an oath to defend. He also thinks you will see things differently because of the choices that you have here.

"From what you say, our job will be a hand dug reservoir, and we will need a portable generator from our Army. We will start working toward that project today if you will agree to help us," said the Fräulein.

Mickey stood looking off into the distance. He was full of indecision and his brain barraged him with thoughts. This is life or death. What good is death? If I really look into my soul all I ever wanted to do was to be of service to humanity. There are children here and they have never done any wrong to anyone. He recalled a pet quote from William White that his dad liked, "Freedom is one thing you can't have unless you give it to others." I have been touched by death twice in these past days, now I am here where I can be productive and safe until this war is over, somewhere there is a reason for all of this, he thought.

In just these few seconds, he realized what he had to do, and do it well he would. He turned to the Fräulein and said, "There is work to be done and I will help you. Let's get on with it."

FIVE

After a restless night's sleep the two airmen moved along the ridge of the mountains they had climbed the evening before. They stayed in the areas that had the thickest brush and tree growth in case there should be a sudden need to conceal themselves. Both men had checked their pockets the night before to see if anything they had would help them through these few days. Farnsworth had found another one of his candy bars, a half a pack of gum, a survival knife and his 45 automatic with its clip. Freestone always carried a couple of packages of peanuts, his zippo lighter and some cigarettes. He had checked out his weapon last night and it was OK. He had a small pad of paper and a pencil. They each had an emergency ration.

"We have got to find some drinking water," said Farnsworth. "I've noticed some large rocks sticking up ahead. Let's check them out for trapped water in the crevice."

They had to crawl on their hands and knees to get over the large granite boulders that formed the rim of the out cropping. Just as they reached the top of the first boulder a cluster of birds flew up from the cavity. They were so startled that they almost hit Freestone.

"What the hell was that? What do you see?" he asked.

"It's a beautiful pool of clear water down there. That's what all those birds were doing down there," answered Farnsworth. "The pool ends at a narrow passage way; it's an overflow."

With the birds and other animals that apparently drank from this source, Farnsworth felt it was pretty safe and he tasted it and found the water to be of good quality. They both had a good drink and refreshed themselves by washing their hands and faces in the ice cold water.

They shared another candy bar and would eat a little of what they had through the days until they could find another supply of food.

Farnsworth finally broke the silence between them, "Let's get rid of the formalities of rank and last names, OK?"

Freestone grinned, "The crew called me Fuzz. My name is Bradley. I was called Brad in High School. What about you Lieutenant Farnsworth?"

"My name is Stanley, got called Stan in the military and it has stuck. So Brad and Stan it is from now on! We need to climb to that high point in the rock formation and see what's around us," said Stan. "I'll go up first, Brad. Stay here out of sight and keep your ears and eyes open. For God's sake, don't even think about using your 45. There is a big stick over there that would surprise someone if they should happen on your position. Check your watch and follow me up in ten minutes. Don't shout or yell at me."

Stan crawled up the smooth surface, using whatever hand and foot holds he could find. When he got to the top he stayed low making sure that he did not expose his position to anyone below. He looked in all directions and waited for Brad to join him.

Everything below looked clear. They had a good view of the valleys on both sides of their mountain. The valley to the south had a highway bordered by a railroad and a small river. The valley curved southwest and several small towns could be seen. The valley to the north seemed to be mostly agricultural with acres of grape vineyards on the upper slopes. A highway seemed to accommodate the different crops by winding from one side and then to the other.

In the valley to the east there seemed to be some kind of industry, for there were tall cylindrical stacks that emitted smoke. Stan guessed the buildings to be more than five miles away. Directly below their position on the north side was a dense grove of pine trees. It would be a good place to hide and rest.

"We need to make some plans for our escape, so let's

check out the pines down there. It will be safer and warmer."

They climbed down the rock formation and entered the pine grove at what appeared to be its center. A giant, fallen tree would hide them for a while.

A sudden noise below caused them concern. They heard what sounded like a truck stop and a door slam shut. Female voices were clear in the valley. Brad and Stan thought them to be caretakers for the vineyards. It was the time of year that required the most care for the growth of the grapes. The intonation was German. They seemed happy and industrious. One womanish voice, by its inflection seemed to belong to the one in charge and was saying something to hurry the others along.

Stan said, "Just hope they don't find our chutes or we may have to use these 45s. Just stay still and not a sound."

It was about an hour later when the words "mittagessen zeit" were heard. The voices drifted down and away. The old truck door closed and the women were gone.

The two men drew deep sighs of relief and decided that since it was late they would sleep there in the hollow of this tree. They would have to be up and out of there at daybreak to avoid being trapped by the workers. Their chutes were bound to be discovered soon.

They ate half of one of the rations and agreed again on the four hour shifts. Stan moved to an opening in the trees that was somewhat protected. The rest of the night went without incident.

The sergeant drove his truck on the bumpy road, high above the valley. The officer riding with him began to complain about the hard seat and the swaying of the truck as it made its way down the winding road into the valley below.

It was a great relief for Sacket when the vehicle finally reached level ground and turned onto the smooth, paved road. His body had suffered from the incidents aboard the Louise

E. Ann and the abuse he had taken from the German guards, and now, tied and bouncing around in the bed of this truck really made him glad that he was in the good physical condition he was.

He really was concerned about what was to come next. He knew he had a real temper and that he was going to have to control it if he was going to live through his capture.

Sacket heard the two men seated in front talking and the word "Americanisur" was all he could understand. It seemed like hours; finally the truck stopped suddenly throwing him against the vehicle interior. A loud voice ahead of the truck shouted, "Halt!" A discussion between the officer and another person ensued. There were sounds of laughter that mingled into the conversation that came to his ears. Someone moved back beside the rear of the truck and into Sacket's line of vision. This had to be a German guard. He could see him. He looked like a prize fighter and the expression on his face was sinister. Sacket was sure he had a temper too.

The guard opened the tail gate of the truck and pulled Sacket by his ropes to the rear with his head facing him. He gave his prisoner a long look, cleared his throat and spit thick tobacco smelling mucus into Sacket's face, then he laughed and yelled some German slang at him. He did not understand what the guard had said, best that way.

The tail gate slammed shut again and the truck moved through an opening. The movement came to a stop and again the rear of the vehicle was opened. There was what appeared to be an office with a big sign on the front.

A guard and the driver of his truck came back and together they roughly pulled Sacket up, forcing him into a sitting position.

The guard untied Sacket's heavy cords on his wrists and ankles and allowed him to sit a moment, both his hands and feet had needles and pins and a numb feeling to them. Five minutes passed and the guard motioned for him to follow into a building. Sacket stumbled but recovered and they entered what appeared to be an office.

Several curious German soldiers came from inside the

building to observe the prisoner. They walked up to Sacket and scoffed at him. They had a menacing attitude about them.

Another soldier came from the building, walked directly to face Sacket and spoke in English, "You are the prisoner of the German Army. We will expect your cooperation. We have an interest in your identity and what your duty is as an American Airman. Follow me into a room further up this hall and we will get started!"

The driver of the truck and the German officer interrupted the plans for Sacket by loudly protesting. They were shouting and there were frantic hand movements, attracting attention in their direction.

Sacket's guard answered the officer in a forceful manner. "My Colonel has ordered me to bring this American to his office. There will be no interference from either of you! The Colonel thanks you for your part in the capture of this prisoner and for transporting him promptly to this facility. He will call upon you to appear before him soon. Stand by until you are summoned!"

The two men left making disgruntled remarks. They drove their truck to the main gate and parked to await the call from the Colonel.

The long hallway that lay ahead of Sacket was bleak. It gave him the feeling of evil. It had dim lighting with at least eight doors on either side. The floor was rough scared wood.

The guard spoke, "I can see that you have suffered today with the loss of your aircraft and your comrades. We are going to try and make your capture as tolerable as possible, even though you are the foe. My commander will want to talk with you. He speaks English and he is a reasonable man and likes some Americans. Treat him with respect and it may go easier for you."

They stopped at the last door, the guard knocked.

"Enter," answered a voice from within.

The guard put his hand on Sacket's shoulder and moved him into the room. Like the hall, the room also was dimly lit, but there was enough light to see quality furnishings. There were pictures on the walls and a few art objects placed

around the room. Sacket immediately caught the aroma of
cigar smoke. There was a man seated behind a large desk in
a swivel chair with his back to the two men. Sacket thought
to himself, this must be the colonel the guard referred to.
Sacket was standing and not a word had been spoken.
Suddenly the officer turned in his chair. Sacket saw a striking
man with short cropped gray hair, wearing glasses and
holding a cigar in his hand. He nodded his head in the
direction of Sacket's guard and a chair was brought to the
front of the desk.

"Sit down," commanded the soldier.

With some sense of relief Sacket lowered himself into
the chair and took several deep breaths.

A low toned English speaking voice sounded from the
other side of the desk. "Would you like to smoke young man?"

The guard who was still near by held out a pack of
German cigarettes and shook one out, then held his lighter
for Sacket.

After several deep drags he looked up and said, "Thank
you sir."

There were several moments of silence, then the officer
spoke in a soft voice. "I am Colonel Hinerick Hibner. I am
the commander of this prison and in charge of all the inmates
here. Your future actions here will make or break your
chances for survival."

The Colonel continued; his voice was friendly but
threatening somehow. "I lived in America for years and I
understand what makes you tick. You are one of 700
American and British prisoners in this camp. Tonight you
will join some of your countrymen. They were captured due
to our ability to shoot them from the sky as you were today.
Your mission in the air was to bomb our cities and kill our
women and children. Our civilians and soldiers have reason
to be very angry with you, but I will do my best to protect
you. You are completely dependent on us for food, housing,
and medical needs."

The colonel's voice became stern. "I only hope your oath
of allegiance to your country will not cause you to suffer or
die. There will be others who will want to interrogate you.

Your actions will make a big difference in your welfare.

"After you have been here for ten days, I will want to talk with you again. I already know a lot about you and your friends and their work. You were stationed at the B-17 Base in Mildenhall, England. Your plane was shot down just a short distance from here, five of your crew were killed. Four of you survived. At our next meeting I hope you and I will be able to communicate.

"It is getting late, so I will send you with your guard. You will have a bath and a short physical examination and then you will be assigned to your new quarters. As they say in America, good luck."

Sacket stood and asked, "Are any of my crew members here too?"

The Colonel smiled and replied, "Your turn to ask questions will come at our next meeting."

Behind him a door opened and another guard entered the room and took Sacket by the arm. Assisted by the first soldier, they led him out of the office, into another building.

This was a room tiled from floor to ceiling. Sacket was told to remove all his clothing and to get into one of the three shower stalls against the wall. The guard turned on a hose and sprayed cold water on him. The shock sent Sacket's body into shivering spasms. A container filled with some sort of strong disinfectant was given to him and he was ordered to rub it thoroughly all over his body, especially in his hair and the genital area. Then he was sprayed again with cold water. It seemed the more his body shivered the more intense the water pressure became. The guards told him that they liked their prisoners clean.

The other guard stood back and watched and gave orders to the hose wielding warden. "Check his hair for the bugs and his fuss for the 'fuss krankheit.' He has some bruises and cuts, but the rest of him looks pretty good."

One of the men tossed him a piece of rough sacking and said, "Get dry and put your clothes back on. The examination is over."

In the mean time other guards had gone through Sacket's pockets and had taken his zippo lighter, jack knife, and the

American Occupation money from his wallet. They had found pictures that Sacket had collected of good looking girls, some he had known, others he had not. There was a full length shot of a movie star, Rita Hayworth. All the guards laughed, made noise's of pleasure, and cupped their hands as if to put their hands on the breasts of a woman.

While Sacket was dressing the guards carried on conversations in German while making hand gestures having to do with Sacket and his girlfriends. He could only accept the verbal insinuations directed at him. He had thoughts of the pain he would like to inflict on these German bastards, but for now his temper had to be kept under control.

One guard spoke in broken English, "Come on now, you bad American, we will take you to your new home."

SIX

Mickey said, "You will be in charge of this project, but let's be friends." He reached out and took hold of her hand, as if he were giving her a gentleman's agreement, and he shook it gently. He sensed the willingness that she returned in this physical contact and there was a look of gratitude in her eyes, even a tear on her cheek.

More and more since his capture he was seeing her as an attractive young woman. There was really not much difference in their ages.

"Please call me Mickey," he said.

Fräulein Reider lowered her eyes and shook her head in agreement. "Yes, I will and you may call me Inga, but only when we are alone. The other's would not understand. Now we must start our project."

At the tool shed, they got a pick and two shovels for the work that was ahead of them. The spot she had decided on to dig the reservoir was just above the fields that needed to be irrigated. The well was only a few yards away and it was on the same level. The problem of extracting the water from the ground was only one of pumping it out. The well itself was already established and had been used before. The big problem was that of electrical power, it had been taken away.

The hard work of digging and putting the dirt in its proper place continued all day with just a few breaks for rest. They had a simple lunch of bread and some cheese, a green pear, and a cup of water that was brought to them by one of the older women. Mickey recognized her, as he had seen her at breakfast earlier in the morning.

While they ate Inga asked Mickey, "Where was your

home and how much schooling did you have?"

Reber had finished eating and took a last sip of water and replied, "I will tell you about that later when we have more time. Now there is work to be done."

He touched Brad's arm to awaken him and excitedly whispered the words, "The Kraut's are catching hell now!" Stan pointed to a convoy below in the valley. "The son's of bitches are running for home!"

The motor brigade was coming to a stop at what appeared to be a park area. The trucks were pulling off the road and were gaining cover under large trees that were on both sides of the road. The sun was ready to rise and the eastern horizon was increasing its orange glow in the cloudless sky.

The two airmen watched from their mountaintop position as hundreds of tiny black specks approached moving toward them in the clear blue sky. Brad was almost speechless as he pointed toward the massive formation moving in above them, "My God! Look at our Air Force would you, they are going to bomb the shit out of them down there! Is there any chance we will get hit up here?"

"Always that chance, Brad, but we are high here and the target is down there. Fighters are always pretty accurate with their machine guns and rockets. Let's hope they have their minds on what they are doing today!"

Now came the sounds of the engines of the flight of fighters that flew near the ground. The first formation to be seen was a group of three P-38s. They had spotted the convoy in the valley below. Just before the planes reached the hiding place of the German trucks, they launched their rockets, then their machine guns were firing into the trucks and tanks. Even at their height and distance the sound of the guns and rockets were deafening. Truck parts could be seen flying through the air. Bodies were everywhere. A tank blew apart. The trees that were once there were gone.

The fire and smoke rose high above the valley and the smell of burning flesh and the heat from the flames that had been delivered by the rockets could be felt even where Stan and Brad were at distance. There was no sign of defense or return fire from the scattered German position. Within a minute another fighter sweep of P-38s descended and dropped their bombs and there was more machine gun fire on the same target. There was no doubt that the convoy had been entirely destroyed.

Farther up and down the valley the same action was being taken. It seemed that the bombers above were passing over the whole scene below.

Stan looked at Brad and said, "Neither of us will ever forget this. It's pay back time!"

The valley, both east and west, was full of smoke and fires from both vehicles and the destruction of buildings. Flames were raging out of control.

No humans could be seen. The toll of the dead must have been very high. If there were injured it was doubtful they could survive for long. There were craters now too from the bombs the planes had dropped.

Stan remarked, "We were lucky today, they sure made a mess down there."

Brad started to speak and hesitated, then lowering his voice he said, "What do we do now?"

Stan, with a half smile on his face, started his reply by shaking his head, "The Germans sure as hell won't be looking for us. They will be trying to find a safe place to hide, the ones that are able to move that is! Their only activity here will be to run and hide. Let's hope they won't come into these hills. I had hoped that we could get out of here today, but for right now I think it is best to stay put and out of sight. Let's open one of those rations and have a little food. For sure we will leave early in the morning, we can make plans while we eat.

When they opened the survival packet they found a plastic bag that could be used to contain and carry water. There was a small packet of dehydrated soup mix.

"I'll go get some of that water from the pool in the rocks," said Brad.

"I'll stay here and keep watch, remember to move slowly and quietly, don't over fill that bag."

When Brad returned with the water, Stan poured it in the container of soup mix and gave it a stir with a stick he had picked up. "It's cold soup and a half of a fruit bar for now."

The morning sun was starting to feel good. The warmth of summer was turning this part of Germany into a place something like what they remembered at home.

"Let's get that little pad of paper and pencil you have Brad and make sort of a diary."

They made some notes of happenings since they had landed.

Stan stood and looked down on the devastation below them. "War is hell!" He looked to his right. "There are a few German's walking along that road. They are heading for the next big town that's on the other side of that narrow pass. They figure that they can find safety farther into their homeland. If they desert the area below us maybe we can find some food and other things we can use in the wreckage of those trucks. We can watch for awhile and then decide what to do."

The guards led Sacket, cold and shivering, from the showers.

The one called Esser, who spoke fair English said, "Don't even think of trying to escape. There have been those who were foolish enough to try. Some have died and some have been severely punished. The prisoners that you are about to join will tell you all about that. You will be assigned to barracks number eighteen. They are all American pigs like you. If you were Jewish, Polish or French you would be sent to another place. You had better be glad that you're not one of them."

As they walked down the main street of the prison,

Sacket realized how large and confining this concentration camp was. His estimate of its size was at least one square mile or better. There were guard posts along a triple barbed wire fence with a high fence beyond that with guard towers manned by machine guns every thousand feet or so. A double set of railroad tracks ran through the center of the camp and a large group of POWs was unloading logs from some of the cars. The men looked haggard and hungry and unfit for the work they were doing. The clothes they wore were torn; some had only rags on their feet. At least ten guards were posted around them and pushed them on with prods when they faltered. One guard was operating a fork lift.

Another group of POWs was loading the empty cars with what appeared to be firewood. Beyond, the sound of a saw mill could be heard. One of the prisoners, a tall thin man, waved his hand in greeting to Sacket. The guard became angry and hit the prisoner across the shoulders with the butt of his rifle for violating the rules of the prison.

Sacket noticed a heavy wooden cross with iron cuffs hanging from it in the yard. It did not take long for him to imagine the sort of torture that was.

Sacket's English speaking guard grinned and said, "Do you see how many of you pigs we have here now. There will be many more in a very short time now!"

Sacket laughed and said, "You will get yours when all this is over!"

His remark brought a hard blow to his back with the butt of a rifle, causing him to fall face forward on the ground.

The guard said, "I should teach you a real lesson," and was ready to assault Sacket again, but the soldier in charge growled something that stopped his aggression and told Sacket to get to his feet and to keep his damned mouth shut!

The three man procession continued on and stopped at the building marked #18. A short, sickly looking American in a worn out flight suit stood in the doorway. He had a bleak expression on his face and said, "Welcome to Grand Hotel. I am the barracks chief and I try to take care of this pile of wood. The gang here call me Klein, or Shorty. Your just in time for chow. Your bunk is the last one on the bottom right."

The two guards that were with Sacket turned to leave. The English speaking one turned to Klein and said, "You had better straighten that one out because he has a big loud mouth and you know what happens to that kind!" He pointed to the sadistic looking cross in the yard.

When they were alone, Klein stood close to Sacket and spoke quietly. "I've been in this place for over a year now. I'll do my best to help you. The others will be coming in a few minutes. Don't be surprised if they don't speak to you at first. We do most of our talking outside while we work. Even then we have to keep our voices down." Klein looked up toward the roof and whispered, "It's bugged!"

Klein had observed Sacket's condition. "You look tired and beat up. Tonight eat what you can and get some sleep. Go back and check out your bunk. I'll be there in a few minutes."

Sacket walked back to the location of his bed. It was made of rough wood. As he moved closer he saw droppings on the floor that had to be those of mice or something larger, he would be very vulnerable since he had a lower bunk. There was a terrible odor around too, and he had the distinct feeling that things were going to get worse.

Klein made his appearance and handed him a threadbare old blanket and pillow. "This is it for now, here is a tin plate, a cup and a spoon. Take care of these cause there are no replacements for now."

Klein and Sacket walked back to the main room of the barracks. The facility had several wooden tables and benches, a few shelves on the wall with one light that hung from the center of the ceiling. All in all it was very depressing.

"Come on out on the front porch and meet the inmates of this facility. Technical Sergeant Gordon Sacket was introduced to the forty-five Americans that would be his friends or uncaring associates, of which some just might be his salvation. Klein gave a few instructions about plans for tomorrow's work.

Klein got the men organized into a line and the weary looking formation of American POWs marched off to a large, smelly building located near the center of the camp. There was a double line of prisoners standing at the side entrance. One line was American POWs, the other of British airmen. Both aisles were moving slowly into the building.

As Sacket got closer to the door, the smell of cabbage and a strong acid odor filled the air. The stench of unwashed bodies was nearly overpowering. He felt ill. His turn in line came to what was described as the "serving table." He held out his tin plate as the others ahead of him had done and he was splattered with a gob of boiled cabbage that was slapped onto his plate, the juice overflowed onto the floor. The attendant who was serving was not paying attention to what he was doing. He was in conversation with another cook who was standing near him. The meal was complete with a chunk of dark, dry bread and a ladle of luke warm, foul smelling liquid that was poured into his cup.

Klein was just ahead of him and said, "Follow me to where our men eat."

Sacket sat down next to Klein and looked down at the plate in front of him with a disgusted look on his face. The man across the table from him said, "You may as well eat up, Sarge. It don't get much better. The Kraut's here are hoping we will all starve ourselves to death. Many have already done that. By the way, they call me Slick. I'll see you soon and we can talk while we are working."

Sacket tried to eat, he found small bugs floating in and around the cabbage and he was sure there was something like what he had seen in the barracks in the bread. He took a bite or two and drank some of the liquid from his cup. He realized that he would have to go slow with the food; it would take some getting used to. When one is hungry enough he can eat most anything.

He looked around and other than a few muffled conversations, there really wasn't much talking. He noticed at least a dozen armed guards walking around the inside of the building observing the prisoners as they ate. The guards were all large and overweight. They were the Fat Kat's of Hitler's super race. They were not in combat fighting the enemy, and they were called the "Braun NASE" brigade by the prisoners in the POW camp.

Sacket ate some, but without enjoyment. The man across the table seemed friendly enough and started a conversation, "How many of your crew made it out and are they OK?"

Klein nudged him with his elbow and interrupted, "He just got here today and he hasn't seen the SOB yet."

Sacket hesitated, watched the man's smiling face, and said, "I wish I knew. I was alone from start to finish."

Again there was another question, "You think your bird and crew made it to their target without you?"

"That's what it looks like," replied Sacket. "A flack burst at my position and blew me out of the waist hatch. The airplane and my buddy's kept right on going. I hope they bombed the shit out of the Krauts!"

The man across from him got up and headed toward the door.

Klein said, "You did OK. Just watch out for that guy and anybody he hangs out with."

Sacket asked Klein, "Who is the SOB?"

Klein replied, "Wait until we get outside. Let's get the hell out of this slop house!"

All the men formed up in a spot that had a number stenciled on the pavement. Most of the men were carrying on conversations in low tones of voice, but they all seemed to be watching for someone.

Klein moved close to Sacket and said, "The SOB is the guy who will interview you in a few days. He will have others that appear to be American or English airmen talk to you. They are spies and they will try and get information from you. Don't be tricked! You did OK in mess hall. You notice he's not here with us now. If you have any questions, now is a good time."

Sacket faced Klein and looked him straight in the eyes. "How do I know I can trust you? When will I meet our American leader that I heard about long before I got into this mess?"

"It will be a while before that happens. It will take some time for you to get checked out, so don't cause any problems. Keep your temper under control and more or less do as you're told by those in charge. Don't help them with any information! Three important words around here are, 'I don't know,'" advised Klein.

"If they find out that they can get what they want from you, your days will become hell on earth. As far as your being able to trust me or anyone else, you will have to decide that for yourself or become a loner. There are some rules covering POWs and they do follow some of them, but for sure not all of them!"

Klein walked out in front of the group and called out, "FALL IN," then "ATTENTION," and finally, "FORWARD MARCH!"

SEVEN

Mickey awoke. For a moment he just lay there in his bed, thinking about the day ahead of him and what he would be expected to do. The thoughts of doubt were constant when he had any free time. How would all this affect his future?

His thoughts were interrupted by the sounds of young voices in the room outside his door. He jumped from his bed and hurried with the process of bathing and dressing so that he could meet the others for breakfast. He greeted the smiling face of Fräulein Reider when she unlocked the door that held him prisoner at night.

Inga said, "The girls have fixed a surprise for us this morning. Come and see."

There was a noticeable aroma of bacon in the room.

When they were all assembled Inga gathered the children around her and they sang a song of grace, thanking God for the food he had provided.

Everyone in the outer room faced Mickey and they all said with Inga, "Bacon and an egg like you have in your home in America."

Fräulein Reider told how Herr Graef's brother ,who was a colonel, had sent him a side of smoked bacon, none of them had tasted such a delicacy for a very long time. It was a special surprise for everyone.

Herr Graef was at the head of the table. He stood up and said, "Let this be one day closer toward peace."

Mickey touched Inga on the shoulder and said, "Herr Graef is a good man and I hope all of you will see a time of peace very soon. You know, Inga, I think about this war's end a lot and I wonder what my people will think of me when they learn how I have spent my time here. Will they understand, or will they want to punish me for collaborating with the enemy?"

"I wish that there was not a conflict of nations and that you were not our prisoner, but under the circumstances I am sure that we are doing what is right and your people will see it that way too one day. If we had sent you to a POW camp it might have meant your death. If you had escaped you might have been killed. I have become very fond of you." Inga became very serious and reached out and touched his hand, she was blushing now and he could see tears in her eyes.

On the way to the farmlands they did not look at one another. Mickey thought about Inga and stumbled to a stop when their formation came to a halt at the fields where all the young people left their line to go to their positions of work.

Inga spoke to Herr Graef and said that she and Mickey would continue on to irrigate the new beans and peas that had been planted just a few days ago. When they arrived at the area, she led the way down one of the bean rows toward the new pump and generator.

Suddenly, Mickey heard the whine and roar of two American P-47 fighters. They were still half a mile away. The two aircraft were diving toward the area with their wing guns flashing like orange lights.

Mickey reached out and caught Inga by the shoulder, pulling her down to the ground and into a furrow between the newly planted beans. The dirt was falling all around them as the two fighters roared over their heads, barely twenty feet above. Inga tried to raise her head, but Mickey held her down, shouting, "Don't move, there will be more!"

After a minute or so Mickey raised his head to have a look. The two fighters had climbed up and were starting a circle that only meant they would make another attack. He saw that back up the road, at the location of the potato fields, that the harvesters were running toward the edge of the fields, leading toward the bordering hill. He raised himself to a kneeling position and started yelling for them to lay down in the fields. It was wasted effort because they could not hear him and kept on running for the hillside and its protection.

The second attack came with the aircraft spread farther apart across the width of the valley. He and Inga were between the paths of the two aircraft and he could raise his head with safety and see the destructive strafing action of the planes. One of them had found the small building used for a tool shed and its supplies. The other hugged the opposite side of the valley where the children had run to.

The small building was torn apart and set afire. Tools and supplies were destroyed. There was a fire burning at another location. Mickey thought it might be the post office. He could not see what had happened on the opposite side of the field.

With the last bomb run both fighters kept on going straight up the valley toward the heart of Germany. Inga was sobbing and Mickey helped her to her feet. She was trying to brush the dirt from her hair and face.

Pointing to the deep marks on the ground from the 50 caliber bullets that had struck ahead and behind them, he said, "They nearly got us!"

Inga started to shake and spoke in a frightened voice, "This has happened to me before, but not here in the fields."

Mickey pulled her toward the road and said, "We've got to see how the others are!"

They both ran back up the road toward the potato fields, the location where twenty young girls, supervised by three, older women had been working. There was screaming and crying. It all came from the south side of the road where the potato crops were growing.

Mickey ran into the field. He saw three bodies on the ground. The first one that he came to was one of the little girls. Her body had been riddled with bullets; the top of her head was blown off. Mickey lifted the body, placed it in the cart, and covered the lifeless young woman with his coat. He spoke with Inga for a moment, then led everyone back to the village.

Mickey and Inga took the cart handle and pulled it down the dirt path to the village. Inga explained to Mickey that their small area had not received more damage because it was hidden beneath some large trees. There was camouflage on the roof top that had provided protection too. The fire had burned out in the little post office building and with a little carpentry work it would be good as new. They would rebuild the tool shed, most of their equipment had been in use in the fields at the time of the attack, so all was not lost.

After they got to the main building they had moved the two wounded women inside and made a place for the dead girl. Herr Graef talked to everyone and explained that tomorrow there would be a person on lookout to warn of any other attacks.

A small ceremony was held that evening before dark for the girl who had died that afternoon and she was buried at the edge of the small village near a beautiful tree.

It had been twenty-four hours since the attack on the convoy. "At dusk we should go down there and see what we can salvage. I think it is best that we stick together." Stan put the signal mirror away in the pocket of his flight suit and told Brad, "We should inspect this area before leaving, be sure we have covered our tracks. Just as soon as the sun drops below the horizon we will move out. Remember, nothing above a whisper."

As the sun dropped below the mountain ridge opposite them, Stan led the way down a small canyon that ended near the site of the destroyed convoy.

When they reached the bottom of the hill they found the road that had led the German's to their death. Stan stopped and pointed to a badly damaged truck that had managed to pull off the road before it had been hit. The driver's and one other soldier's burnt remains were in the cab.

"They never knew what hit them," said Stan.

On ahead were five other burned out vehicles. Two were still smoldering and the bodies of many soldiers lay on the ground where they had fallen and died. Some of the bodies were missing arms and legs and even a head. There was blood everywhere. The destruction had been complete.

It seemed vile to Stan and Brad that they should benefit from the deaths of the German soldiers, but maybe there was some good too, in that they would have a better chance at life with so much death and destruction surrounding them.

They had to move quickly and both men started to take knapsacks off the dead. They looked through one of the trucks and another smaller vehicle for things that would see them through some of the days ahead.

Down behind one of the trucks they started to step over one of the bodies. The man opened his eyes and said, "Helfen sie mir, bitten." Neither of them knew what he had said, but out of fear Stan knew what he had to do. If there was any chance that this injured man might give their presence away he had to be done away with. Stan picked up a jacket that had been blown out of a truck and held it tightly over the German's face until he was sure that he was dead.

Just at that moment the sound of another vehicle was heard up the road.

Stan threw the jacket off in the distance and both he and Brad grabbed the knapsacks they had taken from the dead and headed for the safety of the trees and brush up the hill.

Stan caught Brad by the arm and whispered, "We are not safe yet. Don't make a sound. I hope what we have here was worth the risk we took to get it!

The two men climbed farther up into the hills and got to a spot where they had some view of what was happening below. They rested a few minutes and Stan peered over the edge of their retreat. He could see two trucks and a trailer parked off the road near the devastated convoy. There were about six soldiers and they were lifting the bodies of their dead comrades and putting them into the trailer. Two of the German's made what appeared to be a search of the area around the burnt out trucks and then they all got into their vehicles and headed back in the direction from which they had come. It was well after dark when the trucks and the sound of their engines faded away.

After things got quiet Brad whispered, "Did you see that poor son of a bitch? I will never forget what happened down there."

"He was nearly dead, I just finished the job. We could not take the chance that he might give our position away. That was a rescue party, we can only hope they didn't see or hear us when they arrived. I had hoped that we could leave here sometime today, but it is too dark now to even check out the contents of these bags. Let's rest for now and at daybreak we will pack a few of the things we can use and move out."

"Sounds good to me Stan," agreed Brad.

They were tired. The swift movement down and back up the hills had taken its toll. They had not eaten much for two days now. Hopefully there would be something substantial in the lute that they had taken from the Germans. They each put a knapsack under their heads and slept. Stan rested lightly; he was used to that and he was sure he would hear the slightest noise.

Dawn came quickly and they both were awake. They shook the contents of the bags out and found a half a dozen small cans with the words "fisch and reis" printed on them. There were several pairs of socks, a couple of jack knifes, a first aide kit, and two or three apples. There was a book of poems and a silver crucifix on a chain.

Brad exclaimed, "One of them was a Christian!"

Stan used the knife to open one of the cans of food, "Better eat some of this, Brad. It will give us some energy for the morning ahead."

He checked one of the other bags they had retrieved and divided up the food and other useful items between two of the bags. He gathered up all the remaining things and stuffed them under some large rocks where they would be out of sight. Stan stood up and gave Brad one of the knapsacks and said, "Let's go."

"Just a word of caution," Stan admonished, "if we hear or see anything coming from either direction we will move off the road and into the fields or trees. Be sure you have your 45 in its holster. Don't shout or talk above a whisper. The 45 is only for an extreme circumstance."

"OK Stan, I understand," said Brad.

They carefully descended down from the hill that had given them protection for the last two days.

Stan said, "We will head up that road to the southwest and hope to make it into France in the next day or so."

Stan was in the lead and he gave Brad a thumbs up sign and said, "Good luck, Brad."

Brad returned the signal and said, "I think we are going to need all the luck we can get!"

EIGHT

After returning to the barracks from the mess hall, most made a visit to the latrine. There had been no privacy for the whole day. The plumbing system was in awful repair and by the time it had been used by many it was overflowing into the barracks. There was nothing anyone could do. They had asked that it be fixed, but that kind of a request was useless. The men were told to fix it the best way they could. Shorty had asked permission to cut a hole in the wall and he had been given some extra thick hose to use as a drain to the outside. It worked for a time, but eventually it became clogged and it was necessary that it be cleared. That became a job for some of the men who needed discipline.

When the men could settle down for the evening most of them went to their beds to sleep or talk quietly for a time. Conversations and subdued laughter could be heard throughout the building.

The man in the lower bunk next to Sacket turned to him and in a hard to hear voice asked, "What's your name, Sarge, and where was your home in the states?"

He did not wait for an answer and told Sacket that his name was Bill. "I come from Fort Worth, Texas. I have been here a little over four months."

Since Fort Worth was near his home and Bill seemed to be OK, Sacket reached to shake hands and said, "My name is Tony Sacket and I'm from Denison, Texas."

The two men grinned at each other.

Bill said, "Well I'll be damned. It's a small world. Imagine meeting another Texan in a God forsaken place like this! You know, there are three of us here in Shit City from Texas now.

Scattered laughter broke out through the barracks. Another inmate approached; he seemed little more than a young kid. He sat down by Bill. "They call me Big D cause I'm from Dallas."

Somebody down a ways had heard their conversation and shouted, "Boy will the bull shit get thick now when you three guys get together."

Bill said, "There's a lot to learn around here and we will all try and help you."

Hob nailed boots sounded on the front door steps and a large German soldier with his rifle held in front of him opened the door. He shouted, "All of you shut up, better get these men quiet Klein. Get this place cleaned up. It stinks!"

When the guard left the men all gave him the bird.

"Come on you guys," said Klein. "Let's not cause problems more than we got already."

A few men still sat at the table and most of the rest started their nightly effort to get some sleep on the bare boards of their bunks with their one thin blanket and a thin sort of pillow. As uncomfortable as it was, Sacket fell asleep within minutes. His rest was fitful and throughout the night he heard men crying or calling out to people known only by them. Next to Sacket where Bill slept he heard him call out the name of "Susan," followed by soft murmurs that were not audible.

Sacket was awakened by bright rays of sunlight on his face, then he heard the splashing sounds of water.

Bill swung his legs over the side of his bunk and tapped Sacket's bed with his shoe. "You had better get up and go on outside if you want to wash up. There is only so much water to use and it goes fast."

Klein called down the barracks, "When you're done washing take what water you have left and throw it on the latrine floor so maybe we can help to clean up that mess some."

Sacket saw what the others were doing and took a wash pan given to him by another prisoner and some water from the large barrel that had wheels on its base. Bill had pulled his flight suit down to his waist and was washing his face and arms in a pan full of water. Sacket followed his lead and found that the "pan bath" did make him feel better. He was really not over the cold shower he had forcibly been given on his arrival yesterday.

"You'll take your turn at this chore," said Bill. "You will get up before the others and take that barrel down to the water tank and fill it and bring it back for the others to use. It's summer now and it's not so bad, but when the weather changes and it gets cold, it will be another story. Klein will let you know what the schedule is and explain what you're to do."

Down through the barracks other men were starting to form into lines. Bill said, "Let's fall in. We need to get our plate and spoon."

While they were waiting in line Sacket got Bill's attention and whispered, "Can I trust Klein?"

"Yep, you had better!" replied Bill.

Sacket noticed the lead guard talking to Klein. Bill spoke softly out of the corner of his mouth to Sacket. "It looks like we're going to chow and then they'll bring us back here to go to the can, bet they got a real ball buster for us today. This is the way all the really bad ones start out."

The first meal of the day was about as bad as they got. Boiled cabbage again, roughly ground grain made into a soup and a hot liquid of unknown origin.

Bill said, "Eat it, it won't get any better." And so went breakfast.

They had fifteen minutes to return to the barracks and line up in front of the mess hall. In the return to the line toward the gate the first formation of thirty men began marching to another gate toward the back of the prison that led into the forest. One by one the other groups followed.

Each division had two or more guards, both in the lead and following. The guards carried their rifles with bayonets attached and the soldiers in the vehicles were equipped with machine guns called "burp guns."

As Sacket's group started its march to follow those ahead, he noticed that the first formation had already passed through the back gate. There were more men following. The pace was brisk and he could see that some of those ahead were having a hard time keeping up. The vehicles that were spaced between the units of prisoners were loaded with guards who were shouting out orders to the captives ahead.

Klein was passing the word back to his men in English. "For God's sake, don't fall down or slow up. It's only a couple of miles more!"

The company slowed down and then came to a sudden stop. Klein said, "Some poor son of a bitch up front has fainted and they have dragged him off to the side of the road."

The march started again and it wasn't long until they passed the fallen prisoner. Sacket saw a British airman lying on the ground, a guard was tying his hands and feet.

Bill said, "If the poor SOB don't die they will pick him up on the way back, but he probably won't make it. The Germans don't need any sick or lame prisoners."

Sacket could see that some of the men were limping and staggering. "Some of these guys were injured during their bailout or escape efforts before they were captured."

Finally the men felt paved highway under their feet and the company turned east and stepped off to one side of the highway. A command vehicle with an officer standing in the rear section moved along the roadway. He was giving orders in German, using a megaphone to each section leader who then passed on the word to the men he was responsible for.

It had become obvious to Sacket that each group leader had been chosen for his ability to speak and translate German so that he could communicate between those who were in charge and the prisoners.

Klein spoke to his men, "We are here to repair a bridge. The Germans will tell us what to do and they want it done by tonight! The officer says anyone that tries to escape or shirks his duties will be shot. The sooner we finish this job the sooner we will return to the comfort of our quarters. They say the allied swine that destroyed this bridge with their bombs will only kill their own people if they attack while repairs are being made."

Two trucks with shovels and picks arrived and the guards started handing out the equipment to their captives. There were wheelbarrows that were given to every fifth man.

Sacket's group was ordered up to the sight of the destruction and the group started an endless procession of wheelbarrows filled with rocks and dirt to fill up the bomb craters at the entrance of the bridge.

The German engineer who was the foreman for this work was barking orders to Klein and the other platoon leaders. Sacket had been chosen to push the wheelbarrow to and from the spot off the road where the rocks, stones, and dirt were being collected to the position where they were needed at the bridge repair sight. The only rest or relief that he got was when Klein told him he would trade the wheelbarrow for a shovel that another man had handed him.

Klein said in a quiet tone of voice, "It might make you guys feel better to know that so far this morning several hundred allied bombers have flown over us heading farther into Germany, none of them have tried to bomb this bridge that we are rebuilding."

Sacket stopped and took a long look around him. In the fields on both sides of the bridge, American and British POWs were laboring with difficulty to do what their captors wanted. Watching their every movement with their weapons pointed directly at them were the Germans. The nearest guard with his bayonet equipped rifle moved toward the unproductive Sacket.

Klein shouted, "Get your ass back to work or you will be stuck in it like a pig!"

Sacket moved as fast as he could to keep from being jabbed in his rear end with a bayonet. He started shoveling dirt into the next wheel barrow ASAP. The guard shouted something in German and returned to his observation spot.

When the sun moved directly overhead, a truck with a water tank moved slowly up the line of working men. It stopped every five minutes while the workers shared one of the ladles that was being used to drink from. A basket with stale bread crusts was passed to each group of men, this was considered the noonday meal. The order was given, "Take a piss and get back to work on the bridge!"

Sacket could see that a lot had been accomplished. The two sides of the bridge were coming closer and closer together.

Bill, still shoveling, yelled at Klein, "I have to go to the john, got to take a shit, what do I do?"

Klein motioned to the guard and told him what Bill had said. Laughing, the soldier pointed to the ground.

Klein said to Bill, "Dig a hole and shit in it, but don't take too long."

Sacket said with sarcasm in his voice, "Some people will do anything to get out of work."

The sun was dropping to the horizon and the gap had closed between the two banks of the small creek. A truck crossed the bridge several times, packing down the soil and rocks.

The officer, in his command car, crossed the repaired bridge, turned around and crossed it again. The Germans all gave a cheer while the prisoners muttered to themselves.

The officer said through his megaphone, "We have finished another troublesome task for the Fatherland, Heil Hitler." A cheer by the guards finished this day's unjust German accomplishment.

The return to the prison camp was a disheartened, tired march. At the point where the sick British airman had collapsed in the morning every British and American airman saluted him. He had already been removed. Was he dead or alive? None of them ever found out.

The mess hall had its usual disgusting smell, that of something burnt. Everyone forced down the over boiled potatoes with some sort of a grasslike vegetable on top. The lukewarm substitute for coffee was barely palatable.

Sacket pulled the threadbare blanket over him as he settled down on his hard wooden bunk. There was silence throughout the barracks as each man collapsed into sleep.

For the past two weeks Mickey had spent at least ten hours a day cultivating and irrigating the potatoes and bean crops.

Inga kept reminding him that they were very important food items and that many people counted on them for their very survival. The weather had been very good and the plants were growing well. In another few weeks it would be time for their harvesting.

Inga never lost sight of him from dawn till dark. She was there working beside him most of the time. Every hour or so she would ask him to stop for a short rest and they would have a drink of water. He was permitted time to go to the toilet. He could go fifteen or twenty yards toward the trees and that did afford him some privacy.

The prisoner and the warden, so to speak, had some very interesting conversations while they were on their rest periods and Mickey found himself becoming very attracted to this young and knowledgeable German girl. She had a wonderful voice and smiled most of the time. She was very well built and in excellent physical condition. Even though she wore coverall type work cloths and boots, she seemed very feminine. She was tall, but he was taller by several inches. She had light blond hair and blue eyes. Under the work dress he was sure she had a very desirous figure, full busted with soft white skin. Her lips just begged to be kissed.

After falling asleep these last few nights, he had dreamed of her, that he had touched and kissed her. His hands had caressed her body and had wandered over her thighs, and he had found himself growing with desire. Last night he imagined that she had touched him too and he had awakened with a sudden jolt as he came to a climax.

Mickey was young. He had dated some, but he had not been experienced in the ways of love making. He had been working very hard here and had become more relaxed in these new surroundings. He knew that his body had gained maturity and he was starting to feel some real excitement toward this girl that he worked so closely with. Was he falling in love?

"Mickey, are you all right? You got so quiet. You're not sick are you?" asked Inga.

He came back to reality and said, "No, I'm OK. Do you have a date in mind for the harvest of these vegetables?"

"It will be a week or so yet. They really look wonderful, don't they?" she replied.

They finished their work and headed toward the main building. After they had washed their hands and faces she was waiting for him outside his little room with her hands behind her back, and there was her usual big smile on her face.

"I have a surprise for you. Herr Graef has fixed your wrist watch and here it is."

She held the watch out for him and he put his arm out to her so she could put it on his wrist.

"Even your injured arm is all healed now," said Inga. Without saying a word he reached out, took hold of her shoulders and pulled her body to him. He put his face in the crook of her neck, for she had a certain fragrance about her that he could not resist. His face was close to hers, and he kissed her cheek and then her lips. There was no resistance from her and they clung together in a deep kiss and a warm embrace.

They were both surprised by their sudden reaction to one another, but even more surprised when they heard the voices of the young people and turned to find Herr Graef and Frau Miller standing on the other side of the room. Everyone had smiles on their faces and their happiness showed acceptance of this growing relationship between Mickey and Inga.

Mickey was trying not to show embarrassment and went to Herr Graef, with his arm raised. He had picked up some of the German language these last weeks and he said, "Danke, mein Herr, this means more to me than I can say."

The meal that night was very special. Everyone gave praise to those who had prepared the food of sausage, a special potato salad, and their own home grown strawberries for dessert. Somehow everyone was very sentimental and emotional. The children and adults showed their happiness, some with tears and some with smiles on their faces. Mickey kept looking at his watch and thoughts of his crew and his aircraft commander, Captain McCrea, flooded over him. Without shame he felt the tears run down his face.

Summer was coming to an end. The grass was turning

brown and the leaves on the trees were changing color. The young people around him seemed to have grown. Mickey had not been able to send any letters home. He had asked Herr Graef if he could write those he knew to let them know that he was alive and well and that he was being treated with kindness. Graef said his capture had been reported to the Allied Authorities by radio shortly after his capture months ago.

From the talk he had heard between the people around him he was beginning to understand that the war was coming closer and closer to an end. He had asked Inga what was happening, and she had said nothing. Every day now the number of German soldiers and civilians that passed through the valley heading east into the heartland of Germany had increased.

It seemed to Mickey that the air raids on the cities farther inland were more frequently heard at night. The sky was full of smoke that blew to the west during the day. At night the sky was alight with fires that could be seen for miles. Occasionally, a group of fighter planes would come roaring up their valley, but since that one attack, none had fired their guns.

Herr Graef was taking no more chances that anyone would be harmed. He had assigned someone to be a look out for those that worked in the fields. There was a mission type bell that was to be rung if there was danger of attack. It could be heard all across the valley.

The little village amongst the old trees was never attacked again and Mickey wondered if the Allies had been notified that children were present on these farmlands. They might even know that he was being held prisoner here.

He had discussed all this with Inga and she had said, "I hope that this is the case." She had also said that the German leaders would save a lot of their people and that there would be less destruction of their towns and cities were they to give up now before winter arrived.

Inga said sadly, "Most of us, including myself, have no home to return to, even if we should win this mad, unwinnable, destructive confrontation."

NINE

Stan and Brad left the security of their hills and entered the road below just after darkness took over the land. Both men had watched the cycle of the moon for the days since landing on German soil and they had calculated that it would be full sometime tonight. There was no cloud cover and the light provided by the now full moon would make their travel easier.

They had agreed that they would stay together, but would walk some distance apart so that if there should be an occurrence of danger they could be of some help to one another. Stan was in the lead and Brad trailed him by thirty feet or more.

After about a mile or so with no incidents they came to a fence set back off the road with a gate and some trees beyond, a house was maybe one third of a mile behind the fence. They heard the barking of dogs—thank God the gate was closed. The animals continued their baying. Soon they heard a female voice calling the animals, whatever she said stopped them in their tracks and they became quiet and probably returned to their mistress. If the woman had seen them she might have thought they were just some German soldiers heading toward home.

A few miles farther down the road, the valley widened out and hills were beginning to appear. To their right there was a truck farm and the trees became less dense.

The eastern sky was bright from the light of the large full moon as it rose over the mountains from the east. Just ahead Stan spotted what he thought was a cross roads, then he saw a sign. Brad had come closer to him than their agreed distance, a good thing too because just as Stan started to cross the road to get a better view of the sign they both heard the engines of vehicles coming toward them from the north. Stan grabbed Brad by the shoulder and pointed to the field to their right. Running and jumping across a ditch, they continued on another two hundred feet into the field. The tillage was a cabbage patch of mature growth that had recently been irrigated. They ran parallel to the rows. Stan stopped and hunched down into the muddy ground. Brad knelt down beside Stan.

"Not a sound and don't move!" whispered Stan.

The first of a fifteen vehicle convoy passed and came to a stop midway from their location. The voices of many excited German men could be heard. The word "schnell" was used over and over again by someone in charge. He was shouting orders in a loud demanding voice. He must be an officer, thought Stan.

Stan was on his knees and he could see the cars. They were parked, each packed full of bags and equipment. Would they never move on? There were loud discussions by the men as to the direction they would take. Finally engines could be heard starting and the convoy began to disappear into the direction that Brad and Stan had come from.

"They must be heading for home and safety," Stan said in a sarcastic manner. "It will all be over soon and they just don't know it!"

For safety the two airmen stayed silent for a time, then Stan said, "Let's get going. Use a cabbage leaf to wipe the mud off. I'm going over and see what directions that sign can give us."

Brad followed Stan and they walked up to the sign at the intersection. There were two arrows pointing to the south and one to the north. The top arrow pointing to the south said "SAARBRÜCKEN . . . 41 . . . K's." The other, pointing to the south, read "METZ . . . 85 . . . K's." The bottom arrow read "LUXEMBOURG . . . 79 . . . K's to the north."

Stan spoke in a normal voice as he said, "We will go left and try and make Saarbrücken and then Metz. It will take us three or four days if nothing slows us down. Once we are in France everything will be easier. Let's move on and try and find a place to spend the daytime hours tomorrow."

They had walked at a fast pace for three or four miles on this country road when Stan stopped suddenly and whispered, "Do you hear something, Brad? It sounds like someone singing."

They stood silently off the edge of the road and they both listened intently.

Brad whispered, "It is someone singing and in German too. It's getting closer to us!"

They walked off the road to their left, behind some bushes. Finally they could see.

"It's a German soldier. He sounds like he is drunk; he is staggering and really is not aware of what he is doing. He's not carrying a weapon, shall we jump him or not?" asked Brad.

"Hell no! Let the dumb son of a bitch go. He's heading home like all the rest of them!"

As the two fleeing men stood there not twenty feet from the road, the happy, drunk soldier staggered by, singing and faltering with every step he took.

Stan said, "I hate to admit it, but I actually hope he makes it home."

Several hours and some miles later down the road, the moon was beginning to move in and out of some clouds and the area around them became harder to see. Off in the distance the moon was reflecting on a small lake or pond.

Brad said, "Let's check that place out and see what's there."

They left the road and entered what seemed to be a footpath. The two men walked toward the still visible hills until they came to a grove of tall pines. There were wooden tables and benches scattered all around them.

"This looks like a park," said Stan.

Beyond the trees in a clearing they noticed some small buildings. They walked on to investigate. There were what appeared to be two public toilets. A little further on there were two other shelters grouped around a concrete gathering place.

A little distance farther by the light of the moon they saw another building at the edge of the lake, there were boats stacked neatly up and out of the water beside it. They were in good condition and had been well cared for. The grounds were clean and the trash cans were empty, no one had been here recently.

"Let's look around this place and see what we can find," said Brad.

They walked from one building to another.

"Got any ideas about how to get inside one of these places without breaking a window?" asked Stan.

"My Dad used to leave a key inside our electrical junction box at home," answered Brad.

They looked up and followed the overhead wires to the main building and saw that they ended at a small box on a wall.

Stan said, "I'll take a look inside." He got his knife from his pocket and started to take out the screws holding the cover on the box. Inside was a main switch handle, four rows of fuses, there were thirty two in all. There was a chart with the names and amperage for each of the units.

Stan handed Brad the cover to the box, then lit his lighter so that he could have more light to see by. He checked inside the box completely. "No key in here."

He turned back to Brad for the cover so he could replace it.

"Hey, what is this envelope?"

Brad tore the packet open and sure enough there were two keys, but which buildings did they belong to? Stan moved to the front door of the unit they were standing near and instructed Brad to shield the light of his Zippo and hold it near the key hole. He used the larger of the two keys, pushed it into the lock, it turned and the bolt released with a thump that was decisive. He pushed the latch handle down and gave the door a push and it swung open. The dark unexplored interior with its musty, sweet odor seemed to beckon them.

"Even if there was electrical current we could not use it, too dangerous. We will have to find some candles. Look in your pocket and find a candy wrapper to light so we can have a look around inside here," Stan told Brad.

"I have a bag of peanuts here. Let's eat them and we can use the bag," said Brad.

It took just seconds for them to down the peanuts and Stan held the Zippo to the cellophane. "Hurry and look around. See if you can locate some candles. This thing will burn fast!"

"There's a candle in a holder over there on that shelf," Brad said excitedly and took a few steps to retrieve the treasure.

Stan used the Zippo again for the candle and they placed the holder in the middle of a table.

"OK, so far so good. Brad, go outside and put the cover back on that junction box, just use two of the screws. When you're done, come on back and close and lock the door from the inside. I'm going to see what's here, just maybe this would be a good place for us to stay for a while."

While Brad was taking care of his chore outside, Stan made a careful inventory of the big room. He noticed that all the windows had inside shutters that would keep them from being seen by anyone on the outside.

Brad got done and he locked the door from inside and they continued their investigation of the room. It was furnished with benches and stools that were arranged around tables. The walls were banked with shelves, floor to ceiling. Other than a few carved wooden objects, the shelves were empty. They had to find something to eat soon, even if it was what they had left in their back packs.

In the right hand corner at the back, a small paneled room with a low ceiling had been constructed. To access the room they used the smaller of the keys they had found; it was a bedroom. There were two beds, a foot locker and a cabinet for cloths. There was a toilet and a wash basin in one corner behind a curtain. There was a large pitcher to help flush the toilet.

Brad laughed, "I'm first on the john. It's been a long time since I last used one."

"I don't see any toilet paper, but here's a telephone book that is half used," remarked Stan. "All kidding aside, Brad,

we are not sure we have running water. We may have to
carry it from outside someplace. We won't use the indoor
plumbing for a while. A bush will have to do. Be sure not to
leave any paper around outside," directed Stan.

"We'll try the beds out tonight, but we still need to stand
watch. I think this is a safe place to hide for now. We don't
want to get over confident. Because of the war this park has
been shut down and not used for some time. I think it best
to continue to use these candles for now. If it is safe in the
next day or two, maybe we can open one of the shutters
during the daylight hours. From the dust on things in here it
looks like it's been weeks since anyone was last here."

They decided to eat one of their rations for the night;
they were tired and needed some sleep.

"You sleep first, Brad. I'll take the first guard."

Brad sat down on one of the cot-like beds. It had blankets
that would be warm and comfortable.

Sacket was cold and shivering when he awoke. "Damn these
cold boards don't get any softer in this Kraut hotel!"

Another voice farther down the barracks complained
about the cold morning air. It was the first day of fall and
soon winter would arrive. Several others cursed the Germans,
the war, and their prisoner status.

Klein was up and shouting at all the men he was
responsible for. "It's only going to get worse. Last winter
nearly half of the guys in the barracks died of pneumonia
and malnutrition. Five men were killed by the guards when
they tried to escape. In the year and a half I have been here
nothing has improved. The only chance we have to get out
of this God damned prison alive is for our troops to hurry up
and win the war!"

"There is some good news," said Klein. "Our armies are
about one hundred and fifty miles west of here and the
Germans know that they are losing. It's Hitler and his diehard

Generals who won't stop this suicide attempt, they just keep fighting. I am your leader here and I speak and understand the German language. I hear the guards talking about what they want to do. Some of them want to surrender to save their own skins. Don't be surprised if they become very friendly and don't trust anything they say or do!

"I can talk to you here in this barracks this morning without being overheard by their spies or their electronic devices, do you know why? The electrical power to the whole prison has been out since late last night. The lights on the fences and the guard towers are all off for the first time since I arrived here. They have every walking son of a bitch German guarding the gates and the fences. Take a look out the windows and see for yourself. Even the guards that usually watch this building at night are walking the fence line right now. As soon as the sun is up you're going to see some changes around here, so let's all get up and be prepared for whatever might happen." It was the thought of freedom that inspired Klein's speech.

Sacket noticed that everyone was up and talking in normal tones of voice. Some were even speaking louder and this was very unusual.

Klein called out for them to hurry and get outside. "Fall into formation!"

The only guards that could be seen were far off and they were marching in small groups behind a jeep that carried an officer and a sergeant.

As the sun began showing itself from behind the surrounding forest, a command car with at least fifty marching guards started down the main street of the prison. The Commandant, Colonel Hibner, rode in the rear of the vehicle.

The Colonel halted the procession in front of the prisoners and spoke out in the voice of a well educated English gentleman. "Because something new has come up concerning your status as prisoners, I am going to have all of you remain in your quarters today and maybe for a longer time if it becomes necessary. Your meals and personal needs will be confined to the area in or around your quarters. The

rules and laws as were previously explained to you will be
closely observed and anyone found guilty of breaking any
law will be severely dealt with. Your guards will be
authorized to take immediate action. Any act of disrespect
or any violent behavior will be grounds for painful
punishment. Any attempt to inflict injury or death on any
of my command will mean death to the offender. I would
suggest that none of you try to escape as that would mean
the cross in the court yard and starvation until death. I hope
that we can coexist without any painful or deadly
consequences."

With his last statement to the prisoners, he ordered two
of the guards to position themselves in front and at the rear
of each barracks.

The guard nicknamed "Fatso" by the prisoners had been
ordered to the front of Sacket's barracks and he immediately
started to converse with Klein. He was trying to speak
English, but was unable to carry on the conversation for long
and he finally switched over to his own German language.
His voice was no longer harsh and commanding. Klein
seemed to grow taller and stronger in his appearance and his
tone of voice.

In a few minutes Klein turned to his men and dismissed
them with the order that everyone was to return to their
barracks.

After everyone was inside Klein stood by the front
entrance and spoke to the curious men in his charge, "Yes, I
think Fatso and his fellow guards have seen the handwriting
on the wall. Last night a commando raid on the power plant
up the road wiped out the electrical power to this whole
area. I heard one of the guards say it was the Frenchies and
the American Jews who did it. We have to be real careful
about what we do or say to these crazy Germans. Some of
them will be really pissed off and will be looking for any
excuse to waste any or all of us. It's going to take some more
time and patience to come out of this in one piece. I was
told that there would be food in an hour or so."

Before dark a truck and trailer with six German guards
and four of the cooks from the mess hall came down the

main street and stopped in turn at each of the barracks. The loudmouth cook that everyone despised ladled out a cup of near cold cabbage soup with a piece of hard dry bread to the prisoners in Sacket's barracks. He said, "This will have to do for all the pigs tonight!"

One airman called him a "lard ass Kraut" and threw the soup in his face. The German called the guard beside him and the prisoner was taken outside and cuffed to the wooden cross in the yard. "That will teach him a lesson he won't forget," taunted the cook.

There was nothing any of them could do for the airman, and they would have to look at him and in a sense would suffer the punishment along with him. The night was colder and when daybreak came his body was gone.

The next morning a guard from the headquarters building arrived at barracks #18. It was the clerk that Sacket remembered from the Colonel's office.

He spoke out in a loud voice to Klein, "We have come for the American prisoner, Sergeant Sacket. We will take him with us now!"

Klein beckoned to Sacket, "It looks like the Colonel wants to talk with you. Watch what you say."

Sacket got to his feet and said, "I'll bet it's that God damned Colonel's meeting he spoke of the day I first got here."

Klein said in a low voice, "Be careful and don't kiss his ass."

The clerk told Sacket, "I'll give you ten minutes to make yourself presentable. Try and act cordial, the Colonel wants to speak with you."

While Sacket was cleaning up, Klein said, "Do you need me for an interpreter?"

The clerk said, "That's my job, hurry your man up, it's time to go!"

While Sacket was being marched to the building by the main gate his mind raced with possibilities that might lay ahead. What have I done? What does he want with me? What will the other men think I am doing?

The clerk opened the door and marshaled Sacket down

the same long, dark hallway as he had done on the first day
of his capture. The door at the end of the hallway opened on
the guard's command and he was led into the mysterious
inner office of Colonel Hibner.

Sacket was seated in the same chair as before. He noticed
that the room was illuminated with candles, for there were
no electric lights. The Colonel was seated behind the massive
desk in his chair with his back facing the desk. This too was
the same as the first day, and there was again the aroma of
cigar smoke.

He slowly turned his chair to face Sacket and began by
speaking in a friendly manner. "Before you and I get to the
business of you and your comrades' futures, let me give you
a cup of tea and a cigarette."

There was no chance to respond, the clerk had poured a
cup of fragrant tea and had placed it on a small table beside
him, cream and sugar were offered.

"The tea, cream and sugar with a cookie of my choice
are saved for my guests and myself," said the Commander.
"As soon as it pleases you, have one of my special German
cigarettes."

Sacket tasted the wonderful hot tea and for a moment
his mind raced back to the time many years before at his
grandfather's home, it would be far removed from this
afternoon's tea party. What ulterior motive was here?

The Colonel rambled on about his wonderful experiences
as a young student about Sacket's age. "Most of my education
was gained at universities in America and Great Britain. I
will never forget those days of opportunity and culture."

After a long pause, he spoke in a quiet, tired voice. "What
will become of us all? I am a practical man and I can see
what may be an end to this conflict. Our gallant soldier's
and countrymen have suffered and now they grow tired of
the endless sacrifices that they have endured. The reason I
have called you here, Sergeant Sacket, is this. If you and I
and a few of your intelligent young comrades that are here
in my charge would arrange a meeting with some of your
American officers we might find a way to peacefully
exchange your group of Americans and British for our safe

and orderly surrender. This would end in an honorable solution for all of us. Please tell me what you think."

Sacket could hardly believe what he had heard. He thought back to Klein's news about the loss of electricity and he realized that this might be the opportunity to bring an end to all of the nightmare he and all the others were going through here at Stallage Luft #31.

Sacket sat straight up in the chair and looked the Colonel directly in the face. He spoke softly and slowly, "I must have time to think this out and talk with some of the others. Give me two days and we will need an increase in food, really something decent for all the prisoners as soon as possible. I will return with three men and we will talk with you about a solution to your proposed plan for the future. Remember at least two days and some good food and we will see what can be done.

TEN

As time passed he realized that Herr Graef was actually protecting him from the pain and suffering of a POW prison. None of this had really been his fault. It was circumstance that had brought him to this place in Germany.

"We do have choices," Mickey told himself. "Was I disloyal and traitorous by staying here to help these women and children? Should I have insisted on being sent to POW prison? What would be said by those of his squadron and his friends and family at home, or for that matter the U.S. Air Force. How would they react? Would they condemn or understand the actions of Staff Sergeant Mickey Reber when this was over?"

Every day now there seemed to be more ragged German soldiers who were sick or injured coming up the road from the battlefields of war heading toward what Inga called their homeland. At night, under cover of darkness, small convoys of trucks and weapons of war were heading for the steadily moving Allied attack toward the east.

On several occasions retreating and incapacitated soldiers had stopped and were overwhelmed at the sight of this small complex with its crops and women and children. Because of their exhaustion some had asked to be allowed to remain in this small welcome encampment. Herr Graef would intercede by praising the soldiers for their determination to return to the Fatherland where they could receive the care and food they needed and deserved.

He would always say later, "God be with them," and he would explain to those he was responsible for, "we cannot care for them properly here."

As summer passed into fall Mickey and Inga grew very close. They were young and as the days passed they became more physically attracted to one another. It was evident that they wanted to share their feelings. They wanted to know more about each other's past. How far should their relationship go and what did the future hold for them?

One night when the evening meal was over, most of the young people had gathered outside, under the big trees, to sing songs and tell stories of their families before the war had separated them. Some of the married women spoke of their lives with their husbands and children and wondered if they would ever see them again. Most all of those in the camp thought the Germans would surely lose this war, but they were afraid to express their thoughts of an Allied Victory. There were always the questions, "Where will we go when this war is over? How will the American and British treat us?"

That night Inga and Mickey sat together. Inga looked at him and said, "It is time you know more about me. I hope you will understand why I am here with these people."

In a whisper, Mickey responded, "Your life is important to me Inga and I agree that it is time to share our thoughts with one another."

Inga took Mickey's hand and said, "Let's take a walk." They got to their feet and Inga led the way toward the open fields where for the past months they had worked so closely together. A half moon shown in the sky and they were away from everyone.

Without any explanation, Mickey picked Inga up in his arms. Immediately her arms were around his neck. He walked toward the reservoir that they had built together. When he had gone some distance and he was sure they were out of sight of curious eyes he gently put her down and pulled her body to him. There was that intoxicating fragrance again, he was sure it was natural as there would be no place for her to get perfumes. He put his head on her shoulder, his hand was at the back of her head against the thick braid of her blond hair. Her hand caressed his neck and then reached as far as possible down his back under his clothing.

They held each other. Both had been filled with desire for sometime now and it was doubtful they could control themselves any longer.

Mickey was tall, with broad shoulders, sandy brown hair, and had gray-green eyes. He had a narrow waist and small hips. His body was strong and appealing. He had striking features and was by anyone's standards a handsome young man whose body and mind had matured in these last months.

They kissed softly at first and then there seemed to be an urgency. "Let's go on to the reservoir and go for a swim," suggested Mickey.

In agreement she said laughing, "I'll bet I can beat you there," and she started to run from him.

He chased her and caught her at the pool, with the stars and moonlight shimmering on its surface. It was early fall and still warm with a soft breeze blowing.

Mickey said, "Please let me help you undress."

She said, "All right, but let's both take off our shoes first."

She stood before him waiting. Willingly, he unbuttoned the front of the coveralls she wore and pulled the top down over her shoulders.

Inga was tall, but he was taller. She was slim and with a small waist. She had well developed breasts, and her face was suntanned from her outdoor work, but the skin on her body was fair and smooth. Her hips were pleasantly full, her legs well developed but shapely. Her hands and feet were soft and clean. Her body was well cared for.

Mickey had dreamed of her breasts and her figure. He would never forget that night. Seeing her undressed, she was the vision in his dream. She unbuttoned his shirt and helped him to take it off. He undid the fly of his pants and slipped out of them. They stood there before one another, stripped naked. It took a minute or so to recover from the sight of each other's bodies.

Inga turned and slipped into the water and he followed her. They swam under the pool and surfaced, letting their bodies come together as if they were one person.

"Oh Mickey, I love you so much, don't doubt what I have said. Please make love to me, my body aches for your touch."

Mickey kissed her lips and pulled her to the side of the pool. He got out first and reached to help her up the bank. When they reached the grassy area, he pulled her down. They laid close to one another and explored each other's bodies.

His fingers went over her breasts, down over her stomach and then he was kissing the areas he had touched. His fingers touched her thigh and they slid up until he felt silken hair. Then his fingers moved down and touched a special spot. Mickey could feel his erection growing. She reached for him and felt it too. She positioned herself and guided him into her.

When they had both shared the delight of their climax they just relaxed in each other's arms.

Mickey wondered if Inga had ever been with another man before this. He lacked experience in the art of love, but with this woman to be with, he would have a good teacher. He was sure that he was in love with her. It was time for them to think of the future ahead of them.

They had been in this beautiful spot for little more than an hour and there bodies were dry and it was time for them to dress. Inga finished putting on her shoes and Mickey was smoothing out his cloths and had his shoes on too.

Inga said, "Before we return to the house we should talk while we are alone. I will not rest until you know all of my past."

Now that they had been intimate, it seemed right and honest that they should discuss their pasts with each other. They sat close to one another on an old fallen tree near the pond.

"Please let me be first," said Inga. She thought a moment and began her story. "My two brothers and I were born in a small town outside of Frankfurt. We had wonderful parents. Before the war in 1941 we were all very close, even though my parents both worked we spent as much time together as we could. Mother and Father were well educated and they were in the local political arena.

"In the late thirties my father was made the Bugermaster of our town. He was outspoken and against the Nazi movement and those that eventually became the leaders of

Germany. Even then he was appointed as an ambassador to Argentina. Arrangements were made for our family to move, but it was decided that we children would remain in Germany until the next school year started. My parents arrived in Buenos Aires just before Christmas of 1941.

"During the next eight months we received four letters from them. None of them were handwritten, all were typed. There were no signatures. None of the letters contained a word about their health, there was never any mention of their location or names of acquaintances. This was all so unlike our parents, especially our mother.

"It was in July of 1942 that we got a letter from the German Consulate in Buenos Aires. They told us that our parents had been killed in a airplane crash in the Andes. It stated that their few personal effects that had been found at their home would be mailed to us with more information about their death. The letter was cold and short, had no official seal. There was no address or person that we could contact for information.

"It has been over two years now and I have not been able to find out anything more about them.

"My brothers were inducted into the military service right after my parents left for Argentina and they too have disappeared. I have never heard from either one of them.

"Our country was in need of volunteers to help the many organizations that supported our cause. I left medical school and joined the Hitler Youth Corp. It was natural as most of my medical training had been with children. I had no real choice as Germany needed people in that field of work. Soon I was introduced to Herr Graef who had been put in charge of orphaned children. He has helped so many young people, especially girls. He has placed them in farming communities where they have been safe from abuse of all kinds. All those that work here in the country are providing the food that has been needed by our fighting forces. Nearly all men have been forced to fight this war on the borders of Germany. Only the very old and sick have been excused.

Most of us here do not agree with our leaders or the Nazi movement. It is destroying our country and thousands of human lives, but to resist the Nazis is suicide as there are many Germans who still agree with Hitler and his followers.

"All I want now is to come out of this terrible war alive. I am alone in this world and whatever lies ahead I will do the very best I can to make a good life for myself and those I share it with."

Inga took a deep breath and turned toward Mickey, there were tears in her eyes and on her cheeks. "The story I have told you relates to the loss of my family and why I am here working with Herr Graef, but there is one more unpleasant thing I must tell you. Before I met Herr Graef and while I was in school I was forced to work to support myself.

"One night while I was walking home from work and returning to my quarters I noticed that there were some German officers coming toward me. I tried to avoid them, but they turned and followed me. I guess I seemed attractive to them and they insisted on taking me for some dinner. What could I have done? I had to go with them. After we ate they asked me to go back to their quarters with them. I said I would rather not, they said I had no choice and they forced me to accompany them. There were three of them," she began to shake and cry. "Mickey, all three of them raped me. I was a virgin. That is the only time I have been with other men."

Mickey put his arms around Inga and comforted her as best he could. "I am so sorry, Inga, you have suffered so much. I do understand all that you have just told me. Don't think any more about the German officers. It does not make any difference to me. I am angry that these men hurt you so. I would never do that to you or anyone else."

He dried her eyes and said, "Now it is my turn to tell you of my past life. I was born in Buffalo, New York. I am an only child. My grandparents came to the United States from Germany and Central Europe. My mother learned many of the German traditions and we practiced lots of them in our home.

"Although my grandfather came from Germany, he was an American and was not influenced by the frequent requests of the new Fascist German Government that started in the United States. He was determined not to have anything to do with what he called the 'new set of gangsters.' He used to say, 'The fools that follow these mad men will only aide in the destruction of the Germany we once knew, you would think that the last war would have taught them something.'

"I was a Boy Scout at age ten and was taught about fair play and honesty. Each summer vacation I attended camping trips to the forest of the northern parts of the United States. I worked on grandfather's farm some each year and earned money to pay for a bicycle and later earned money for my own car. Granddad taught me some about farming and promised one day that his farm would be mine. He was alive and well when I left the U.S., but who knows now?

"When I graduated from high school everyone wanted me to go to college to become well educated. They said that would prepare me for my future, so off to college I went!

"It was 1942 and I was a sophomore at the university. One day my best friend and I took our girlfriends to a dance across Lake Erie, there was a resort called Crystal Beach in Canada. We had a wonderful day and a big band was playing a lot of the new popular favorites. Lots of the songs were about the war and the men and women fighting it.

"It became very noticeable that most of the young men dancing were in uniform. The Army, Navy, and the Air Corps were well represented from both the U.S. and Canada. June, she was my date, asked me, 'When are you and your friend Don going to join up?' She squeezed me a little tighter and said, 'You would look so handsome in a uniform.' I guess Don's date, Midge, may have asked him a similar question because we talked about enlisting later that night, after we took our dates home.

"It was late that same night, we walked the streets, found a small coffee shop and talked about the glamour of the military until 6:30 a.m. A young sergeant who was waiting for his bus back to his base, had some time to kill so he came in for breakfast. We saw him and asked him to join us. He seemed happy to have company. His first question to us was, 'What are you guys doing out of uniform?' Don and I looked at each other for a second and I said, 'How do we join up?' The sergeant looked at his watch and, laughing, said,

'In about a half an hour the enlistment office will be open at the Post Office.' He wished us 'good luck, hope I'll see you both around.'

"College did not seem very important to either one of us any more and at 8:00 a.m. we entered the enlistment office at the Post Office. All the rest was a matter of standing in line, filling out questioners, taking tests and going home to face the wrath of both our parents."

Mickey turned to Inga. "Someday I will tell you the rest of my story." The moon was still bright and the glow of the early evening was still with him. "I do have one other thing to say. I have only touched one other woman. I have never been in love as I am now. Inga, before this beautiful night ends I want you to know that you're the most important thing in my life and if you will have me I want to be your husband."

Inga put her arms around Mickey and again there were tears in her eyes, but this time it was from happiness. When she could control her voice she put her head on Mickey's shoulder and whispered, "I love you more than I can say and I will be your wife."

Their evening ended in long lingering hugs and gentle kisses. Mickey went to bed with his thoughts of Inga and their future life together. It promised to be one of inspiring mental growth and a life long companionship that would be filled with physical pleasure, if their time spent tonight was any judge.

What a strange world this was, to go through so much and to have come so far to find the one girl in the whole world that he knew he could love and cherish for the rest of his life.

Inga fell asleep with thoughts of her future life with Mickey. She might go to the United States with him or they might even stay in Germany. What an ironic situation this had become. It was as though he had fallen into her life from the heavens. She knew that her life with him would be one of mutual understanding and growth in all things and certainly one of shared passion. She could still feel his touch from their early evening of love making and she could hardly wait until they would be together again.

A thought crossed her mind. There could be a chance in the near future that there might be a child. She would not mind because it would be Mickey's and she was sure that if for some reason he had to leave her he would return. They could have a beautiful son or daughter. Should she discuss this possibility with him?

ELEVEN

Stan and Brad had made the decision to stay at this Analgen. Stan had read about such places somewhere in his college studies. This was a place of rest for the upper class Germans, somewhere they could bring their families or friends to spend some time away from their regular duties and if necessary prying eyes. He felt that it would be safe and so far in these few weeks that they had remained hidden, no one had attempted to enter the area. They felt safe and it was comfortable, but the rooms were closing in on them and soon they would venture to the outside.

On occasion the two men had opened the shutter a crack on the front of their building. They had heard the sounds of numerous trucks, even motor bikes heading in the direction that they had come from. Nothing ever seemed to go east. There had been times when some of them drove into the Analgen and parked under the thick pine forest to hide during the day. Stan and Brad were always on the alert with their 45s, but so far no one had bothered them. Was this place Verbieten?·

The men they could see walking were the once proud and victorious Germans who were now tattered and unkempt. They all had a tired, beaten look about them. They were always looking into the sky, watching for the increasing Allied planes that came overhead daily. At times this was cause for alarm for Stan and Brad too.

Stan's anger was sounding almost paranoid and many times a day he would say, "Let's hope these stupid bastards will not forget who brought this hell back to them," and then he would comment, "They will forget and a new Hitler

and a generation of godless, selfish people will start
something like this war all over again." Stan had majored in
political science and he had some strong view points. "With
all of their education in the world of politics and science the
German people keep right on making the same stupid
mistakes right down through history."

One night a convoy of German antiaircraft guns, their
support equipment, and the men it took to operate the large
type 88s pulled up into the park near the highway. Stan felt
useless so far as the defense of his country went.

"I wish we had some way to wipe them out. We would
never have a chance if they knew we were here."

They both were awake all that night, wondering if any
of those Germans would investigate their location.

The next day at about eight in the morning the German
gun crew started the rapid firing of their guns. This went on
for over an hour. It must have had an effect on the Allied
aircraft above because there was a retaliation flight of A-26
Bombers that appeared. Because of their location it was hard
for Brad and Stan to see what was taking place.

When Stan heard the first run of the bombers he said,
"Get under one of these tables, Brad, and stay put until it's
over, just in case they overshoot their target. We will have
some protection if there should be a hit."

There were six low level bomb runs on the antiaircraft
gun emplacement. There were loud explosions and the
building shook violently and then there was deafening
silence. It was Stan's guess that the German defense near
the road had been totally destroyed

"It's over," he said.

Later that day, after sun down, a small group of retreating
trucks stopped at the scene of destruction. They lingered
only a few minutes.

The next morning, Stan unlocked the door and cautiously
looked out. Everything was quiet, but there was smoke in
the air and the offensive odor of burning flesh was present.
Cautiously Stan moved up to the smoldering mess. All that
remained were dead bodies and blown up equipment. The
newly used allied weapon was napalm. Between that and

the rockets, the charred dead lay where they had fallen, nearly everything else had been consumed by fire.

Stan returned to their building. "They clobbered them with napalm. They didn't know what hit them. I guess it was a total loss because the patrol that stopped didn't do anything but look. The dead were still there, burnt to a crisp and nobody cared. Their mothers and fathers, wives and kids and friends will never know what happened to those men."

That afternoon Stan suggested they catch some fish down at the small lake. They had the boat house to shield them from view. They caught several beautiful trout, made a small fire, and cooked the fish on a willow stick.

"How much longer can we stay here, Stan?"

"The nights are getting colder and we are going to see it snow real soon," replied Stan.

The two men had searched through the building they were hiding in and had found a large case of canned food. There were vegetables, mostly cabbage and beans. Since they had the trout that were abundant in the lake and always easy to catch they had managed to eat well. They had found a source of fresh water outside their location and carried that inside in a container that they found in the main room. So far neither had been sick, so they assumed their supplies of food and drink were good.

One day while fishing near the boat house Brad heard the voice of a German just outside the door of the building. Stan had trained him well; he stopped what he was doing and took a few quiet steps toward the half open door and looked through the hinged part of the door so that he was hidden. He saw a German soldier with his back to him, he was holding a hand gun and had it pointed directly at Stan. The German soldier was talking rapidly and pointing to the ground.

Stan was talking loudly, "I don't understand you," as if to warn Brad about what was happening.

Brad picked up a boat oar and without making a sound stepped through the doorway and with one swinging move pounded the outstretched arm of the German with the oar. The surprised German turned toward Brad. The blow on his

arm had caused him to drop his gun. Brad swung the oar
again at the soldier's head and the German fell to his knees.
Stan was on top of the soldier and had grabbed the gun from
the ground. Brad continued to beat the man on the head with
the oar while Stan stood up with the gun in his hand.

The German was lifeless; his head was a bloody mess. "I
think he is finished," said Stan.

Brad threw down the oar and stood there. He was shaking
and had a look of terror and panic on his face, "Oh my God,
I have never killed anyone before!"

"I'm sure he is dead and we have to get rid of his body
right now before more Krauts come around."

Stan shook his head and said, "You saved my ass, Brad,
but we don't have time for a funeral for this man, so let's
weight him down with stones and feed him to the fish."

They carried the dead German to the end of the little
pier and found enough rocks to fill his pants legs with and
tied the ends closed and rolled the corpse into the water.

Brad was still stunned by the whole incident. Stan led
him back to their building. "You stay here and be quiet, I'm
going to look around outside and see if our friend was alone."

Stan made a thorough cautious search of the outside area
and found the dead Germans only belonging. He had left his
motorcycle near the entrance to the park.

He had stopped there in search of fuel . . . Stan checked
the saddle bags on the bike and found handwritten messages
from the units of the battle fronts west of here. He had been
a courier taking the word of the war zone to the safety of the
headquarters farther east in the homeland.

Stan put the messages in one of the pockets of his flying
suit and pushed the cycle to the water's edge and into the
lake. He considered using the bike, but when he checked it
was out of fuel. It would have been of no use to them without
gas and it might have somehow connected them to the death
of the soldier if it was found.

When he returned to their hideout he found that Brad
was still troubled over his part in the killing of the German.
"Brad, you have got to realize that what you did was what
you should have done. You saved my life by doing it. What's

the difference in killing the enemy with an oar or the bombs we help to drop on them? You will always remember what we did, but you will realize as time passes that we were trained to do what we did. That man would have shot the both of us if he had the chance. The politicians back home will say it was making the world safe for Democracy."

"You're right, Stan, and we are here to tell the story and that man in the lake is dead!"

Somehow Brad seemed to change. In this first big confrontation of his life he had grown up.

The Colonel stood up from his chair and smiled at Sacket. "You know, Sergeant, an American prisoner does not tell me, the Commander of this Prisma, what to do!"

Sacket raised his right hand as in a salute and said in a quiet and friendly way, "I meant no disrespect, Colonel. I just want to say that if you and I are going to make the ending of this war more beneficial for all concerned you have to understand that there will have to be some change in attitude and principles by all who are concerned here.

"The prisoners are all very hungry and they are angry at the treatment they get from some of your guards. We all suffer from the cold at night. The smell of the barracks from the overflowing latrines sickens us. It is getting colder and we do not have the proper clothing. Some of the prisoners need medical attention now before they die and the rats have got to go!

"We have reason to believe that this war will end soon. What I am trying to say to you is your future and that of your staff will depend on what happens to the prisoners and their surrounding conditions, after all you're in charge here. I am sure that you understand what I have said. When I return to the prisoners with a promise from you to provide them with proper food and the kind of treatment your men would receive from the Allies if they were in our position, there will be a much better chance for you and your people to get the fair treatment from the Americans that you want when this war is over. The actions that you take in the next day or two will make the decisions for all of us."

The Colonel took a handkerchief from his pocket and wiped the perspiration from his forehead and in an act of contemplation he blew his nose. He stood there for a long moment, looking directly at Sacket before he said, "You can go back to your barracks and tell the men who you will choose to meet with me day after tomorrow that I have decided to comply with their requests for more desirable food and that I will give consideration to the other complaints that you all have."

Colonel Hibner called to the English speaking orderly and told him to escort Sergeant Sacket back to his barracks. "Sacket, you and the three men of your choice will be called back to this office in the time that we have agreed on. I would say that we both have a lot to accomplish in this next day or two. You are dismissed!"

On the way back to the barracks the orderly said in dismay, "I would never have believed that this could happen. What makes the Colonel act this way? He seems like he is afraid of something."

Sacket smiled and said, "He knows this war will end soon and he is sure that Germany has lost the battle."

As Sacket entered the barracks, Klein and its other occupants were waiting just inside the door. Klein excitedly pushed him to the table. They sat opposite each other and the others crowded around to hear what was going to be said.

Klein said, "The power is still off so they can't listen to us. Tell us what happened."

He told two of the men to keep watch over the front and back doors to watch for any curious guards that might have an ear out on their conversation.

"OK Sacket, what gives?"

"Things look good but, it is sort of complicated and it's going to take a lot of work," smiled Sacket. "The Colonel can see that Germany is losing the war and he is trying to soften all of us up for the rotten treatment we have had and our obvious dislike for his country. He asked me what I thought arranging a meeting with the Allies that would be of benefit to him and his men in exchange for the repatriation of all the prisoners here . . . What it all comes down to is that he wants to surrender to the Allies before there is a formal end to the war so that he can cover his butt. I told him that I would have to talk it over with all of you and the rest of the prisoners and our camp leaders, that includes American and British, before I could give him an answer.

"If we are going to do anything we have to move fast. There will be a meeting day after tomorrow in his office. There will be at least four of us. I told him that he would have to improve our food and living conditions and he agreed and it will start today. I did not give him any names, but I thought of you, Klein, as you speak German and have been in charge here and you have more time here than most of us. Then I thought the Senior Officer for both the American and the British would be best. Now, what do you think?"

Klein put his hand on the table. "I'm in favor of giving this a try. How do the rest of you guys feel, yes or no?"

All the men crowded in and around the table and replied in the affirmative. "Let's go for it!"

"Good ideas on those to attend this meeting, Sacket," complimented Klein.

Klein went to the front door of their barracks and called out to their German guard, Fatso. He explained to him that Sergeant Sacket had permission from Colonel Hibner to have a conference visit with Lieutenant Colonel Howard.

Fatso scowled in a disbelieving manner and said, "We will see about this," and he gave directions to another guard to see if in fact this was the truth. In less than five minutes the guard returned, vigorously nodding his head to the affirmative.

There was a short discussion between the guards and then Fatso approached Klein and said, "Our commander has given his permission for you and Sergeant Sacket to go to the barracks of Lieutenant Colonel Howard and you may go alone. We will not accompany you. I will notify our Commander when you both return."

The two men arrived at Colonel Howard's barracks to find that the guards who were usually posted there had already been notified of their Commander's permission for an intended meeting between these prisoners and their captive officer and that they were free to enter his quarters.

"Notify us when you have finished so that we can let Colonel Hibner know that this meeting has been accomplished," said the English speaking guard.

The first thing that Sacket noticed when he entered Building #10 with Klein was that there were all officers imprisoned here, even so there was very little difference from his own barracks.

A very thin tired looking captain met them just inside the door and asked, "What can I do for you, Sergeants?"

Klein took the initiative and said, "We have Commander Hibner's permission to speak with Colonel Howard. We need to see him now, it is very important."

"Come this way," said the Captain. "The Colonel has been sleeping, he has not felt well for the last day or so."

The group took a few steps down a very short hallway and at the first door on the right the Captain knocked on a door and entered the room without waiting for acknowledgment. The room was very small with a small wooden framed bed and one high window. There was one chair in the room and a small table, no other light except that from the window. The room was small, dark and dingy.

Colonel Howard came to a sitting position on his bed. He looked sick.

The Captain said, "These two airmen have permission from Hibner to talk with you. I am sorry to disturb you, but they say it is very important. They came to our building without an escort of guards and that is very unusual that they be allowed to do that."

It took a moment for the Colonel to gather his strength. Soon he got to his feet and said, "It is good to see you two, from the looks on your faces you do have something of importance to relate."

Klein spoke first and he introduced himself and Sacket. "It is important Sir. I am the Barracks Chief of Building #18 and I am fluent in German. I have been here in this prison for over a year and a half and would welcome any chance there might be to put an end to this damned war and have all the men who are imprisoned here to be set free to return to their families. Sergeant Sacket will explain what he has been told by the prison Commander and of some of the things that have been agreed to by both of them. Go ahead Sacket, tell Colonel Howard what happened today and why we have come to see him."

There was an hour of explanation by Sacket and some questions asked by Howard of both Sergeants. "When will we meet with Hibner? Do you have some plan in mind for the repatriation of these many prisoners? Can we trust Hibner? Will he carry through with his promises?"

"Only time will tell sir, anything is worth a try. He promised improvements today and if that happens we really think he is sincere," said Sacket.

"You two have acted very wisely and I will contact our British counterparts and let them know about the intended meeting with Hibner and find out how they feel about his desiring preferential treatment from the Allies in exchange for the return of all these men who have been so badly mistreated for all these months. I will contact you as soon as possible as I realize that time is of the utmost importance. I assume that we have authority to communicate when we need to," said Colonel Howard.

"I would suggest, sir, that when you are ready to see us that you ask your guard to give us the message and we will get here on the double, no matter the time," said Klein.

"I will do that, Sergeant. I do hope Hibner will improve both the prison conditions and the relations with the prisoners. To prove that he is sincere some different food, starting tonight at dinner would really help to prove that. I thank you both for your efforts. It is an outstanding effort and, if achieved, will be of benefit to all of us."

The news that something big was going down had already started to travel through all the barracks, American and British as well. The German guards assumed different personalities and they were seen huddled in groups throughout the prison grounds. There were smiles on their faces. The frequent entry and exit of the German guard personnel could be seen at the Headquarters Office.

There was an aroma of something different escaping from the mess hall that drifted throughout the grounds of the prison. It was definitely not the usual sickening smell of boiled cabbage. Several large trucks from the Quarter Master Supply Office were making their rounds dispensing large bundles of gray and green blankets that the men in the barracks had needed for such a long time. There were clean uniforms and boots of various sizes given to each barracks chief for his men. Hoses, like those used on Sacket when he first came, with a disinfectant so that the latrines could be washed down were laid at the door step of each barracks. Two doctors made the rounds of each building to check on men that might be sick. They administered medicine where it was needed.

It appeared that Hibner really was serious. The real proof came at dinner time when the men in line were served meat and potatoes. The servings were not large but they were adequate. There was an apple and some kind of a hot sweet drink that put smiles on the faces of all the hungry, near starving prisoners.

Sacket said to Klein, "It really looks like the old son of a bitch is going to keep his word. Look there, the mess Sergeant and his fat cat cooks even have smiles on their faces."

Everyone slept that night with the hope that they would soon be released and they dreamed of reunions with their loved ones.

TWELVE

After making his daily inspection of all the crops, Herr Graef found Mickey and Inga alone, just inside the tool shed. He had not deliberately spied on them. The shed door was partially open and he had heard them discussing some of their hopeful plans for the future. He had quietly retraced his steps back to his office. He was really pleased with this budding relationship. He knew that Inga, in all probability, had lost her family and that after the war's end she would not have a soul to return home to. It would be wonderful if she had found some one she could really share her life with.

He was fond of Inga and thought of her as a daughter, and since she did not have a father of her own to talk to, maybe it would be of comfort to her to have some one to confide in. The war was rapidly moving to a close and he felt that it was his responsibility to talk to her now.

He left the office and saw Inga and Mickey in the distance getting some materials to take back into the fields. He called to her, "Inga, can I speak with you for a few minutes?"

"Of course, Herr Graef," and she turned to Mickey, "will you please go on ahead of me. I'll be a few minutes. We have discussed our work for the rest of the day and you can go proceed with it."

Mickey smiled and whispered, "Don't be long, I'll miss you," and he took the small wagon and pulled it in the direction of the fields. All the while he would be in plain view of both Inga and Herr Graef.

Inga walked back to where the elderly gentleman stood and they both turned to face in the direction of the fields. They could watch Mickey as they were talking.

"Inga, I must tell you that I feel very responsible for you and the young people who are here in my charge. It is as though you are all my children and your welfare has become very important to me, so I felt a great need to discuss the future with you.

"I have noticed how well you and young Sergeant Reber are getting along. You two, working together, have provided an efficient irrigation system that has helped us to be more productive. Even in such times as we now live in some of us can find some moments of happiness." He was looking at Inga with a slight smile on his face.

She was thinking to herself that Herr Graef must have seen or heard her conversation with Mickey earlier and she felt like a child and she began to blush.

Herr Graef continued as if he were her father. "I am sure you realize that, as a young German woman facing life alone in this country, you would have many complicated decisions to make when there is an end to this war, and you know that it will be over soon. How will you and the Sergeant handle it? Have you discussed this probability with each other?"

"Herr Graef!" said Inga in surprise at the bluntness of his question. "I can only say now that I want a future with Sergeant Reber. He is the kind of man that I have dreamed about all of my life. Yes, we have talked about our feelings for each other and we are very much in love. I appreciate your interest and concern on my behalf. Please help me. I want your suggestions. I don't want to make any mistakes."

With this opening, Graef felt he could give Inga his opinions and fatherly advice. "Now is the time for you two to start making your plans for the future. Just remember, he is a soldier and he will have to return to his countrymen and whatever rules they set down for him. This may require some sacrifice for the both of you. When the time comes you must not delay his repatriation in any way, as his future will depend on its outcome. No matter where he is sent or what he is asked to do you must stay in contact with him. Separation will be difficult for both of you, but it will make or break your future relationship.

"I am sure that the other young people here can recognize a growing bond between you, but for now I would not discuss this matter with any of them. You must continue your normal duties and you may use my office on occasion so that you can discuss your future plans. When you do, the others must consider that it is strictly business.

"I have only the very best wish for both your happiness and your future together. You may tell Mickey that we have had this talk and that I have said you should both be very discreet about what goes on between you for now. You both have my blessing.

"Thank you for caring about us, Herr Graef, and I will talk to Mickey as soon as possible." Inga turned, and while she and Graef had been talking Mickey had drifted from their view.

Mickey had some work to be done in the upper potato fields that bordered the forest, he leaned on a shovel he had been working with and stared into the trees. The thought came to him that he could escape into the woods and make his way to the West and the invading Allied Armies. He was alone and for the first time nobody knew where he was. The daily gossip said that the Allied Armies were near the German border to France and they would be entering Germany very soon. At the upper end of the potato field there was a pathway entering the forest both he and Inga had seen it and had talked about it on several occasions when they had been working. She had once commented, "That pathway could be an escape route for you, but I hope you will forget about that possibility. I have heard of prisoners trying to flee. Our police and armies will stop at nothing to capture and punish escapees. Please don't try! Herr Graef and all of us think of you as a good and kind person. You have helped us so much by being here, we are all grateful to you. You are an American who has cared enough to sacrifice your own freedom for our survival and I have fallen in love with you."

Mickey stood and looked out across the small valley with its vegetable crops. On the opposite side of the valley he could see the young girls picking the beans while the older women put the filled baskets into a large hand cart that would be taken to the village for sorting.

"I have made my choice. I have been over and over this and now I have Inga to consider, we can have a wonderful life together."

He reached down and picked up the digging fork that was used to uncover potatoes and went to work as though he were attacking an enemy. He had to get all this indecision out of his head! The weather had been good and this harvest would be a really productive one. The first fork full produced many large, well formed potatoes.

The second digging was interrupted by someone running toward him. He stopped and looked up to see Inga, her hair was streaming softly over her shoulders. He laughed and reached out to grab her. She was flushed and out of breath from the long run she had made up the hill to his location.

"You're here," she said as she took hold of his arm.

"Of course I'm here," he put his hands around her waist and pulled her to him. He just held her until she had time to catch her breath and then they kissed. She was very warm and had that special personal fragrance about her that he loved. What a wonderful passion for each other they shared.

Inga became very serious. "Come over here and sit with me on the grass. I want to talk to you about the conversation I had with Herr Graef."

She told him about the concerns the kindly man had and of the advice he had given her and said, "It is time for us to make some plans for our future."

"I agree with all he said, especially the part about being careful while we are around the others. You can believe it or not, but while you were gone I gave our involvement a lot of thought and I too had decided that we should keep what is between us a secret. I am sure that the love we have for each other is real and that one day we will be able to share the rest of our lives together. There are bound to be lots of problems for us to settle and we will surely have to be separated for a time, but as soon as I am repatriated I will start to make plans for you to join me. Tonight I would like to have some writing material and I will make a list of some addresses in the U.S. and some phone numbers so that you will be able to contact me. I will speak to Herr Graef and give him my Headquarters Squadron and the address of my parents so that he can help you.

"I promise you, Inga, that I will make every attempt possible to communicate with you just as soon as I am free to do it. I want you to write down this address for me too. Does mail come here to the camp?"

Mickey and Inga felt secure in their relationship after their discussion. They would begin to make plans to be married and they would share a life together as man and wife. Inga would be a part of his family. She hoped they would like her. They would raise children of their own, they would be happy.

Their final kiss that afternoon was interrupted by the sound of a three plane formation of Thunderbolt P-47s streaking down the valley on their flight toward the coast and home. Although they had not fired their guns or rockets the effect of destruction was very clear.

Brad became more and more dependent on Stan's advice. It was as though he had become his teacher. Only once had Brad said anything about them killing the German soldier; it was an act of defense and he had learned from the experience.

The two airmen were thinking more about what they were going to do when the Allied Armies got closer to them, "Brad, we have winter coming on and we will have the problem of surviving the cold. We need to think about our food supply. Things have been great because we could depend on the fish. We can even do that when it gets colder, but it won't be as easy."

Neither Stan nor Brad had explored the park any further than the road or the area around the building that they had hidden in for the last eight weeks. They were both anxious to move out toward the Allied invading Armies.

"Oh for the day we can safely join our American forces again," Brad had said.

"I really feel we would be crazy to give up this place until it is safe. If we are not careful we could still be captured or killed by the Germans or even mistakenly killed by our own advancing troops. I think we should try and explore the rest of the park, farther away from the road," suggested Stan.

There had been lots of evening hours for the men. They had talked about their friends and families. Girlfriends had been a part of the conversation. Neither was seriously involved and, since Stan was the older, he had much more experience.

They had explored their futures and what they would do when they got home. Stan wanted to complete his education and was determined to become a lawyer. Brad had been to flight school and had been copilot on their last flight, but since he had seen the planes that had flown over them he had taken a great interest in fighter type planes and had said, "If we get out of this alive I'm going back to flight school and get into something really exciting! I'm really glad that I'm with someone who has had as much experience as you, Stan. I would hate to think of what might have happened if it had been someone of my age and expertise. You have saved our butts over and over again and I am grateful to you.

"Thanks, Brad. I appreciate your vote of confidence. Now let's think about what we will do in the next day or two!

"Across the lake there are some more buildings and I saw a road that headed into the hills beyond, there may be something important over there," said Stan thoughtfully. "We can take one of the boats across the lake. There will be a full moon tonight and that can help us in our search for another place to lay low for a while longer."

That evening, before darkness fell across the park, they shared a can of kippers and another can of beans. This had been one of the more tasty foods they found in their building.

When they had finished eating Stan said, "We will cross the lake and hide the boat on the other shore. Remember—"

"I know," said Stan, "no talking or unnecessary sounds!"

"Very good, Brad, you're learning a lot about lessons in survival," complimented Stan.

It took them only a few minutes to get one of the boats near the storage area and slip it quietly into the water. They each had an oar. Brad sat at the stern and used his as a rudder, while Stan sat in the bow and used a lot of energy to pull the boat through the water with as little noise as possible. It took them just a matter of minutes to get across the small body of water. They hid the boat in the willows along the shore and proceeded on to investigate the buildings that they had seen from a distance from the opposite shore.

"These are cabins," Stan said quietly.

The first one they came to had a small wooden sign up on the front wall near the door that read "EIN" and a name that read "GRUN HAUS." They walked further, following a winding road into the forest, passing at least another ten cottages. All were numbered and named like the first. The last number was "ZWOLF" and its sign read "RUHE."

The two men walked on a little further beyond the cabins and there the path opened onto a long narrow field that Stan estimated to be over a mile in length, as they came to the end they found what appeared to be a small hanger that was tucked back under some tall pines. It appeared not to have been used in months, as there were high grass and weeds grown up around its exterior.

With the brightness of the full moon they were able to see other objects. A tall pole with a wind sock stood out and shown white in the moonlight. A Nazi Swastika that had been painted on the sliding front door of the building was weather worn and faded. It was obvious that this was a small airfield and that it had not been used in a very long while.

Stan whispered to Brad, "Remember the name we used for this place? Analgen? It is a VIP private hideaway! Let's walk back to those cabins and see if we can get into one of them, might be a better place to stay hidden than where we have been."

They came to the last of the twelve cabins and walked all around the outside of it. It was shuttered with a lock on the door just like the main building across the lake. There was a difference, as there did not seem to be any electrical wiring with these units. They looked everywhere they could think of that a key might have been hidden.

Brad whispered to Stan, "Do you think the key to the other place might fit this door?"

Stan replied in a sarcastic voice, "That would be too easy, but we will give it a try."

He took the key from his pocket and pushed it into the lock on number twelve cabin. The lock clicked and sprang open.

"Well, I'll be damned," uttered Stan. "These Germans are champions at efficiency."

"They're thrifty too," said Brad.

Stan pulled the key out of the lock and he had to give the door a really hard push inward to get it open. The smell of mothballs and chemicals was strong and the interior was pitch dark.

"We will need some light. Brad, look around and find something that will burn easily. There are some small pine twigs on the ground over there. They will have pitch in them and should burn long enough for us to see something inside here."

Stan entered and used his zippo for some light and Brad was right behind him with the twig he had asked for.

"I brought some more too just in case we needed them," said Brad.

They got the twig ignited on the first try and they had time to look around the room. On a table there was a holder containing a candle. They got it going and there was sufficient light for them to search the entire room.

The objects that stood out most were large oil paintings. They were hung on three of the walls of the room. The subjects were men and women of the past. Their clothes and hair styles put them in the early nineteen hundreds. The rear wall had shelves and a cupboard. There was a small stove and a sink that took up one corner and both showed signs of having been well used. In the front of the room was a bed complete with blankets and pillows. It had been covered with a sheet to protect it from dust. There was a large painting over the bed.

"These paintings are real works of art, Brad, and they probably are very valuable."

Stan looked further for pictures and on the little table by the bed he found one of a man and his lady. The man was a German officer with medals on both sides of his chest. He looked familiar to Stan. In the cupboard they found a few bottles of what appeared to be very expensive brandy. Several boxes of matches had been placed inside a glass jar. They would have been safe from the dampness; that was smart. Salt and pepper and a container of sugar were found in glass containers as well.

"There seems to be only one room to each of these places. We have done a lot tonight and while we still have some moonlight, I think we should return to the place on the other side of the lake. We can talk when we get over there about what we should do, stay over there or move to this spot."

It was midnight and the moon had moved across the sky to the western horizon. They found their boat and noiselessly moved across the water to the other shore, lifted the little boat to its place, and walked to their building. They entered their hiding place and locked it up from the inside. Both men had become used to the darkness. It became easier to deal with after these months of adapting themselves to night vision.

Stan was always the last one to bed and the first up each morning. He took it upon himself to make the plans for each day and they did what he felt was necessary for them to do to prepare for the future. He never used the term "escape" because he thought of their positions as evasive. He kept reminding Brad that they were Aircrew Officers and that they should continue to think and act as they had been trained. Professionals.

"Hey Brad, I think it is about time we used the scissors and this razor we found to make ourselves presentable. We need to change these socks of ours and take some kind of a bath before we begin to rot. We can do that at lake side in the morning. I'm beginning to feel like a hippie with this long hair. How are you as a barber? I'm not much good, but

I can put a bowl over your head. Did we find some underwear in those German duffel bags? Take a look in the morning cause these I'm wearing are shot! I'll let you give me a shave and I'll do the same for you, even if we just even these beards up a little."

Brad had gone to sleep and probably did not hear a word that was said. "All in good time tomorrow," yawned Stan.

"That boy doesn't know it yet, but we are going over and take another look around at those cabins tomorrow. I've got a hunch we are going to uncover something really big!" Stan said to himself.

It was late afternoon and nearly all the prisoners had eaten and had returned to their barracks. Klein continued to hold his men at attention in front of the mess hall. He had sent a message by one of the guards to request permission from the prison Commander that they be allowed to meet with Colonel Howard and Squadron Commander Owens. This meeting was very important to all the men. Time is short and they needed every minute they could have. Sacket stepped forward and handed the guard a paper with the names of those who would be attending the meeting the next day.

In just minutes, six German guards returned with Colonel Hibner's orderly. He spoke in German to Klein "We are here to accompany those men who will be at the meeting tomorrow to the location of your choice. Other guards have been sent to escort Colonel Howard and Commander Owens to your requested conference."

Klein dismissed his men and he and Sacket turned and walked with the guards to Colonel Howard's quarters.

Just as they arrived Commander Owens and his aid came from the other direction and all six men formally greeted one another with appropriate salutes and then the introductions were made and, finally and less formally, they shook hands with each other.

A spot there in the middle of that field in front of us is suitable," suggested Owens. The other men agreed, but Klein asked to be excused. He spoke to the guards and asked that they be given at least fifty feet so that they could have complete privacy. In an attempt to be good-natured, the guard said, "OK, and good luck," and directed his men to move back the distance.

All those involved in this evening's important meeting formed a circle and sat on the ground. Howard spoke first. "I would like Sacket and Klein to explain how this all came about and of the request that was made by Hibner. Let's drop the formalities of rank as time is very valuable. Sacket, will you please begin."

"Yes sir," and he spent ten or fifteen minutes telling the story of his capture and ill treatment by the Germans. He spoke of the first talk he had with Hibner. He told of his last conversation with the prison Commander.

"I feel that he is certain that Germany will lose this war and he wants an easy out for himself and his men. In turn he is willing to turn over all the prisoners here to the Allies. To be blunt, he wants to save his ass!"

Klein commented on these last two days. "I have been here for over a year and a half. Up till now there has been nothing but cruelty. I am sure that you understand what I am saying. There has been a change in the way we are all being treated by the guards and officers. I am sure that this is because of the impending defeat of the German Armies and the Nazi Government.

"I believe that tomorrow we will hear of a plan that Hibner has thought up and he will expect us to help him present it to the Allied Forces before the war has officially ended. He has already mentioned to Sacket how forgiving and agreeable the American's and British have always been. He will have some sort of a plan to exchange all of us for a guaranteed surrender and he will hope that the action against himself and his men will not be as harsh as if he were to be captured and turned over to a war crimes court for inhumane treatment," commented Howard. "What is your opinion, Owens?"

"We must be very careful of these insidious Germans. I too have been interviewed by Hibner. For over a year now he has been searching for a weakness in any one of us that he could use to his advantage. Our military rules of conduct say that during war time we cannot promise the enemy any benefits without first getting authorization from our Commanders in Chief."

Commander Owens further assessed the prisoners' position. "Our welfare will be thought of only if it fits into Hibner's plans, but if he and his Command want to surrender to the Allies with our help we may very well be able to accommodate them. It is my opinion, like yours Sacket, that Colonel Hibner is scared and wants to save his own ass now, before the rest of Germany is defeated. He has a lot of pride and does not want his image marred. He will expect us to be easy on him and his men, especially when it comes to reporting the type of treatment these prisoners have received while in his care. Whatever happens tomorrow we must all be unified with our requests and not quibble over small details.

Klein stood up and was thoughtful. "It seems that we are all expecting him to come up with some sort of a plan. Should we have one of our own if we disagree with his?"

"Good point," Sergeant. "If that should be the case I feel that we could ask for one more day to make some sort of a decision. Do you all agree?"

Everyone said yes and that they felt Hibner was eager enough to come out of this as clean as possible and that one more day would not make a difference to him.

Commander Owens made the final statement, "Because Howard and I are in charge of our respective men, we will make the decisions for the rest of you, is that agreed?"

"Affirmative," said the rest.

After several hours the meeting between Colonel Howard and Squadron Commander Owens and the enlisted men came to an end. Klein called the German orderly and the guards over. "We are ready to return to our quarters. Tell Hibner's orderly that we are prepared to meet with him late tomorrow. Be sure that he is told that we all appreciate the improvement in the food and the extra things that he has done to make all the men more comfortable. I don't know if any of the rest of you noticed, but that torture device in the form of a cross has been removed from the front yard. Good night everyone and may tomorrow bring us all success!"

THIRTEEN

Since ten o'clock last night, after Inga had kissed him good night, Mickey had been locked in his room. She had secured him as her prisoner in more ways than one—he was in love with her. He had crawled into his bed and was soon dreaming of the beautiful German girl that was his captor. The sounds of voices from the large outer room had soon subsided and all was quiet.

A large sedan, the type used by German officials, and two soldiers on motorcycles turned off of the highway that ran in front of the valley and turned into this small community headed by Herr Graef. It was after midnight, sometime around two a.m.

The vehicle came to a stop at the entrance to the large stone building and the driver had honked the horn several times. The noise from the bikes and the persistent honking horn woke nearly everyone. It had been a strict rule made by Herr Graef that no children or adults would rise from their beds unless he asked them to. They were under his supervision and had complete trust in him; they would always follow his instructions.

Herr Graef was up. He put on a heavy robe and got into some slippers. He tied the belt around his waist and placed a Luger hand gun in the pocket of his robe. There came a loud knock at the door, it sounded as though the door were being struck with some sort of an iron object. He unlocked the heavy door and slowly opened it.

Two soldiers stood outside. They were armed and appeared to be very angry. "What is the meaning of this late night intrusion and why do you appear so hostile?"

The rear door of the sedan opened and out stepped an officer, "I am General Smitt." With a wave of his hand he dismissed the two soldiers at the door saying, "We are here in our country now and these guards and this driver of mine have been in France far too long now."

"I am Herr Graef, the Commandant of this children's refuge and state farm."

Walking up to Herr Graef the General extended his hand in a gesture of friendship and said, "I am on an important mission to the heartland of our country. We left the battle zone this side of Metz at sundown this evening. My men and I will be driving straight through to our Headquarters later this morning and we are in need of some food and fuel for our vehicles."

Herr Graef smiled and shook the General's hand. "You are welcome here and we will do what we can to provide you with some food and a little fuel. You must understand that we too have shortages. We have barely enough fuel to run the motor that operates our reservoir, and we have no electricity. All our food is grown on our acreage. We have over one hundred children that have been orphaned, housed and maintained here. Most are young girls. I will escort you to that small building across from us and the women will provide you and your men with a meal in our dining hall."

Graef got a lantern and led the five men across the street and showed them into the building that normally served as a storage place for the potatoes and other vegetables. He got them seated and poured them each a glass of cider. It was a national drink and a treat for these men. Herr Graef raised a glass with them and toasted their health and victory for this hard fought war.

As Graef left to return to the main building he overheard the General saying to his driver, "Make sure our gas tank is full!"

When he got to the main building he saw that Fräulein Reider and Frau Miller were up and dressed.

"We have some German soldiers to feed and they want what gasoline we can spare. They are waiting in the storage building across the street. Try and satisfy their appetites for food and I will give them a ten liter can of fuel. We want to hurry them on their way. Remember, don't get into any long conversations with them and nothing must be said about Sergeant Reber. Keep them out of this building! If they become a danger to you or to our facility call me immediately! Be very careful of yourselves!"

The two women and Herr Graef entered the storage house, they found their guests enjoying the cider.

"I'll have another glass of cider," spoke the General.

The two soldiers and the General's driver had finished their drinks and showed pleasure in their surroundings.

Inga and Frau Miller stepped into the small kitchen and began cooking a dinner of fried potatoes, beans, and a small amount of sausage. Soon the food was served to the hungry men.

One of the soldiers said, "We have not had a meal like this for a long time and we have not been around such beautiful German women as this since we went to France," and he looked at Inga with desire in his eyes.

Herr Graef said, "You will be glad to be back in the Fatherland. I hope you have good food and get lots of rest when you reach your home and your families."

"You have a full tank of fuel and Frau Miller has made some sandwiches for the rest of your trip. I know that you must be in somewhat of a rush," advised Herr Graef.

The General hesitated before speaking again, "I wish we had good news to tell you about our efforts to drive the Allies back into the sea, but because of the great losses of men and the shortages of equipment, our forces are being overwhelmed on all our fronts. Some of our leaders are ready to give up and stop fighting. We really wonder what we will face when we return to our homes. The leaders of Germany are fools and they are ready to abandon their country, they are not to be trusted any longer. We thank you for your hospitality, Herr Graef, but we must go now."

They took the extra food and boarded their respective vehicles and left.

One of the soldiers riding a motorcycle said, "With beautiful young women like that we should have stayed for the rest of the night."

Mickey had been wakened by the honking horns and realized that something unusual was happening. For the sake of Inga and Herr Graef he thought it best not to reveal himself. It was an hour or so before he usually got up, so he had time to give some thought to his actual repatriation. He must give Graef addresses and phone numbers and his home squadron in England. His thoughts were really confused when he considered having to leave Inga. How long would it be before he would see her again? With these last thoughts on his mind he fell asleep again.

He awoke suddenly and dressed as quickly as he could. The sound of the door being unlocked and opened was always at the same time as it had been since the first morning of his capture.

This morning he and Inga met in the doorway, but today Inga came inside his room and closed the door before she embraced him out of view of the others.

She said, "We must remember what Herr Graef said, be discreet."

"That's going to be difficult," replied Mickey.

Inga gave him a sweet but brief kiss. "I'll see you later up on the hill, Mickey Reber," and she left his room.

When Mickey entered the other room he asked, "What was all the commotion at the main door last night?"

Inga spoke in a louder voice than usual. Everyone in the room turned to listen to her and she told them all of last night's visit by the General and his three men. "While we were serving them some food they each spoke of how badly the war was going for Germany and they said the Allies were entering our homeland. The General even referred to his country's leaders as fools and deserters and said the German people had lost faith in their leaders."

"I have great concern for Sergeant Reber," said Herr Graef, "I think it is best for you to stay here with us until your countrymen arrive. These last days of the war can be dangerous ones for all of us. Our soldiers will become desperate and they will be a threat to the children and all of us who make our homes here. Mickey, until your American forces pass through here, we should all go into hiding."

Mickey agreed and said, "Now we must get all of the food possible in from the fields because the cold and snow will be here very soon. I noticed that the temperature got down into the thirties. If it goes any lower everything will freeze. We should all start to bring wood to the storage shed by the door for the fires that we will have to depend on for heat."

"Those are very helpful suggestions, Mickey, and we will get started as soon as we have finished breakfast," said Herr Graef.

"Herr Graef, can I have a word with you before we start to work?" asked Mickey.

"Of course. Is something troubling you, Sergeant Reber?"

"Yes, by this time my parents have to know that I was captured and that I was taken prisoner. When I am returned to the American Military Authorities I want you to understand that I will make every effort possible to communicate with Inga. Tonight I will give you some addresses and phone numbers for my family so she will have them for some time in the future. I will write to my parents and tell them what has happened here as soon as I reach my headquarters. I think I will be taken to France first. As soon as it is possible, I will start proceedings so that Inga and I can be married and, of course, I want to take her back to the United States with me. Please believe me, I have only her best interest at heart. I love her very much and I want to spend the rest of my life with her. It may be many months before we can see each other or even talk to one another. Please don't let her get discouraged."

Stan was the first one out of bed and inside their hideaway it was very cold. He could see his breath when he exhaled. He opened the shutter on the highway side of the building and he could see the falling yellow leaves from the trees outside.

The signs of winter's approach were everywhere and the colored foliage formed the clouds of winter's near cold spell.

Brad rose from his warm bed with his usual morning lament, "God, I wish that I was at home."

Stan looked over at his shivering companion and said, "Quit your bitching and let's get dressed! We have a lot to do today. It's cold outside, but we have warm clothes and food. We're lucky to have the necessities.

"It's not warm in here, Brad, but I've been thinking that it might be safe to build a fire in one of those cabins across the lake. The pines that those cabins sit under would conceal any smoke coming from the fire place. Let's go over there today and see what we can find."

The lake was not calm as it had been yesterday. It was violent with wind whipped waves, but they made the trip with little trouble and hid the boat again in the willows. Stan had made an anchor with some rope and rocks and they had secured the boat to an old fallen tree that was nearby.

They entered the pine forest that concealed the cabins and came to one near the center that they felt would be safer. One sign read "SIEBEN" other read "BEFEHISHABER"

"Don't have a clue what those signs say, Brad, but let's see if this key opens the door."

Brad took the key from Stan and put it into the lock. Sure enough, the bolt turned and as they pushed the door open there was the same musty odor coming from it as the other cabin they had gone into yesterday.

They had come prepared this time with candles from the place across the lake. With some light in the room they both stood looking around them in utter amazement at the sights in front of them. Three of the walls were covered with large and small framed pictures. Most of them were photographs.

The interior of this cabin was much the same as the other one, except that this one seemed to be better supplied with food and fire wood. There was even some coal. They started to look closely at the pictures on the wall and found that most of them were of military officers and group pictures of soldiers and navy personnel. Beside the front door was a large oil painting of Adolph Hitler. There were other, smaller paintings of notable people in Hitler's command. A small plaque over the picture of Hitler read "VATER."

"I'll bet that Hitler himself stayed here," said Brad. "There's a lot of things here that our Intelligence people will be interested in," commented Brad, "and my guess is that we are going to find a lot more for them to look at. We must tell the proper authorities about this place when we get back to civilization."

The two men checked out two more of the cabins, both were nearly the same on the inside except they did not have all the pictures as the one marked "SIEBEN."

It was getting colder and darker outside, so they decided to stay the night in the first cabin they had entered yesterday. It was supplied with some coal and fire wood and was warm and comfortable.

"How come you chose this one, Stan?"

"Because it is most central of all these buildings, Brad, and it's not as likely that someone would check it out. Just call it a hunch, Brad!"

After darkness had settled in on them, Stan built a very small fire, it felt good and it lit up the room. While Brad was bringing in some more fire wood from outside, Stan heated a can of beans mixed with corn.

Brad said, "That sure smells good!"

"It is different from what we have had in a long time," said Stan. "Let's eat and enjoy this sort of a celebration."

"Brad, while you clean up here I want to look around outside, try and find a good place to take a crap. You can do that too when I come back."

When Stan came back, Brad was filled with excitement, "I found something unusual and I want you to have a look at it."

"OK Brad, I think we are safe here. Other than a slight smell of smoke downwind of the cabin toward the lake you can't see any sign of the fire or any evidence of our being here. You go on outside and do what you gotta do and I'll take a look at what you found."

It was a hand carved wooden box with an intricately

engraved top. It was locked and the only way to get it open was to pry and break the lock. Stan shook the box. It made no sound. What should he do?

"Maybe it is best if we take this box with us. It might be something like Pandora's box. No telling what is in it."

When Brad came in Stan told him what he thought.

Brad said, "It's OK if we can keep our curiosity under control. Anyhow let's forget it for now and take advantage of these nice beds and blankets. How will we know when the sun comes up? It's so sheltered by the trees outside."

"Our fire will burn down by six in the morning and it will get lots colder in here. Sometime tomorrow we can move our stuff over here from the building on the other side of the lake, does that sound OK with you, Brad?"

It had been two weeks since they moved across the lake and life was better here. There had been no uninvited guests and nothing had happened to cause them concern. The weather had become colder but there was no rain or snow.

The number of Allied airplanes continued both day and night. One day while fishing, Stan counted large formations of both fighters and bombers. Sometimes the fighters had flown down to almost tree top level. He wondered if they had seen him. Was this the time to use the signal mirror? It was as if the planes were hungry for the sight of the enemy.

It was not far across the lake and Stan and Brad could see the German soldiers walking toward their homeland. They were frightened and ragged. After watching them from their distance Brad had said, "Those poor sons of bitches are not goose stepping now!"

FOURTEEN

It was colder outside now and light snow had fallen for the last day or so, leaving the grounds of the prison camp white and bleak. The men were glad to be inside and, since less work detail was required of them, they were more comfortable than they had been in many months.

Christmas was just a week away and there still had been no word from the Camp Commander, Colonel Hibner, about his meeting with Commander Owens, Colonel Howard, Klein, and Sacket. Had he been bluffing? Was this just something else to torment the men with? In the dead of winter would everything go back to the conditions they knew before the talks? Some of the men were getting desperate and out of hand. Would they be repatriated or not?

The commanding officers had visited with one another on two different occasions to see if either had information that was new. Sergeant Klein had talked with the other barracks chiefs to see what scuttle butt might have been passed down to them by the German guards. Nobody knew a damned thing!

There was one difference that all the men noticed, they were not restricted as closely to their barracks as they had been and it seemed that the fence lines had less guards than before. In fact there were fewer guards than ever before, even Fatso had not been around in a week or more. Something was going on, but what?

On Christmas morning, Colonel Howard and Squadron Commander Owens were notified that they were to be at the headquarters building to meet with Colonel Hibner. Four hours passed and the entire camp came alive with gossip.

Everyone's curiosity was peaked. Klein and Sacket stood on the front steps of their barracks and kept watch toward the headquarters building, as they were sure that was where the news would come from.

At noon, Colonel Hibner's orderly came out of the watched building with the two captive commanders and four guards. The six men walked the length of the street and stopped in front of each barracks. A guard entered the building and came out with its chief, and he fell into the line that was being formed with the two officers. When they came to building #18, Klein was instructed to join the growing formation of men.

"By the way Sergeant Klein, the Colonel wants Sergeant Sacket to come along too. Call him quickly!"

"Come on Sacket, on the double. Let's go!"

It was cold outside and puffs of air could be seen by the prisoners at the windows of their barracks coming from every breath taken by these special men who left their foot prints in the snow covered ground, who were on their way to hear the news that would surely affect the lives of every man in the entire prison complex.

The formation of twelve prisoners was marched to the mess hall. There was still no electricity, but the hall was brightly lit with lanterns. Three long tables with benches had been set up so that they were facing a speaker's stand. Each prisoner found a seat at one of the tables. Sacket noticed that the guards had weapons, but none were pointed toward any of the captive men and the guards all seemed to have a perceptive smile on their faces.

A guard gave the order for everyone to stand and come to attention. Chairs slid back with a scraping sound and all the prisoners stood up. Colonel Hibner with another German Officer entered the room. Hibner came to the front of the room and stood behind the speakers stand.

He nodded his head at the orderly who told the men, "You will all be seated. There will be no distractions in this room while Colonel Hibner is speaking."

"This meeting has been called today as a result of a conference that I have just had with Colonel Howard and

Commander Owens and of discussions I have had with Sergeants Klein and Sacket. Your barracks chiefs are here because they represent the men in their particular quarters. I want to introduce General Herman Schmidt who will assist me following today's meeting," spoke Hibner.

He turned and gestured to the tall, thin, severe, bespectacled German officer who held his uniform cap under his arm. He quickly stood and came to attention.

"You have my permission to speak General Schmidt."

"I think it is only necessary that you men know that I was at the meeting with your officers and that I am aware of the decisions that have been made. I will do all I can to be of assistance." With a click of his heels, he saluted Colonel Hibner and quickly sat down.

"I have become very concerned for your health and that of all the captives held here in this prison. The quality of your food has been improved. These last weeks I have issued orders for warmer blankets for the winter. Each barracks has received a small supply of coal to warm its interior. It has become very cold so there will be less manual labor required by the prisoners. For those of you who were sick, you have had medical attention. I am sure that you have noticed a more relaxed security in the surrounding area of the prison. This does not mean that it would be easier for any one of you to try and escape or cause any trouble for myself or my command. We still stand ready to perform harsh and deadly punishment for anyone breaking the rules of this prison camp!"

Following his last statement Hibner stood looking around the room at the faces in front of him, as though he were waiting for what he had said to be absorbed by his listeners. Hibner took a minute to again survey the room and continued to speak, "Depending on the battles between our armies, I am planning an honorable exchange for all of you here in this prison for the peaceful surrender of myself and my personnel. In the event that your countries' armies reach a point some twenty miles from this prison, we will meet them with a representative from yours and my ranks and surrender all of my men, including myself, for the safe repatriation of all the war prisoners in this camp."

A thoughtful expression came onto Hibner's face and he continued to speak, "I should explain that I chose Germany in this unfortunate war, but I have always admired and have been inwardly jealous of your two countries. I will stay in contact with all of you and keep you appraised of any new developments. If action is to be taken, you will hear of that too. I give each of you and your men credit for the trust you have put in your leaders and for the loyalty and service you have given to your respective countries."

Hibner had given these men a true compliment. He turned his head and gave a nod to the Guard Esser who called everyone in the room to attention. As Hibner left the speaker's stand he was saluted by all the guards in attendance. There was an expression of defeat, yet relief, on his face. All the men in the room felt they had won this round, but still it would not do to cross the Colonel. He was still very much in charge.

Outside the German Sergeant Esser spoke to Colonel Howard and Commander Owens. "Haupman Snyder also speaks English. The two of us will forward any new information about your possible repatriation. If you have need to contact each other let your barracks guard know and he will make the necessary arrangements."

The prisoners had formed a line outside. It was cold and the daylight was fading. Some of the men were shivering. Esser noticed the condition of the men and instructed the guards to return them to their barracks.

He held Klein and Sacket and spoke to them, "If these plans come to pass, all the men here, prisoners and Germans alike, will have the both of you to thank for their freedom and a lesser punishment for us. I have heard that Americans are not vindictive and that your prisoners are treated much better than ours. You will have our thanks and gratitude. All the Germans here hope you're successful in your efforts."

That night, in each of the prison barracks, there were sounds of jubilation. Full discussions of the day's proceedings were probably the best Christmas gift any of the men could have had. As everyone settled down for the night one could hear the sounds of Christmas carols being hummed ever so softly. The moon was full and the stars shone brightly above the prison. This night the men were full of hope for their freedom and a return to their families.

Christmas morning was here! The children and their elders had done everything possible to make this a very special day. They would begin it with a special breakfast.

As Herr Graef left his office and bedroom he saw that the kitchen was alight with lamps and the women were working feverishly with the preparation of the morning meal. Some of the children were busy putting the final touches to the large dining table.

Some of the girls had put on the one dress they had brought with them. They were all growing so fast that soon they would be too small for them. Nothing went to waste and things were passed down to the smaller children, even the worn dresses of the women went to the larger girls; they might have needed alterations, but that was not a problem. A snip here and a seam there and the dress was good as new.

All the young people were in the large room and as Herr Graef entered they all chanted, "Merry Christmas, Merry Christmas, today will be a day to remember!"

Through the closed door to his room the sounds of celebration had reached Mickey's ears. He was up and dressed in the freshly washed but worn flight cloths he had come to this place wearing. Inga had retrieved his uniform and had mended the tears and torn places. He was surprised, what a Christmas gift! He was lucky to have such a thoughtful and caring woman in love with him.

He had a gift for her too, he had carved a small ring out of wood for her. He had spent his free time polishing it. He knew that he would soon have to leave this place and this would be something for her to hold onto until he could get back to her.

It was colder outdoors now and Mickey was sure there would be a fire in the huge fireplace. As he opened his door the sun was starting to streak through the east windows. The silver rays of light shown horizontally across the big room and onto a Christmas tree that had been decorated by the children. It sat in the corner of the room away from the fire. It was a pine and its fragrance filled the whole room, making this day even more festive. It reminded him of the holidays he had spent at home with his mother and father.

Inga and Frau Miller, assisted by some of the other girls, were placing the food on the table. It smelled delicious. Herr Graef brought in two large tin containers that were decorated with paintings of dolls and ribbons. Mickey thought it was the kind that his mother used to put candy and cookies in and he was sure the children were in for a real treat. Herr Graef reminded Mickey of Santa Claus. The old gentleman was full of smiles this morning. The only thing lacking was the long white beard.

At the table there were little place markers, each with a name on it. All the children were so happy. Each had done her best to be as pretty and clean as possible and they all had big bright smiles on their faces.

Even little Willie's face shone with the light of the holiday spirit. He had grown so much these past months. He was really a different boy from the sad lad that Mickey had first known and he was very bright too. Mickey was teaching him some English and some simple arithmetic. He looked at the boy with pride and he knew that one day Willie would really make something of his life. "Just look at this life I have helped develop," he said to himself.

Herr Graef was at one end of the table and Frau Miller at the other. Each child found her own place and stood behind her chair. Mickey and Inga were seated next to each other and there were smiles of approval by all those who were at the table.

The large table overflowed with traditional German foods. Little cakes and cookies, sausage, enough for a serving for everyone. An egg apiece was a special treat, with some homemade jam for the "fresh from the oven bread." A special hot German potato dish was placed at either end of the table. Warm cider filled each cup. Herr Graef gave a blessing for the abundant food and for the safety that had been provided all his children.

He thanked his many friends, especially his brother, a general in high command for sending such wonderful foods that would make this day special for these children in his charge. "The special foods we have had today would have been impossible except for the kindness of those who are in high places."

The outdoor temperature was becoming very crisp but the two large fireplaces kept this big room very comfortable and the festive foods had warmed the bodies and spirits of everyone. Mickey had learned more and more German and the children were now speaking some English. Very interesting conversations were going on. Inga made all the necessary translations in both languages so that everyone could understand what was being said.

Herr Graef finally opened his canisters that had been on the table. The children and adults alike were delighted when they found it contained candies and other special treats that were typical of special days in Germany.

When everyone had their choice of candy they seemed to settle down into the comfort of this warm enchanted room. Herr Graef stood up and asked that they all give him their attention for a few moments.

"I want to thank you women for the wonderful meal you have provided. It took a lot of extra work and we all want you to know that we appreciate it. I feel that I must tell you what is in my heart," continued this kindly gentleman. "Very soon now we will see great changes in our lives, in fact, that of the entire world. We should all be prepared for the things to come as they will affect all our lives. I think of each one of you as an individual and no matter what happens I am sure you will make good choices and decisions for your futures. You have had good discipline and proper training, don't let anyone change your thoughts on what is good or bad, or what is right or wrong. Be your own person!

"Now, I think it would be interesting if any of you who

would like to would tell us something about yourselves, and then the younger children have been practicing a few songs for today."

Mickey and Inga both told of a special holiday with their families. Herr Graef shared a childhood experience with his family and then came the songs. The final one was sang in English and they all giggled their way through "Jingle Bells." It was a wonderful day and everyone was having so much fun.

The rest of the day and evening were spent with Frau Miller telling about the birth of the Christ Child Jesus. When she had ended her story she said, "I hope and pray that each of you will spend next Christmas in a peaceful and joyful way."

The moon was bright and the night air very cold. Mickey found a warm coat for Inga and he put it around her shoulders and asked, "Please come outside with me for a few minutes?" he had that look in his eyes that she could not resist and she wanted very much to be in his arms. She yearned to be kissed by the man she loved so much.

They did go outside but not far from the building. "I have a small gift for you, Inga. I love what you gave to me. Thank you for mending this uniform for me, it really means a lot to me. It is very possible that I will need it soon, when it is time for me to leave you for a while."

He took the small ring he had made from his pocket and slide it onto her finger. "I know that we will have a time of separation, but I promise you that it will be as short a time as possible. You will never be out of my thoughts, I will pledge my love to you with this ring as though we were already man and wife. I love you with all my heart, Inga."

She looked up into his eyes, and there were tears on her cheeks. "You are so thoughtful, Mickey, and I pledge my love to you. I will wear this ring from this day forward and will live for the time we can be reunited."

She raised her face to his. He traced her face with his fingers as though he were an artist putting something on a canvas that he did not want to forget and then he kissed her lips, barely touching them at first and then fiercely, searching her mouth with the tip of his tongue. Then he touched her lips, just tracing them with his tongue as if to memorize the feeling of her mouth.

"I love you so much, Inga. I don't know how I am going to manage without you even for a short time."

They hugged once again and he drank in her special fragrance.

"I can never forget how wonderful you smell to me."

That night Mickey and Inga dreamed of one another and shared their complete love in the secrecy of their dreams.

As darkness fell over this part of Germany, the sounds of war in the West became silent.

FIFTEEN

Stan was up first, and he had dressed as warmly as possible.
They were doing OK, but the condition of their clothing was
not so good. Their uniforms were worn and the socks and
underwear were a mess. They had washed them some at the
lake, but as Stan had remarked, "Let's face it, these things
have seen better days." Their boots were thin and at times
their feet got so cold and wet that Stan thought aloud, "I
hope that one of us doesn't get frost bite."

He had checked the small calendar in his wallet every
day since they had bailed out of the Louise E. Ann, the
fourteenth day of June, with a small X.

"God, I hope this will all be over soon and we can get
back to civilization."

Today's date was December 25th, Christmas Day.

"Ho, ho, ho. I wonder if Santa Claus is going to come
down that chimney?"

There was a small mirror on the wall over the wash basin
and as Stan looked into it his face peered back at him. He
had been well built with dark hair and hazel eyes, good
looking in a rough sort of way. His face and body had changed.
He had lost at least twenty pounds, and his face was very
thin. The hair that he had always kept short was longer and
it sure was not the military cut he had been used to. He felt
his arms and shoulders, and his stomach and hips. They were
firm, but much thinner. He had been in good health and so
far he had no aches or pains to complain of.

"Guess we have really done pretty well with food cause
neither of us has had constipation problems and we have
been more comfortable than most might have been in a

situation like ours. This war has got to be over soon and with any luck we will be found, or find our way back to our units. We have just got to stay with it!

"I can't complain to Brad, he is doing OK and he really has grown up a lot over these last months, but he just might lose it if he really knew how up tight I am. We have got to get out of here and see what is around us!"

Stan stood looking out of one of the windows of the cabin they were in. He shuddered, as it was really cold out and there was a light snow falling.

"It would be so easy to just forget it all and stay right here and do nothing. Got to get our butts moving and explore this place today.

"Hey Brad, wake up. It's the 25th of December. Merry Christmas and all that good stuff. Let's get something to eat and have a look around outside!"

Brad rolled over on his bed. "God it's so warm and nice here, I hate to get up. It really is Christmas. That means we have been around this place for six months. Do you really think we are going to get home, Stan? I have so much I want to do. I had a girlfriend once and I would sure like to see my parents. Do you ever wonder if your family is still alive? I sure do."

"Yeah, I know what you mean Brad, and yes I have had all sorts of thoughts, but we just have to keep thinking that things will turn out OK. Come on now get dressed and we will eat something and get out of here for a while."

Brad was up and was the first to open the front door of their cabin. "God it's cold outside."

"I know it, Brad, but I want to know what's west and south of us."

Brad, who had begun to assert himself more, said, "Instead of climbing that hill to look around, why don't we leave here tonight and move to the west or even the south and try and make contact with our armies. I'm getting tired of just sitting here on my ass waiting for something to happen."

Stan closed the door and became very serious. From a distance he looked Brad straight in the face. He was doing all he could to control his voice and temper. "Number one,

Brad, we're still operating in a military manner, that is the reason we have been able to survive this whole gaggle so far. Number two, you have no real plan or sound idea of how to go about our repatriation or safe escape to the west. I have not restricted you at any time from talking about possible ways to get out of this area alive. Our staying here, in safety, far outweighs the danger of penetrating the German side of the battle zone. If you have noticed there is little or no activity on either the German or Allied side here now. It may be just a matter of days until the Allies advance toward us and we will be here waiting for them. You're not thinking or planning, just anxious to be out of here and if we were to follow your thoughts we might even get ourselves killed!"

Brad shouted, "OK we will do it your way, but if something doesn't happen soon I'm going to go on alone, to hell with it!"

Stan held back what he really wanted to say. "Come on Brad, we're friends and fellow sufferers and after this is all over we can go our own way, but for now we really need each other. Let's get out of here and see what's on top of that hill. Maybe Santa Claus left us a real surprise up there."

They made ponchos out of one of the blankets, ate something, and got as warm as possible. They locked up the cabin and started walking toward the snow capped hill on the other side of the runway.

Brad seemed a little ashamed of his outburst and followed Stan a few paces behind. He stopped to pick up two long sticks and caught up with Stan. "We had better take these with us. This snow could really be deeper than it looks."

"I believe you're right. Good idea Brad," praised Stan as he took the offered pole.

The air was crisp but invigorating.

Brad said, "Is it OK if I lead the way? I spent some summers in Colorado as a Boy Scout guide."

"Sure," agreed Stan.

At the beginning of their uphill climb the snow as only a couple of inches deep, but after they reached half way up the hill the snow became deeper and more difficult to wade through.

"These hiking sticks really do help. Thanks Brad."

There were no trees on the uphill slope, but the low brush began to slow them down.

At about eight hundred feet above the park below they stopped to catch their breath. Stan remarked to Brad, "I would say that we are about halfway up. The brush is only about waist high and we are partly visible to anyone below. These ponchos are white and should give us a little protection. See the highway in front of the park, Brad. It leads to some kind of a village that is about three miles southwest of us, come on let's get going."

After another half hour of climbing they finally reached the top. Far to the west there seemed to be low clouds of dust or smoke.

Stan began talking in a quiet voice about what they were able to see. "Have you noticed that we have not seen any large formations of Allied aircraft? We have not heard the sounds of battle from the west, but the prevailing wind today is from the east. Whatever is causing all of that smoke or dust is on the ground. I would say we are about forty miles from what ever is going on."

Brad held his hand up to get Stan's attention. "Look what's up there behind us. I wonder what's in that building?"

Stan turned to look and said in an excited voice, "Let's go have a look!"

As they approached the building they saw that it was partially hidden in a heavy growth of small trees.

"It looks like these trees were planted to hide this structure," said Stan.

The building was constructed of bricks and stone and had shuttered windows all along its sides. The two men walked all the way around its outside. At the rear they found a shed that was full of large containers. There was a paved road in front of the shed and it seemed to run down the hill, with the snow it was difficult for them to know what direction it took, but the snow with no tracks showed that it had not been used for a long time, at least in the time they had been hiding there.

They went back to the large building and at the rear there

was a steel back door that showed no signs of recent use.

"Let's check the front door and see if we can get into this pile of brick," said Stan.

"We can try the front windows if the doors are locked, but we will have to pry off one of the shutters," suggested Brad.

"It is ridiculous to think that these keys might work again, but we will give it a try," said Stan.

Of course the keys did not open the lock.

"Must be something of real importance, maybe even classified, for them to have this way up here. Look at all this steel on the doors and, really, it has very few windows."

When they pried one of the shutters off the back window they found that the steel framed windows had been placed for security and they would be difficult to enter.

"Can we break the glass?" asked Brad.

"We can try," said Stan.

He took a large rock in his hand and covered it with his poncho to protect his hand. He swung the rock several times at the glass of the window. Nothing happened. Stan walked back to the shed they had found, found a steel crow bar, and went back.

"Stand back, Brad, while I give this a try."

He hit the glass with all his strength and finally, after three tries, it shattered. Stan cleared the jagged glass from around the frame and reached through and unlocked the window. It swung open inwardly and provided a two by three foot opening.

"Let me go in first. I'm thinner than you," said Brad. "Just give me a boost."

Stan agreed and hoisted Brad up to the window and Brad got through with no trouble.

"Now that you're inside, and if everything seems OK, go to the rear door and see if you can open it. It looks like it should slide open if it were unlocked."

Everything became quiet, so still, it worried Stan. "Brad are you OK?"

He listened for an answer and still Brad did not speak.

"God damn it, Brad, if you're all right say so!"

"Yeah," whispered Brad. "I'm OK. I just needed to get my bearings. It's really dark in here. It will take me a few minutes to find my way to the rear door. When I am there I will signal by knocking on the inside and give a try at opening it a little, do you hear me, Stan?"

"Yeah, good work, Brad. I will go back and wait to hear your signal. For God sakes, be careful!"

It seemed like it took forever, but finally there was a knock on the steel door and suddenly it slide open exposing Brad standing there with a grin of pride on his face.

With the door open slightly and with the light from the broken window there was enough brightness for them to see by. There seemed to be several rooms inside this structure. The area they were in seemed to be some sort of a communication center as there was a lot of radio equipment.

"They have everything here to receive and transmit radio signals. Somewhere outside there must be some big antennas. We'll look for them later," said Stan.

At one end of the room there were two big doors that would indicate two smaller rooms. Both were locked.

"Wonder if the keys to these rooms could be hidden somewhere in here?" queried Brad.

"Let's take a look around and see what we can find, Brad," answered Stan. "You take that side of the room and I'll look over here on this side."

They searched their areas with no success. Finally they came to the doors themselves. There was a two foot space between the openings and there were two pictures in simple but tasteful frames. The one on top was of Hitler and the one below was of Goebbels.

"What do you think, Stan?"

"I'll bet it's under the one of that son of a bitch Goebbels," replied Stan.

"Well what are you waiting for, take a look and see if you're right," taunted Brad.

Stan reached up and took the picture from its hanging place, and sure enough there were two keys on a leather thong hanging from the picture's support.

"How in the hell did you suspect that, Stan?"

"Just guessed, but Goebbels was in charge of propaganda and this place and the people who operated from here were under him. Now let's see what's inside these locked up rooms."

Brad had been exploring the outside room and had opened some cupboards under a counter. "Hey Stan, you will never guess what I have found."

All of a sudden there was a strong beam of light in Stan's face.

"What the hell is that?" he yelled.

"There are several large flashlights under here. How's that for a break?" said Brad happily.

"Great, that is really something. Here, let me have one so that I can see what is in this room. You go ahead and explore further outside here if you want to, no telling what you will come up with," said Stan.

The first room that he opened was not what Stan had imagined it would be. There was every kind of weapon imaginable in this German arsenal. It contained pistols, rifles, machine guns, all kinds of knives, an assortment of explosive devices was neatly stacked in boxes and metal containers. Explosives, such as mines and grenades, were well marked and identified. Ammunition for all the above weapons had been placed next to or with matching fire arms.

"God damned, would you look at this," said Stan in a shocked tone of voice. "There is enough stuff here to blow this whole place off the face of the earth!"

Brad had come in behind Stan, "Look here, a Luger six. I have always wanted one of these! Shit, what a trophy this will make!"

Stan just laughed and said, "We should check out the other room and then we will come back here. Put the gun down for now. We know that these weapons are here and they may help us later on."

They closed the arsenal door, but did not lock it.

"OK Brad, open the other door."

The first thing they saw when they flashed their beams of light around the room was a large map, showing Germany and the bordering countries. It took up one whole wall and had several hundred pin held tags stuck in the map. Each tag had a number placed on it.

The other three walls had filing cabinets lined up against them, a rough guess was maybe seventy five or more in all.

Stan opened one of the drawers and said, "Each card has a name and an address on it and it gives a description and a few remarks about a person. There must be literally thousands or maybe millions of people identified here."

"What the hell are we going to do with all this stuff?" asked Brad.

"I think I know what it is all about," remarked Stan as he checked some more of the cards in the files. "This whole place has to be kept just as is for our forces."

He closed the cabinets he had opened and shown his flashlight around the room to be sure it was just as they had first found it and told Brad to get a knife or two. There was no need for guns, as they had their own 45s and still had enough ammunition.

After Stan had locked up the second room he directed Brad to clean up all the broken glass and close the shutter from the outside. "Wait outside the back door for me, Brad, and I'll be there in a few minutes. Keep your eyes and ears open for anything unusual. If you see or hear anything knock on that steel door and I will hear you."

Stan went back to the room with the weapons. He had second thoughts about what they might be able to use. He found a canvas bag hanging on the wall. He placed two Lugers in the bag with ammunition they would use. He chose two automatic guns that were retractable and easy to carry and ammunition for both. He put a box of six hand grenades and a much prized pair of German binoculars in the top of the bag. He threw the automatic guns over his shoulder, closed the bag, and departed the room. He locked the door behind him and put the key in his pocket as he had done with the key from the file room.

Brad had done his work and was waiting outside. Stan set the inside lock on the door and met Brad outside as the iron door snapped shut behind him.

"I wish we could blow this God damned building sky-high, but there is too much evidence against the Nazi's to destroy what they may need to convict them at later war trials."

They took a last walk around the building and noticed several wire cables coming from the roof. "Those will lead to some antennas and probably an electrical source."

The obvious location was a grove of taller trees beyond the building. They followed the cable to the grove of trees and found the antennas hidden and camouflaged by heavy plant growth. A small structure in the trees held an engine driven generator.

Brad asked, "How can we fix this so it won't run?"

Stan smiled and said, "Take off the oil cap cover and we will each pour a couple of handfuls of dirt into the engine crank case."

This done, Stan wiped off the contaminating evidence on the engine itself and put the clean oil cap back in place. "That will destroy any engine, Brad. Come on, let's get out of here!"

The day's activities had been exciting and they had not really noticed how cold they were. Stan knew that they must return to the safety of their cabin to get warm and find something to eat.

"These binoculars will be great. We can keep an eye out for anyone that might show up on top of this hill."

"They had an uneventful trip back to the cabin, ate some kipper snacks and had a drink of water. They felt safe enough to sleep tonight without one of them keeping watch.

"Hey Brad, Christmas was not so bad after all, wonder what the rest of the world did today?"

Both men had been asleep for several hours when all of a sudden Stan came awake with a sickening start. How damned lucky they had been today, what if that building or the surrounding area had been mined? He drew a sigh of relief, no use thinking of what might have happened, just thank God the worst had not. It would seem that fate had been on their side today. What about tomorrow?

SIXTEEN

It was very cold outside, but there were no clouds in the sky and the sun had melted the snow. Klein had put his blanket around his shoulders for warmth and had been out in front of the barracks talking to two German guards for at least two hours. This sort of fraternization would not have been possible just a few weeks ago, but Hibner's plan had been disclosed to all his personnel and they had decided without exception that their surrender was by far the best way to survive this war that all Germans at this prison knew to be a lost cause.

The latest news from the front said that the German army was being driven back into its homeland. The Allies had crossed the boarder at Aochen in the north and Saarbrücken in the south, not far from this prison facility.

Sacket came out on the porch. "What the hell is going on, Klein? Are there any new rumors floating around?"

"It's obvious that there are more fighter bombers flying to the west every day, and one of the guards said that it was impossible to travel on any highway during the daylight hours, and at night daylight flares were being dropped.

"Yeah, I remember hearing about those million candle power flares that were used for night attacks. One can light up the sky brightly for a mile around. They are awesome weapons," stated Sacket with a knowing shake of his head.

The two men were as anxious as all the prisoners in the camp for information about this pending exchange of Allied prisoners for all of Hibner's German personnel.

"The big question now is how is this going to be accomplished?" said the thoughtful Klein.

"These damned guards are driving us all crazy with their questions about what their treatment from the Allies might be. It is all I can do to keep from telling them that they are going to get their asses kicked and their noses rubbed in their own shit," said Sacket vehemently. "But you know as well as I do that this war has been fought because of the inhumanity by the Germans and their partners in crime."

New Year's day came and went, and it was January 1945. There had been two meetings in Colonel Hibner's office with the British and American officers. There had to be a good plan for making contact with the Allied armies and a decision made as to where the repatriation would take place. Would there be radio contact or would personnel contact be a wiser move? There was danger on all sides of thought.

The danger from the Allied side was that an eager, on rushing attack might see the surrendering Germans as a still dangerous enemy to be dealt with by death on sight. The danger from the German diehard gestapo was that they may want to kill the defenseless Allied prisoners and punish the traitorous German soldiers and the Commander of this prison.

These were weeks of anxiety for all the prisoners. Some of the men got unruly and verbal and there were some examples of the rule that Hibner held over this camp. One man was shot and killed by a guard when he ran for the fence.

"Poor stupid son of a bitch, if only he could have held on for a few more days," said Klein. "We have all got to stay busy. I want to see this place kept spotless and anyone who gets out of line will have me to deal with if Hibner doesn't get to him first! That's an order, do you all understand!"

At least the weather was cooperating a little more. There had been little or no rain. The days were still on the cold side, but there was sun and the men could get out and exercise after they had completed their work assignments. The food was regular and had improved considerably. They were warmer at night and were threatened less. All considered, things had changed for the better and that gave assurance that something would eventually happen that would be for the good of all.

The second week in February, Hibner called a meeting in his office and ordered the American and British officers be in attendance.

"There has been a decision made," said Hibner, "as to how the first meeting with the advancing Allies will be made. The plan will involve two men. One German and one American will be given the privilege of going to the front lines. Both men will be dressed as medics and in the uniforms of their own countries. They will use their own discretion as to where they will cross the battle zone and turn themselves over to any Allied soldier, preferably the American Army. It is anticipated that these two men would ask to be taken to the nearest intelligence officer or officer in charge. They would explain their situation and elucidate to that person that the safest way to make contact with their commanders and the Prison Commander is to fly over the prison camp and drop instructions for a safe and orderly surrender of all German personnel in exchange for the repatriation of all this camp's prisoners, American and British alike. To identify the prison there will be a large bull's eye made and painted red in the center of the camp's yard. They need not fear weapons being fired from the ground. They will have freedom of flight and landing.

"Whoever these two men are they will have to memorize all their needed information. Nothing can be written down because there is too much danger that a message could possibly fall into the wrong hands in the event they are captured. They can give the location of the prison as being six miles east of Saarbrücken on the road between Saarbrücken and Kiaserslautern.

"Now we have to make the decision as to who will be chosen for this mission. That will depend on the answer we get from this board." Hibner surveyed the room. "I will give you some time to contemplate, although I feel that the decision is an easy one."

"Let's not waste time," said Colonel Howard as he stood up. "For the Allied American my choice would be Sergeant Sacket. He was a part of this original plan from the start. He is in better physical condition because of his more recent capture and the short exposure to the lack of care experienced by other prisoners."

"I am hopeful that any experience you may have had here at this prison will be softened by my attempt to return every man here to his home," responded Hibner. "I agree with your choice of an American if it is your choice too, Commander Owens."

"Good choice, Colonel Hibner, and he gets my vote!"

Hibner spoke again, "For the German soldier to accompany your American I will send Stabsfeldwebel Esser. He is a Master Sergeant and speaks fluent English. He has been in my service for over a year now and I trust his judgment. You are free to return to your quarters now and talk to your men about today's discussion." Colonel Hibner stood up and offered his hand in a gesture that seemed to acknowledge his part in bringing about this mission that would bring freedom to his prisoners.

Hibner's face was more friendly and relaxed than these officers had ever seen it. He even offered them each a cigarette in a gesture of friendship and understanding.

Colonel Howard and Squadron Commander Owens stood up and Colonel Howard spoke for both of them. "I assure you that we will cooperate fully with this plan now that we know what is intended for all of us. We must be allowed to call a meeting of all our men today before it becomes dark."

Colonel Hibner assured them that he would provide a place for the requested meeting, and he would send a message within the hour, sooner if possible.

Sergeant Esser accompanied the officers back to their quarters and said, "I have been instructed to give you all the help you need for this afternoon's meeting. Good luck, gentlemen."

"Before you go, Sergeant Esser, would you ask Sergeant Sacket to come to my quarters?"

"I would be happy to do that, sir, but I think you would have more privacy meeting with him outside in the open field," said Esser.

"Good idea, Sergeant. I will wait for him there."

"Hey Sacket, Colonel Howard wants to see you out on the field, get your ass in gear and see what he wants!"

"OK Klein, I'm on my way. Don't get shook up in the heat of the day!" And Sacket ran out of the barracks and over to the field across from the mess hall.

"Sergeant Sacket reporting, sir, what can I do for you?"

Howard explained about the meeting that had taken place earlier. "You and Sergeant Esser have been chosen to take the lead parts in this mission. I am asking you now if you would volunteer to participate in this plan. It may not be without danger to your life and you should consider it carefully. If you don't want to do this say so now and we will choose someone else."

"As you know, Colonel, I am a regular in the service of my country and I would be honored to be a part of this mission. I realize how important this will be to every man in this prison and I will do all in my power to gain their freedom and get them home. I will do my damnedest to achieve what is expected of me and I will cooperate with Sergeant Esser one hundred percent. Yes sir, I accept this mission and thank you for your confidence in me."

"Thank you, Sergeant. I will see you at 0700 in the morning for a briefing meeting with Colonel Hibner. You acted in just the manner I had imagined you would. Very shortly there will be a meeting of all the men confined here, on this field."

As Sacket and Howard faced the mess hall they could see the men had already begun their march to the field. There were some seven hundred of them in all.

The sun was fading and the air was cold as the men fell into a standing formation in front of Colonel Howard and Squadron Commander Owens.

Howard spoke with as loud a voice as possible. "Today a decision was made on how to effect our release from this prison. Two volunteers have been chosen to take part in the mission; one is American, the other is German. The Germans here realize that the only way that they can surrender without being killed or punished is to cooperate with us and the Allies."

The Colonel took a long deep breath, "The Gestapo and diehard elements of the German army could come down hard on all of us if we don't plan this action with great care. For security reasons I feel it best not to reveal any more of the plan now. As soon as the mission is under way I will have more information for all of you. For now let's keep the talk about all of this quiet. It is cold and you may return to your barracks. I will keep you appraised on the progress of this assignment. Thank you and good night."

As the men were marching back to their quarters not a voice was heard, but their faces were full of smiles and their hands were raised in the V for Victory sign.

At the farming community the potatoes and beans had been harvested and stored in the under ground vaults that had been built in the sides of the hills next to the small village. The cabbage had been pickled and put into large vats for the winter storage. The few cows and swine had been given access to the barn near the location where Mickey had first been captured. Their winter food supply of dried grass and crop tops had been bundled and stored in the barn. It was winter and a time for rest. Any repairs that would be needed to equipment would be done now to be ready for the spring planting.

At breakfast this particular morning Herr Graef had mentioned the sounds of the approaching Allied Armies to the west. "We must be ready when they get here. We should not panic or show fear. Above all we will not show any hostility. The troops that may come could be American, English, or French. It is my opinion that these oncoming troops will treat us fairly and will provide us with the information we need to go on with our every day lives." Herr Graef stopped and took a long drink of the hot liquid in his cup. "We should all hope that there will not be a battle here at our village and that our armies will not be near to engage the Western Allied forces in combat. Should there be a battle here we will seek shelter in some of the underground vaults that have been built into the near hillsides. The concealed cellar should protect us from an air attack."

The girls at the table were finishing their breakfast and were listening carefully to this old gentleman that had only their best interest at heart.

"When it appears to be just a matter of a few days from an attack we will take food and water and go into the vaults. It is also important for all of you to know that Sergeant Reber is now and always has been my prisoner. He used good judgment by not resisting anyone on the day of his arrival. I did not turn him over to a prison that normally holds captured Americans. It is your responsibility to speak of him as a laborer in my custody. If and when we go into hiding he will be brought along as our prisoner. Is that understood?"

Everyone shook their heads to let it be known that Herr Graef's words had been acknowledged.

Because of the frequent low level fighter sweeps up and down the valley, nearly all outdoor activity was kept to a minimum during the day and after dark. The hills were covered with snow and the valley was stark and white. It was cold outdoors, and most of those in Herr Graef's charge were busy indoors trying to prepare for whatever they thought might help with their survival. White flags of surrender had been made and placed in hidden spots so they would not attract the attention of any retreating German army units.

In the past weeks several small motorized convoys of Germans were heard passing the village at night. A man and his wife leading two large draft horses and a couple of cows had stopped at the entrance to this settlement and had asked for food and water for their animals.

Herr Graef said, "I will bring you a bundle of dried grass for your animals and there is a road side water trough where they may get water."

The man took half the grass and stuffed it into some canvas sacks on the horses' backs. "We thank you for your kindness. We are from a small farm about 25 kilometers west of here. The Western armies advance was only a few kilometers from us when we left. We are looking for a safe place to the east. These few animals are all we have left of a large herd."

Feeling sorry for the couple Herr Graef told them, "The farther east you go the more mountainous it becomes. You would do better to stay in this valley. There is a large flat pasture about two kilometers ahead and you can put your animals inside the fenced area, off to the south side of the road. You will find two stone buildings and you and your wife may stay in one of them. Both structures are empty now and no one will disturb you."

The man said, "We thank you for your kindness. We will repay you somehow someday."

Before they left, Frau Miller came out with two loaves of fresh bread and said, "The war's end is near and sometime soon we may all be able to start our lives over again. Take care of those beautiful horses and we wish you both well."

Mickey and Inga were in the main room of the building with the girls. They were playing a game that gave everyone a chance to participate. The game had to do with geography and questions and answers. Everything possible was done to help educate this young group and they were really very knowledgeable. They were very interested in what other people did and what the rest of the world was like. They spent hours talking and asking questions of Mickey about the United States.

The game ended when Frau Miller said it was time for everyone to retire, and she reminded them of their plans for tomorrow. Everyone left the room and Mickey and Inga were left alone to enjoy each other's company.

Today Mickey had noticed that Inga had dressed differently than she usually did. Instead of the coverall type cloths she had worn in the fields she was wearing a long, rather heavy skirt with a warm long-sleeved blouse that looked like a tunic top. He could not see beneath the skirt, but she appeared to be wearing heavy stockings with a sandal type shoe on her foot. She still wore her hair in what was called a French braid. It kept her hair neat and close to her

head and he was sure that it required little care and it always
looked beautiful. She had wonderful features and her skin
was so smooth and clear. Just looking at her now made him
love her even more. I could make love to her all day long, he
thought to himself.

"Inga, I have to get serious for a few minutes. I know
that when I leave here it may be a very long time before we
see each other again. The laws will say that we cannot
communicate and not knowing where you are and not being
able to speak or write letters to you will be of a constant
concern to me. For whatever good it will do I have written
down my family's address for you on this piece of paper.
Please know that I will tell them of our relationship so they
will understand that we intend to marry one day. I should be
able to contact them by letter or telephone soon after I am
repatriated. I swear to you that we will be reunited some
time in the future. God, I wish I knew when that would be.
Just thinking of a separation from you is more than I can
bear," he reached for her and pulled her close to him.

When he turned her face to him to kiss her she pulled
away. "Not here, Mickey. Let's wait until we can be alone,"
she whispered. "I have noticed one of the older girls watching
us. She thinks a lot of you and she is of an age that she is
fantasizing about you. I don't want to make her jealous or
hurt her feelings."

"But Inga, I love you and I want to make you my wife,"
said Mickey.

"I know Mickey, but fifteen and sixteen-year-old girls
can really have some strong feelings. Let's go outside for a
few minutes."

Mickey and Inga went outdoors so that they could say
good night in the privacy of the cool velvet darkness of night.
There was no moon and they held each other closely. Mickey
felt her breasts under her shirt and put his hand up the bottom
of her heavy sweater; he reached up until he felt the velvet
smoothness of her breasts and the erect nipples.

She sighed with pleasure, "I need you tonight, Mickey.
Please make love to me."

He nuzzled her ear and a special place at the side of her

neck that he knew she loved to have him touch and kiss, then he drank in that special fragrance from her skin. There was a small banister on the building and she turned and sat on it, making herself just a little higher. She pulled up her skirt and put the sweater she was wearing around his shoulders so that they were protected and warm. Mickey had all the freedom he needed with her body and he undid his pants and pulled her to him. As he entered her body she sighed with delight. They clung together in ecstasy for some minutes.

"I love you, Inga," he sighed and he kissed her in that special teasing way that she loved so much.

She pushed his hair from his forehead and kissed his eyes, the tip of his nose and then his lips. "We are so much in love that it just does not seem fair that we should have to be apart," she said and buried her head in his shoulder.

After a few moments more of shared passion they kissed, took each other's hands and returned to the inside, each going to his or her own bed to dream of their love.

Mickey awoke during the night thinking of Inga. We have been intimate and we are well educated enough to realize that there could be consequences. What if there should be a child? God, I would never want to leave her alone in a difficult situation like that. I do want children with her and I would want to know if I had a child. I must talk to her about this. It is very important!

SEVENTEEN

It was early in the morning. They had eaten what was available. "God I will be glad when I can really eat what I have been dreaming about. Some bacon and eggs and pancakes and hot cereal with raisins and some really good hot coffee," said Brad. He got up from the table and took his usual morning trip outdoors.

They were still not using any of the facilities in the cabin. It was cold and taking a shit outside got more difficult every day. While he was gone Stan cleaned up some; he would go when Brad returned.

"OK Stan, I'm back. Go see if you can find a tree we have not used yet," chided Brad.

Stan left and Brad had time to look at himself in the mirror as Stan had done some days before. "Damn it, I am getting so thin." He felt his legs and arms and his torso. "But all this climbing that we have been doing is sure keeping us in shape."

He noticed that his face was thin, but it seemed to Brad that he had matured. His eyes were very blue, set wide apart on his face. High cheek bones came from an Indian relation, way back somewhere in his genealogy. His sandy blond hair was long like Stan's. He was tall and angular.

"Well not so bad for all I've been through. When I get back to the world I'm going to eat every damned steak I can find and put some meat back on these bones, and we will make it back if Stan has anything to do with it!" he told himself.

Stan came in and made a serious, flat statement, "We had better start keeping a watch for any Germans that might come searching our area while they are in retreat. I have been thinking that it would be best for us to stay out of sight of either side until the Americans arrive. While I was outside I sort of checked out our position and I think the safest place for us to be is up on top of that hill where we can see who's coming and who's going where. With all that ammunition and guns up there we could make it really rough for anyone down here in this location. Let's pack some of our food and some blankets and take them up there today."

"I sure do hate to leave this cabin. It's been so warm and comfortable here. Guess you're right though. It is best to be prepared and now probably is as good a time as any to move along. OK Stan, is a blanket apiece enough? And what about all that stuff we brought back with us day before yesterday?"

"We will take one Luger apiece and hide the rest under the beds. There is plenty more where that came from and we will want to use the bag to pack some of these things in. It is cold outside and it looks like it might snow again so let's travel as light as we can.

"We are going to get through this survival experience, Brad. You have changed a lot, thanks for agreeing with me about moving. I know that sometimes it seems easier just to do nothing and hope for the best, but if we do the right thing we are going to make it back."

They packed what they needed and Stan went to the door and cautiously opened it. More snow had fallen last night and the air was much colder than it had been yesterday. The cloud cover was low in the sky and it looked as if it could start snowing again any time.

"One thing, Brad, when we get up there we are going to have to pry open that same shutter again and put you in the window again. Is that OK with you? We have the keys to the inside rooms but not the main building."

"Yeah, I can manage that," said Brad cooperatively.

As they walked to the base of the hill they were going to climb they could hear the sounds of motor vehicles out on the highway. The air was cold and crisp and the acoustics made sound around them very sharp, but because of the trees between them and the roadway they could not see the small convoy that was moving past the park.

It took them better than an hour to climb the hill that just the day before had only been a few minutes' walk. The pack they were carrying and their ponchos and the new snow had really slowed their progress. They stopped to rest for a few minutes and Stan pulled his binoculars from the top of the bag and positioned them for his viewing. Up the road the German convoy was now in clear sight.

"I can see that there are mostly heavy guns and some support equipment and men in those trucks. That can only mean they are heading for the high hills or the river for their next defense move. Damn it! I wish we could let our forces know what's going on. They could put an end to all of this with just one good shot from the artillery."

"Could we do anything about it, Stan, with all that stuff up on the hill?" asked Brad.

"Let's get moving, Brad. Maybe you have a good idea there."

When they reached the stone and brick building, they entered just as they had discussed. Brad opened the back door just enough to get them in. They put their supplies in the room with the filing cabinets. The flash lights were just where they had left them and would be very useful.

Brad was curious about the contents of the cabinets and opened one, took a card out, and read it. It was written in German, so he did not know what it said.

"Wonder what in the hell this is all about?"

Without thinking he put the card in his chest pocket, closed the cabinet, left the room, and locked the door behind him. He looked carefully around the room and went outside where he found Stan watching below with his binoculars.

"I locked up the place and I'll help you watch the country side below," said Brad as he came up behind Stan and reached down for the second pair of binoculars that was near Stan.

Stan pointed toward the south and whispered, "There is a large command car with two motorcycle escorts heading this way from that town you can see."

Both men concentrated their binoculars toward the oncoming escorted vehicle. It was traveling slowly and seemed to be searching for something on the right side of the roadway. It passed the park area and the cars speed slowed even more and finally it stopped at about one half a kilometer farther along the road. They were watching the car with intent interest.

"Shit Stan, what do you suppose that guy is looking for?"

"Keep watching, Brad. God damn it, he has found a gate! There must be some kind of a road there, where are they going and who is that in the car?"

They continued to watch. The car had disappeared under some trees that covered that part of the park.

"Oh God Brad, I'll bet I know where he's going to end up," said Stan.

"You got it, they are going up a back road that will bring them right up here where we are now!" said Brad. "How are we going to cope with this one, Stan?"

Stan motioned to Brad. "Let's move over toward and into that thick growth of trees near the small building where the power unit and the antennas are. That will give us some cover and our ponchos will act as camouflage. We will stay right there and see what happens."

Just as they got to the tree cover they were surprised to hear the sound of a small engine airplane. They looked up and at the base of the low swirling clouds there came a small observation aircraft. It was turning very sharply in a steep bank. Turning into the wind the aircraft settled down over the far end of the runway and made a three point landing.

"That pilot really knows what he is doing. I'm going to be that good someday," said Brad. "The snow on the ground did not even bother him. He's got to be a real ace."

The aircraft taxied to the small hanger and its engine shut down. Before the propeller had quit turning there was another sound, that of the large powerful command car. It roared onto the other side of the runway with it lights flashing on and off and spraying snow from under its wheels, and it came to a stop near the now still aircraft.

Brad and Stan were so intent on viewing this incident that they had forgotten any fear they had. Both men had their eyes glued to the sight in front of them. Just as the car got to the plane's landing sight the hatch like door swung up and open and the pilot stepped down the small ladder type steps. He was waving and then saluting the officer who had climbed from the rear of the staff car whose door slammed in a slight breeze that had caught the chauffeur off guard. Even from this distance the noise and voices of the actors in this play could be heard.

"Would you look at that, Stan," said Brad, and they observed the pilot and officer patting one another on the backs.

"We're both on time and I like that," commented the officer.

"That's the man in the picture, it's Goebbels himself," said Brad in an excited voice.

"Right," said Stan who put his finger to his lips. "Calm down and be really still, this is no time to mess up!"

There was about five minutes of friendly conversation between the two men below, but it was in German and even though it could be heard it was not understood.

The pilot looked at his watch and propelled the thought-to-be Goebbels toward the airplane. Before climbing aboard the officer waved and shouted "auf wiedershen" in the direction of the chauffeur. He stepped into the aircraft; the door closed. The plane's engine was started and in less than a minute it began to move toward the far end of the airstrip. There was no hesitation, the pilot turned the plane onto the runway and began his take off roll, leaving wheel marks in the light snow and with only two hundred yards to get off the ground the small airplane leaped into the air and began its climb up and through the thick overcast clouds. Within just seconds it was gone.

The limousine and its motorcycle escorts left the area as they had entered, leaving their tire marks in the snow they drove slowly until they reached the roadway boarding the park and turned to the east.

He's headed for the homeland," Stan said. "I would guess that Goebbels did not want to chance the rest of the trip to his headquarters by car. We did get a close look at the son of a bitch, didn't we, Brad?"

It was 0700 in the morning and Sacket left his barracks to meet Colonel Howard for their early morning briefing with Colonel Hibner. When they arrived Squadron Leader Owens was already there with Sergeant Esser. Colonel Hibner was at the door to greet them and had a cup of hot tea waiting for all the participants of this morning's meeting.

The tea was finished and now it was time to get down to business. Hibner was seated behind his heavy mahogany desk of which the surface was polished, neat and uncluttered. This office looked as though it had care every day. Not a thing was out of place and even with the dim light from the lanterns there did not seem to be dust anywhere.

There was a knock at the door and General Schmidt who had been at the meeting in the barracks came in. He had some packages with him. "I have the items you requested Colonel Hibner."

Hibner stood and spoke, "Come in, General. These items will complete our materials for this mission. Now that we have decided who will make the contact with the Western Allies I feel it is of the utmost importance that we proceed and with great haste. Colonel Howard, now is the time for you to give Sergeant Sacket the information he will need. He must know what he will do and say after he and Sergeant Esser make contact with the proper officials of the Western Allied Armies."

The next hours were spent briefing Sacket and Esser on the route they would take to the point of Allied contact, their method of travel, personal information about the prisoners held at this prison by the Germans, names of the German officers who would cross over to the Western Allies, and the method of confirming the instructions for the repatriation of Allied prisoners in exchange for the surrender of the German officers.

"We hope that both of you men have the ability to memorize the information that has been given to you. It will not be possible for any of it to be on paper because if for some reason you should be captured by Germans this whole thing could blow up in our faces," cautioned Colonel Hibner.

The only break in the meeting came after several hours and that was for a simple lunch. There was a good wine to toast the success of this forthcoming mission.

Sacket and Esser were to be outfitted with uniforms of their respective countries and told that a vehicle was being prepared and serviced for their use.

Colonel Hibner raised his hand to get the attention of the men in the room. "The time I have selected for your departure is to be at 0600 Wednesday morning. The weather forecast is for rain and fog. This will eliminate any low level air attacks on the part of the Western Allies and the movement of tanks and artillery by our armies will probably be away from their battle zones. We estimate the fighting will be at a minimum and defensive on the part of our forces."

Colonel Howard asked to be heard and his request was acknowledged. "After you two men have made contact with an officer in charge you must explain to them what our positions are here as prisoners. They must understand that we are all in danger of being moved or worse, eliminated. Those in charge must know that all here, including the Germans, will cooperate completely with whatever course of action they recommend, whether it means staying here or moving out in the direction of the battle zone.

"We will prepare a message zone in the shape of a large bull's eye that will show from the air. A man or message could easily be parachuted into or close to that area. We will all be watching closely day and night."

Squadron Commander Owens stood up and walked over to Esser and Sacket and shook their hands. "My men and I all thank you for what you're doing and we will pray for your safety and the success of your mission. You are brave and honorable men!"

Sacket stood and turned to face the Officers and Esser. "I want all of you to know how honored I am to have been chosen for this mission." He put his hand on Esser's shoulder and said, "I'm glad you and I will be together on this wild ass adventure. We have the details, I'm ready to go," said Sacket eagerly.

Esser stood and remarked, "I agree with everything Sergeant Sacket has said. We both thank you for this opportunity to be of service." He turned to Sacket and extended his hand. "Grundlich gluck, as we say in German," and the two men shook hands.

Colonel Hibner stood and said, "I agree with Sergeant Esser's words. You two men rest for the remainder of this day and tomorrow and you will both be on your way very early Wednesday morning. Now, you should all return to your quarters. If something should change or if something new should come up between now and tomorrow evening feel free to contact me. If there should be some reason to abort this mission you will hear from me. I have asked that General Schmidt assist me in Sergeant Esser's absence for I want him to be completely rested to begin this important assignment. Good afternoon gentlemen."

Back at Sacket's barracks all of the men had just finished eating dinner. Everyone was either sitting or standing around talking about what they imagined this plan would be to get them out of this prison camp. It was amazing what some of them had come up with. One thought helicopters would land and just whisk them back to civilization. Another said the gates would just be opened and they would be free to go out on their own. Some were still thinking it was all a hoax and nothing would happen at all.

As Sacket approached Building #18 he knew he was going to be deluged with questions. Klein was the first man he saw as he came through the door. It was just a matter of seconds and he was noticed by everyone in the room and they began to crowd around him.

"Tell us everything that was said."

Klein said, "Give the guy a break. He has been over there all day. Let him settle down for a few minutes."

"It's OK, Klein. They are all anxious to hear about this exchange program. I am tired, but it can all be told in a matter of minutes and then I'm going to hit the sack.

"Well here it is! Wednesday morning Esser and I will leave

here in an ambulance and we will be dressed like medics. One German and one American. We will follow the road from here through Kaiserslautern, then on to Saarbrücken where the battle is now being fought. Esser will be driving and do all the necessary talking. I will be in the rear of the ambulance under a blanket posing as a wounded soldier. There is rain in the weather forecast, so we should have little or no opposition due to fighting. Once we have crossed into Western Allied held country we will surrender ourselves to the American authorities. Then it will be my job to identify myself and Esser to an intelligence officer or a commander in charge of that area. We have had to memorize all the necessary information about this mission. We don't leave until early Wednesday. So far as I know none of the other guys know about this yet, and I think it would be best not to let it get out of here until after Esser and I are on the road, just in case there should be a leak outside this camp. I will do everything I can to accomplish what is expected of me. I know how important this is to all of you."

Sacket was feeling lots of emotion and said, "If you guys don't care I'm going to try and get some sleep."

There were sounds of praise from the men in the room, but not a word of the plan was spoken by anyone that night. The barracks were quiet earlier than usual and it seemed that everyone man slept better than he had in months.

God I hope this is one of my last nights in this damned bed, Sacket thought to himself as he laid down, fully clothed, on his wooden bed. He forced himself to sleep and dreamt of his warm comfortable bed when he was a boy at home.

During the night Klein threw an extra blanket over him and he slept warmer than he had in a very long while.

Tuesday came and went. The men asked no questions of him and there were no new problems that needed the attention of Colonel Hibner. He did not see Esser that day. He got off by himself and went over and over the plan until it was imprinted on his brain. He was not really a religious man, but he prayed some too. "Please let this go off without a hitch, so many men are depending on me. I feel so responsible and, if it is within my power, let me get everyone out of here and home again. Please let this work for the good of all concerned. I'll even thank you in advance, God, for any help you can give Esser and me."

He exercised some and talked to Klein about things that were unimportant, but not once through the day did he allow his thoughts for the coming days to be interrupted. The prisoners in their ragged clothes continued to do their daily chores around the barracks. The work they were all doing was keeping their minds occupied. Everyone's nerves were on edge. Klein even had some of his men out sweeping the porch, and then there was the least desirable duty, that of keeping the latrines clean and helping clean up in the mess hall.

Dinner came and it was time for bed again. Soon he would be on his way out of there. He was relaxed this night and surprisingly slept very well.

The next thing he knew someone was shaking him. "It's 0430 hours and time to hit the boards."

He looked up into two faces over him and recognized Klein and Colonel Howard. With real effort he sat up and accepted a steaming cup of coffee. He didn't know where it had come from, but it was welcome and tasted great.

He dressed in the fatigues of an American medic. There were well worn boots that were his size. Howard had an officer's leather flying jacket that he had scrounged from one of his men. Sacket put it on and Howard slipped a Red Cross arm band up his left arm.

"You're a doctor now. The jacket and the arm band may influence the enemy, just in case."

Sacket's uniform was complete with a garrison cap. One would never know to look at him now that he had been in captivity for six months. He was six feet tall and a lot leaner than he had been when he first arrived. Dark hair, deep set eyes, and a contagious smile made him very attractive. He was cooperative, but had a temper that had gotten him in trouble many times in his life.

As he left the barracks everything was quiet. Klein came out with him. "They all want to respect your request and have told me to wish you God speed and good luck," and with a pat on the back Klein was gone.

Outdoors there were clouds in the sky and it had warmed enough to melt the snow, leaving puddles on the grounds around the barracks.

Sitting in front of the barracks was a German ambulance, red cross and all. Sergeant Esser, dressed in German fatigues, was in the driver's seat waiting for him.

"Get up here in front with me, you can move to the back after we get down the road near the front lines."

Sacket got in and looked over at Esser. "Let's get this show on the road!"

As they drove the ambulance past headquarters, Colonel Hibner walked out to the vehicle and saluted both of them and said, "Last night two German guards who were ready to escape and inform were shot and killed. I feel sure that we can proceed with safety. Good luck, gentlemen." With a salute he turned on his heel and was gone. The guards opened the gate and with a salute waved the ambulance on. It had begun to rain and Esser turned the windshield wipers on. This mission had begun.

As Esser turned their vehicle onto the road that led to Saarbrücken he said, "We will drive slowly until we get to the battle zone, there might even be a road block. I will tell you when you should get into the back. It is important that I should do all the talking, even if you should be personally confronted."

"Yeah Esser, I remember all that and the rest too. You sound like a broken record, but I know that you're just trying as hard as I am to keep all this stuff in your head," said Sacket.

"I think it is time for you to get in the back now, and no matter what happens, not a word! You're wounded and very sick, OK!"

The two men traveled quietly on down the road for about ten miles. They saw only a few small villages; there were no signs of military occupancy. They approached an intersection with signs and markers that told of conditions ahead. There was a barricade. Two German soldiers with rifles stepped out into the path of the ambulance. The rules of the road were not to use headlights and with the rain Esser had barely stopped in time. One of the guards had a large flash light and shown it from one end to the other of the vehicle, the second guard was standing near the barricade. An official conversation was in progress between the guard and Esser, who was on the driver's side of the car. Esser pulled his identification papers out for him to see, meanwhile the second German was holding his flashlight so the beam pierced the interior of the ambulance. Sacket was on a bed in the rear and every now and then he moaned.

The identification papers and Esser's explanation seemed to satisfy the rain soaked Germans and they stepped back and waved the vehicle through the checkpoint.

Daylight began to show in the east and the threat of exposure was becoming more imminent. Esser increased their speed, but the rain had started to turn to snow, which was just one more hazard for these men to contend with.

They drove on for some miles. Esser kept a careful watch on the road and spoke softly back to Sacket. "We are passing German troops and their equipment on both sides of this road. They appear to be digging in for a stand here in this small valley."

As they rounded a gradual turn in the road, Esser saw two German Tiger Tanks, one on each side of the road. There was a German soldier standing in the open hatch looking toward the Western Allied enemy. This must be the German first line of defense and I have got to get through it, thought Esser.

Without hesitation Esser turned on his siren and flashing red lights and accelerated the ambulance. The German tanker trooper turned in surprise and waved the ambulance through the opening between the tanks.

Esser could hear the man in the tank shouting at him, "Do you know what's ahead? You must be crazy!"

As the ambulance widened its distance from the tanks behind him and the flashing lights of what appeared to be small arms fire, he noticed that the fiery tracers were all going over his vehicle on either side.

"God damn it Esser, what's all that racket? It sounds like all hell has broken loose!" screamed Sacket.

"I think we are nearly there, so get your American uniformed ass up here in front with me," called Esser to Sacket.

It took only seconds for Sacket to climb forward into the right seat. They were about one mile from the German line of defense and Esser slowed down expecting to face an American check point and guard.

They drove for another mile at slow speed. American equipment and soldier's began to appear on both sides of the road. They passed up and over a small rise and a jeep with about ten soldiers around it stood in the middle of the road. The soldiers all had their weapons pointed at the ambulance.

Esser turned off the engine. "Now it's your turn Sacket."

The guard said, "Turn off those lights and that damned siren and get out here with your hands over your head, both of you, on the double!"

Sacket jumped out of the ambulance with his hands up raised and spoke to the Staff Sergeant who was approaching him with his rifle pointed straight at him and Esser, "God damned am I ever glad to see you. I am an American. This German Sergeant and I have just escaped from a German Prison of War Camp."

The Staff Sergeant said, "Yeah and I'm Clark Gable, you two come with me. I'm taking you both to our command post and we will see who you two really are! Don't even think about doing anything funny or you may have some real need for that ambulance you were driving!"

EIGHTEEN

Last night the sky had been brightly illuminated in the southwest and the sounds of war were very noticeable. The distant sounds of explosions came one after another in quick succession and could be heard and sometimes felt. All the children lay awake, listening in fear to the frightening sounds and thinking of the imagined but real destruction.

This morning Herr Graef, Inga, and Frau Miller were sitting on the floor with the children, trying to reassure the youngest and older ones alike by answering their fearful questions. "Will there be fighting here? When will the war be over? Will the Americans kill all of us?"

Inga spoke out loud and said, "I think the Americans and English soldiers will be like our friend Sergeant Reber. You all know him well, he is a kind and gentle man. Herr Graef and I both speak English and when the Americans get here Mickey will be here too. I think he will be able to tell his friends what we have been doing here on our farm and he will help them to understand that we are no threat whatsoever to them."

Young Willie, the only boy in the group said, "I am a German and my uncle always told me, 'Just remember Willie, you are a man and you must always fight for your country.' I have never forgotten that, what shall I do now?" The tears streaked down his face and he got up and went to sit near Herr Graef.

The older man put his arm around the boy's shoulder. "You have been helping your country to feed its many people all these months, Willie, and that is far better than shooting and killing with a gun. When all of this fear, hate, and

suffering is over and the really good people of Germany
prevail and they are at peace with themselves and other
nations, you will see how really important your work on
this farm has really been."

Willie turned his face toward Mickey, "If you have to go
away, will you try and come back to see all of us again? I
will really miss you."

"Yes, when the war is over and everything is calm again
and I have the permission of my country's officials, I will
make every effort possible to get back to this part of
Germany," said Mickey looking directly at Inga.

The next afternoon it became colder outside with clouds
that hung heavier and lower over the valley. Just after dark
it had begun to snow again and there seemed to be a thick
fog covering everything. The military traffic was very light,
just one or two vehicles had been seen during the early
evening, probing the fog and light snow on the roadway in
front of this small community.

"If the weather stays like this until the day the Western
Allied Armies come up this valley and there is not a battle
going on I think it would be wise for you and I to be sitting
right out there on the roadway to meet them," suggested
Herr Graef to Mickey. "All the others will be safer hidden in
the bunkers on the hill, but only if there should be a sudden
outbreak of gun fighting. We might be taking a risk, but let's
you and I go out there in the morning and spend a few hours
seeing what is passing our village. That is really the best
way to gain some insight on how the Germans and Western
Allies are doing in this war."

"As your prisoner you have been good to me, Herr Graef,
and when this war is over I hope the future will allow us to
be life long friends," said Mickey with real emotion in his
voice.

As it became daylight the next morning the two men ate
some breakfast. They dressed as warmly as they could. Inga
had found some homemade heavy underwear and some extra
warm hand knit socks for Mickey to wear under his regularly
worn flight suit. She brought him a helmet type headgear
that covered his head and face to shield it against the cold.

For the past six months Herr Graef had been dressed in the official uniform of a General. Mickey had not realized the insignias on his hat or shoulders were that of a General. The uniform he wore was the informal version of his rank. All during the time since Mickey had been captured, he had assumed the position of a gentleman civilian, probably because of what he was now in charge of or maybe what he had been doing prior to the war. Because of his great respect and love of others, it was not hard to understand what a kind and compassionate person he really was.

Herr Graef slipped into a heavy uniform overcoat and put on a similar head and face cover to what Mickey was wearing. Each put a blanket around his shoulders and the two men went out the door into the cold, snow-like fog.

They walked with difficulty to the road and found shelter in a little roadside stand that had been built at the entrance to this little farming community. The two men talked softly for more than an hour about politics and what they were going to do in the event the Western Allies should appear on this road.

Herr Graef reached inside his overcoat to a pocket, removed a small pen light, and handed it to Mickey. "Keep this for an emergency and be sure it is out of the sight of others. Try it to make sure you know how to use it."

Reber pressed the on button and pointed its light at his wrist watch. "It is 12:15," said Mickey.

Suddenly Herr Graef put his finger to his lips and it seemed that he was listening intently for something. He stood and peered out of the open side of the stand and looked up the road.

Then Mickey heard the sound too. It was a person walking toward them in the snow. There was the distinct sound of boots crunching and scuffing in the snow and then an occasional cry or whimper. "Hilfe mich, belieben hilfe mich," and then more scuffing in the snow.

Herr Graef slipped out of the stand and waved to Mickey to follow him. Coming toward them in the middle of the road was a single figure. The person wore the heavy winter overcoat of a German soldier and a hooded head covering instead of the regular hat worn by the German military. The man was hunched over, looking down and ahead. He was struggling to stay on his feet.

Herr Graef called out, "Stopfen," and the soldier stopped. He did not take his hands out of his pockets, but he raised his head to look directly into the eyes of Herr Graef.

There was a conversation in German and finally Graef said, "Let's take him into the stand and get out of this falling snow."

Mickey took the soldier by the left sleeve and led him inside. With the pen light he looked at the soldier, who was very cold and despondent. Graef told the soldier to sit down and relax and he checked his military identification. Graef took the blanket from his own shoulders and put it around the German soldier who flinched in pain as his right arm was touched.

"This poor man has been walking all day from a place near the battlefront where his Panzer Troop was nearly wiped out by the Western Allies artillery. His tank and two others were destroyed. He has a bad wound on his right arm and he says his other crew members are all dead. He did not want to be captured, so he was trying to return to his home town that is located just a few more kilometers up this way at a place called Shifferstadt. I don't want to leave him here in his condition. He would never make it through the rest of the day. Let's take him to the big building and have one of the women dress his wounds and feed him something hot."

"Mickey, you help him get up to the big building and I will go ahead and get things ready for him. If he tries to talk to you answer him in English and see what happens. Check him for weapons. I don't think he has any."

Graef disappeared into the falling snow. It took Mickey several tries to get the injured man to his feet and after they had begun their difficult walk to the main building, Reber asked the soldier, "What is your name?"

He repeated the question several times and finally the soldier turned to him with a strange expression on his face and said, "Mein name is Herman. Are you an American?"

Reber was half carrying, half dragging Herman by the

time they got to the door of the building.

As the two men entered the warm interior, several of the women were there to help. Reber got the cold and injured Herman onto a folding cot located in his room.

Frau Miller asked Reber, "Will you help me to take off his over coat and other clothing. We must be very careful of his right arm. I'm not sure, but I think it may be broken."

She had been right. The arm was broken in two places and there were several deep cuts too. Two of the women began to care for Herman. Frau Miller set his broken arm and dressed several deep cuts. They made him comfortable and warm and got him hot food and drink.

One of the women said to Herman, "At least you're safe here and the war is over for you now."

Inga came into the room and put her hand on Mickey's shoulder. "It is nice of you to share your room with this man. I want to talk to him and find out more about him. Herr Graef thinks we might get a better idea of when the Western Allies will be in this valley by the answers he gives me."

After Herman was settled in bed, Inga went in to talk with him and was in his room for more than an hour. When she came out she related the information she had heard to Graef and the others. "His name is Herman Schultz. He is twenty-five years old and he was born and raised on a farm near the little town of Schifferstadt. His father and two brothers were all in the military and he has not seen any of his family for more than three years. He had been trained and fought with the Panzer Command, and had just recently been promoted to Staff Sergeant. His battalion has been fighting in France since the Western Allied invasion. They had been given orders to move on to the East. It was impossible for them to go farther as they had run out of fuel. He said they just had to sit there in one place and they were surrounded and destroyed. All of his enthusiasm and devotion to Germany has been lost. He told me several times, 'All is kuput! Now all I want to do is go home and hope that I still have some family left.'

"I'm glad we found him when we did. He could not have made it much farther up the road. He would have frozen to death," said Mickey with concern in his voice.

Stan put both pairs of binoculars back in their cases after they had watched until the last of Goebbels' limousine had vanished from view on the roadway below.

"That's going to be one to tell our grandchildren, Brad, probably the closest either of us will get to a God damned son of a bitch of that caliber," said Stan showing his distaste for the higher German officials.

Brad turned his head skyward. "Stan it's going to snow a lot more now, so let's get into the building and plan on staying the night instead of trying to hike back down that hill."

"Good idea, Brad. No use either of us getting sick at this late date. We have blankets and some food. You go ahead. I have to take a leak, and then I'll be right in."

When Stan came back Brad had been investigating some of the other cupboards in the larger of the three rooms. He had closed the shutter from the outside. There was a small stove in one corner that had a supply of firewood near it along with some coal. He had a fire going and the area of the stove was warm and comfortable enough. He had found some candles and had one or two of them lighted. Not a lot of light but enough to see by, he thought.

Stan came in and was pleased at the progress Brad had made. "I think there might be a couple of fold-up cots under that counter, Brad. Apparently the Germans had spent some nights here too."

"Yeah, it looks like they had enough supplies to stay here for as long a time as was needed. I'll bet if we check out the rest of these shelves we just might find some other things to eat too. I'm going for a walk now, be back in a flash."

Brad left the building and found a nearby tree that suited his needs, then walked to the edge of the pine forest that protected the stone building from the view of anyone below in the valley or even in the area of the cabin they had stayed in. He looked up at the smoke that was coming from their fire inside the building and it could not be seen. It was dissipating in the trees before it could rise above them. At the edge of the tree line he could look out across the valley and beyond. Although the clouds had lowered to only a couple hundred feet above the hill tops, there were flurries of snow coming from the dark gray overcast and the ground in all directions had been blanketed in a white shroud.

Stan came outside and joined him. "See Brad." He pointed to the south west. "There is a town about ten miles away. That highway in the valley below curves in that direction. That means that the retreat of the German army will be followed by the advance of the Western Allied armies from the direction of that town. What a beautiful sight that would be to watch!"

The sun was gone and darkness became more pronounced. There was an occasional bright flash that they could see beyond the town. Because of the wind's direction the sound of artillery could not be heard.

The two picked up another sack of coal and a canister of water that had been stored near the generator shack by some foresighted Germans and went into the building and closed and locked the large door that had been opened just enough to allow entry.

Brad and Stan talked a little about their families at home, and talked about the crew of the Louise E. Ann. They still wondered about their fate and hoped for a reunion with at least some of them when all this was over. Stan was still desirous of becoming a criminal lawyer and Brad could talk of nothing else but being an Air Force pilot.

"Guess we better turn in early. I want to be on deck to see what happens when this war starts moving again. If the weather clears tomorrow, things just might start to happen. The Air Force will be doing its job and the tanks and artillery will be moving again and the infantry will be pushing the Krauts back farther into Germany. That could mean you and I will be free again and maybe very soon now!" said Stan.

The men slept well that night. They were warm and felt safe. Stan could not help but think of the night he awoke feeling panic at the thought that this very building might have been rigged with explosives. They had opened every door and had moved so many things around that he now felt sure they were safe from that sort of catastrophe. Best err on the side of caution; he would have a closer look at things outside tomorrow. The one place they had not gone was into the hanger itself and something told him to be wary of that building and the surrounding area.

When daybreak came Brad awoke, yawned and stretched. As he pulled his blanket down from over his head he noticed how warm the room was. In the past few months his breath had shown as vapor when he had exhaled at this hour of the morning. He looked toward Stan's cot and realized that he was not in it. He sat up with a start at the noise he heard, metal and wood were being moved at the other end of the room. What in the hell was going on?

Neither of them had ever relaxed enough at night to undress and they slept fully clothed, right down to their boots, just in case they had ever had a problem that would have necessitated their leaving their immediate area. Brad walked quietly to the end of the room with his Luger in his hand.

He noticed that the door to the weapons room was open and, just as he got even to the door, Stan came through it carrying a wooden box.

"God you scared the shit out of me," screamed Brad. "What a relief, what in the hell are you doing?"

"I got to thinking about our helping our forces out when the time comes. That might be today or tomorrow. It's going to come one of these days and soon now. Let's get a couple of these machine guns put together and have the ammo for them ready to use."

It took the rest of the morning to select two guns, and get them cleaned and assembled. Stan was a sharp shooter and knew a lot about fire arms, but all the directions for these were in German so he really had to work with them slowly to be sure he had them put together properly. Brad could load a hand gun and fire it OK, but he lacked the expertise, without assistance, to do this on his own.

"Let's put one of these guns on each side of the hill out

there and cover them until they are needed. We can put ammo with each unit."

One box of ammunition was loaded on each gun and two other boxes were placed by each just in case they were needed.

The weather had improved. The snow and rain had stopped. There were breaks in the clouds that let the winter blue sky show through. The wind had stilled and the temperature had raised to well above freezing. The war was in full swing again and the sounds of the big guns were much closer. With the clearing skies, flights of P-38s and P-47s were again searching the valleys for the enemy and P-51s were in hot pursuit and patrolling the air above the clouds for adversary aircraft.

Brad watched the sky with a real growing desire. "I can't wait until I can get back in school again. I'm going to be the best God damned pilot there is one of these fine days!"

He turned his eyes towards the valley and saw smoke and fire. "Hey Stan, those fires have started in just the last few minutes. It would really be a bad day for a drive in the country."

"The sky is nearly clear to the north. I'll bet the British are giving them holy hell up there!" said Stan victoriously.

For the rest of the day the air traffic remained busy and deadly, while the roadway traffic in the valley was limited to a couple of bicycles that were headed east.

It was about an hour before sunset when a single P-38 seemed to fall from the sky, it was headed toward the park with smoke streaming from one engine. "He seems to be on fire and in trouble!" said Brad.

"He's too low to make it over the hills on either side of the valley, he is looking for a place to land, Brad!" said Stan, running to the edge of their hill to get a better view of the ill fated aircraft with smoke and now flames coming from its right engine.

"He's seen the runway Stan and he's heading in that direction, he's going to try for a landing." Stan had started to run down the hill toward the runway below.

"Get a gun and follow me down there, now damn it!"

The plane made the approach and had augured in on the end of the runway, collapsing its landing gear, and it slid to a stop half way down the short air strip. As Stan ran towards the crippled and still smoking P-38 he saw the pilot push back the canopy and climb out of the cockpit onto the left wing and in panic he jumped to the ground and started to run.

In frantic pursuit, Stan ran after the pilot. "Don't run, I'm here to help you! I'm an American, I'm an American!" he kept shouting.

The pilot heard Stan shouting at him and turned to see who he was. Within seconds Stan in his ragged flight coveralls had run up to the plane and the amazed pilot.

"Come on, follow me to safety. I'll explain what's been going on when we get up the hill," said Stan.

The pilot, who wore Captain's bars, nodded his head and with an astonished look on his face started to run along side of Stan up the side of the hill toward the stone building in the distance.

The snow was starting to melt, the men slowed their run to a walk, but kept a steady pace. When they reached the top of the hill, Brad appeared before them with a gun pointed directly at them.

"Take it easy, Brad. It's OK, let's get inside and explain to the Captain what we are doing here," said Stan.

"I can't believe what's happened here. This has got to be the damnedest experience I have ever had," said the disbelieving pilot.

Brad closed the building's door against the cold evening air. "You're the luckiest son-of-bitch pilot in the world, sir! And now that you're here with us, I am beginning to believe that we are going to make it out of this God forsaken place."

It took Stan a few minutes to catch his breath and calm down. "Brad, check outdoors and take a look up and down the valley. We just better hope that no one else saw the plane come down on that landing strip."

"OK Stan." Brad put the gun he had in his hand in its holster.

The Captain was still breathing hard from his uphill run,

but he was laughing too and said, "Where in the hell did you two guy's come from? I'm Captain Bill Wilson and when I get the chance I want to buy you both a drink. The crew chief of my plane is going to be royally pissed off. That old bird has over one hundred missions on it, and damn it, I had to get hit over Haiserslautern. It's just a few air miles west of here. I didn't have to bail out, thank God! I've seen this valley with that small runway several times before on low level runs, but I never saw any signs of life down here."

Stan stood up and said, "I guess now is a good time to introduce myself. I'm Stanley Farnsworth, 1st Lieutenant, United States Air Force and the other man is 2nd Lieutenant, Bradley Freestone of the United States Air Force. Six months ago we were shot down over Germany and bailed out, we were a part of the 8th Air Force out of Cambridge, England and our plane was the Louise E. Ann, a B-17 Bomber. There is still much to tell, sir. Get your breath back and let me check outside to see how Brad is doing and have a look around. Just take it easy for a few minutes and I'll be right back ASAP!"

Stan found Brad at the edge of the hilltop surveying both the park and the airstrip below. "Thanks Brad, you're doing a good job. I have told the Captain who we are and how we came to be here and our organization in England, but I wanted to check on things out here and he needed time to take in his landing and us. We will both talk to him in a few minutes. I see the fire on the P-38 has gone out. Have you seen anything or anybody?"

"The only thing I've seen so far have been a few people walking on the roadway below. I'm not sure if they are civilian or German military, and no body came to check on the airplane. The town to the southwest looks like its all on fire. I still say that Captain is one lucky son of a bitch!" commented Brad.

"Let's go inside, Brad. We will open an extra can of beans and put a little extra coal on the fire for our guest."

As they entered the stone building together, Stan patted Brad on the back and said, "We just might get through this damn war yet!"

NINETEEN

The escape was over, but now the real work had just begun. It was Sacket's position to convince the Americans at this station that he and Esser were for real. They did not have much time and with these Military Police, who were extremely conscientious about their assigned duty. The task of getting through to the commanding officer of this station was not going to be an easy one.

"I'm going to have to be a real silver tongued mother to pull this one off," Sacket told himself.

"The both of you put your arms up and lay against the top of the hood of that jeep and spread your legs apart," yelled the sergeant in charge.

"Search them," the sergeant growled with authority. Meanwhile, there were three other GIs who all had their guns trained on them. It was cold and raining, but that did not make a difference to any of these men who were used to all kinds of weather and who were dressed for it as well.

After a few minutes of rough, but thorough searching, the Sergeant said, "You and the German can explain this wild story of yours to my Lieutenant. Tie their hands behind their backs and put them in that weapons carrier and get going. Hey Sergeant James, you take over here. I'm going along for the ride so that I can hear what these jokers have to say. Esser had done exactly what he had been ordered to, he had not said a word.

"I only have one thing to say right now," said Sacket, "There are many lives at stake here. We are not armed and we have come to try and accomplish a mission that was assigned to us. We realize that you have to do your job in the best possible manner, and I would not expect you to do otherwise. I am Tech. Sergeant Gordon Sacket of the United States Air Force and I ask that you take us as soon as possible to your commander. What we are trying to do here is of great importance!"

"Yeah, sure, but first we are going to have to see my Lieutenant," insisted the Military Police Sergeant. "Get this fucking carrier moving!"

One of the guards in the vehicle said, "We have been picking up a lot of you Krauts lately, but this is our first time to find an American dressed like a medic, arm band and all. Hey you guys, this German is dressed like that too, and where did you two get an ambulance like that?"

The ride was about ten minutes. They bounced around torn up roads that were full of holes. Sacket saw several bomb craters that had been roped off. One might have swallowed up a vehicle as large as the one they were riding in if you were to come up on it in the dark. The carrier entered a demolished town that was still smoking and burning from artillery shells and the surrounding buildings were mostly bombed out rubble.

The driver pulled up in front of what appeared to have been a hotel. The Sergeant got out and walked around to the back of the vehicle and with a laugh in his voice said, "You both get your asses out here. You're going in to see some of our big brass, after you see my Lieutenant that is. This just might be your lucky day because the big brass just arrived here this morning from headquarters."

With the last comment from the Sergeant, Sacket and Esser both had smiles on their faces and Sacket said, "It always pays to go to the top when you've got troubles."

Sacket had a real temper and he was doing all he could to control himself. He was becoming more agitated and angry with the attitude of this butt kicking Sergeant. "You know Sergeant, you just might be surprised when all this is over. You may wish you had given this situation a little more consideration. You might have even gotten a campaign medal and another stripe and it just might work out that your Lieutenant won't really be happy with the way you have handled Sergeant Esser and myself."

"You want to bet? He's going to reward my actions for bringing in someone like you and this Kraut that's with you!"

With the last remark Sacket and Esser were escorted into a building that was in better condition than most of those around the area. The windows had been blown out and the once polished hardwood floors were scratched. There were piles of trash and glass that had been swept up in an attempt to clean the mess up. It was doubtful that someone would do anything but demolish this building after the war was over.

"OK, this is Lieutenant Meadow's office. Wait here until I tell him what's going on here."

The Sergeant entered the office and his voice and attitude changed immediately, "Staff Sergeant Kirk Sanders, Military Police, requests permission to speak with Lieutenant Meadows."

There was a clerk sitting behind a table who looked up and gave the Sergeant his attention. "I'm sorry Sergeant but the Lieutenant left some hours ago and will be gone until tomorrow."

"I have a problem that needs the attention of an officer in charge. We have a man outside that says he has escaped from a POW Camp and he came into the area in a German ambulance, accompanied by a German Sergeant. He says he has urgent business and needs to talk with someone in charge. What should I do? Is it OK with you if I throw the two of them in a lockup until the Lieutenant returns tomorrow?" asked the Sergeant.

The clerk thought for a moment. "We do have all those officers who are having a meeting in the big room. Maybe we had better check and see if they are willing to talk with them. Give me a few minutes and as soon as they stop for a coffee break I'll go in and see how the General wants to handle this."

"I have three guards and myself and those two prisoners in the hall way. We will wait out there until you can check with the higher ups."

"It should just be a few minutes, Sergeant, and then we

can make a decision," responded the clerk.

Sergeant Sanders came out of the office and back into the hallway. "You guys are sure lucky because Lieutenant Meadows has left the area and won't be back until tomorrow so the clerk is going to check with the big brass about your big problem. If they don't want to handle it, we may put you in a lock up for the night!"

"God damn it to hell," said Sacket, losing his patience. "We have got to talk to someone tonight!"

He had seen the clerk go through a big door to their left and without hesitation he broke loose from the guards and turned his back to the large door and pushed it open.

"Come on Esser, we are going to get into this room and speak to someone in charge instead of a this wet behind the ears Sergeant who acts like he's God's gift to the military." Both Sacket and Esser had moved so fast that their guards did not have time to restrain their actions. The door to the meeting room sprang open and all six men were standing in front of a desk that had five colonels and a general seated behind it.

A first Lieutenant rushed up to the Sergeant and his prisoners and said, "This had better be something really important, Sergeant. You have all interrupted a serious meeting here."

The clerk was standing behind the General, "I was just about to tell you about this, sir. I am sorry for the intrusion. Guards, take charge of these prisoners and remove them from the room!

The General put up his hand. "Let's have some order here. Maybe we should hear what these men have to say."

Sacket stepped forward and looking directly at the high brass seated at the meeting table. "You had better bet your sweet ass that seven hundred American and British lives depend on what you're going to do about the information we have to tell you!"

Now all eyes and attention were focused on this dirty so-called American airman with his hands tied behind his back, who had spoken in such an insubordinate manner to all the officers in the room. A Colonel who sat next to the

General stood and pointed his finger at Sacket and said, "You are out of order and rude, but there may be good reason for your insubordination. Now that you have the attention of everyone in the room I suggest you tell us who you are and what did you mean by your last statement regarding American and British lives? Gentlemen, I suggest we take some time to hear these men out. Give us your name and your reason for being here."

Sacket had stood his ground and was still in the foreground. "Thank God, and you, sir. I am Technical Sergeant Gordon Sacket, Serial number 19178857. You are going to find this hard to believe, but I have been a prisoner of war for more than six months now and I have been sent on a mission from Stallage Luft #31. The man with me is Master Sergeant Esser from the German military. We both have very important information to give you from both the officers of the Allied prisoners and the German Prison Commander and his men that could mean freedom for all the camp prisoners, more than seven hundred in all, sir."

The General stood up. "Just a minute. I have some questions that need to be answered before we can proceed. Who is your American Commander at Stallage Luft #31 and who is your German Prison Commander?"

"Lieutenant Colonel C.J. Howard of the 397th Bomb Squadron, USAAF and Colonel Hynerick Hibner," replied Sacket. "Sir, I was taken prisoner on the 28th of June, 1944."

"What is your place and date of birth and what is your mother's maiden name?" questioned the General.

"My birth date is 10/14/22. I was born in Denison, Texas and Welch is my mother's maiden name, sir. I was shot down over Germany and I was a part of the Air Crew of a B-17 with the 390th Heavy Bomb Squadron, 8th Air Force, Cambridge, England. The Louise E. Ann was the name of my aircraft and Captain Ian McCrea was the name of my Aircraft Commander, sir!"

The General turned to his adjutant. "You got all that information, Lieutenant?"

"Yes sir," came the reply.

"Get on the wire immediately and verify it, ASAP! I want

answers within two hours. Get on it now!"

"Yes sir," and the Lieutenant was out the door. "Guard, untie their hands. Do it now," ordered the General.

"In the mean time," continued the General, "you guards are to see to it that these men get some food. They are to be treated with respect. Do you understand Sergeant?"

"Yes sir," came a sheepish reply. "See to it that these men are allowed to clean up and get them some other clothes, on the double. I want them back here in two hours. When we get verification we will start working on the plan these men have that could mean freedom for our honored war prisoners. This story is so strange that I have a feeling it is the real thing. One for the books, gentlemen," and he smiled at everyone present in the room.

Sacket and Esser were whisked to a temporary field hospital a few hundred feet away. They had hot showers and got clean clothes. Sacket was issued a new army fatigue uniform.

"What shall we do with the stuff you were wearing?" asked a PFC in charge of clothing.

"Save it to be used as evidence," said Sacket.

Esser was issued a new army fatigue too. The only difference was that it had a large letter "P" stenciled on the top and bottom.

"Wonder what Colonel Hibner would think of this?" said Esser.

"Don't worry about it. You look great, and besides, if the Colonel has his way he will be wearing the same thing one day soon now!

"Hey Esser, you speak great English. Don't be afraid to speak up and get your two cents worth in. You are very knowledgeable and any ideas you might have would be worthwhile and of benefit to the officers in charge here and to our men in Stallage Luft #31, OK?"

"I will be of help any way I can, Sergeant Sacket. You have so far been very successful."

"Yeah, but you got us through those German lines. I thought we were done for when all those bullets started to fly back there. We make one hell of a great team!"

"Hey Sergeant, you and your friend Esser are due back in the meeting room. If you're ready we will escort you back. I really gave you guys a rough time. I guess I have been in this theater too long. Fighting this damn war and being away from your family really doesn't improve your disposition any, and then we are always watching out for sabotage or some other sort of enemy activity. Some of these German women have come over here trying to get our troops involved with them for whatever reason they might have and you got to know they are up to no good. Anyhow, I really hope that the powers that be in that room up there can help you and those guys in that prison camp. Good Luck Sergeant, and you too Esser."

When they got back to the room there were five more enlisted men with pads of paper and pencils ready to take notes, and there were two Captains from Intelligence that would know how to handle this very sensitive assignment. There were K-rations on the table and two big thermoses of hot coffee.

"Sergeants, sit down and eat something and have something to drink and we will proceed as soon we get the report back on the information you gave to the General."

One of the Colonels spoke in a powerful voice that demanded the attention of everyone in the room. "It has been two hours since we sent off our request for information and we should have word any minute now. I want all of you who are responsible for taking notes to be ready at a moment's notice. There will be no distracting conversation once this meeting has resumed! If any of you have any questions, now is the time to ask them."

Just then the door opened and in came the young Lieutenant that Sacket had spoken to with disrespect. He was followed by three Sergeants, all four men had approving smiles on their faces. The Lieutenant moved over to the Colonel in charge and handed him a set of papers. The Colonel read the text twice and placed the documents on the table.

"Because of the serious nature of this mission that involves the lives of Americans and British, and from what I now understand also Germans, it will be called 'Operation Rescue' and it will be classified as 'Top Secret.' Everyone in this room is involved and if there are any leaks it will go very hard for the person or persons who take any of the ensuing information outside. Is what I have said here understood?" spoke the Colonel in a magisterial tone of voice. "Now that we have received the necessary information that confirms the validity and identification of these two men, we will proceed with Operation Rescue.

"Sergeant Sacket will you come forward and join us here at this table. Please start at the beginning of your experience and tell us all what the concerns are regarding the American and British prisoners, and the German prison officials and their personnel." With a wave of his hand the Colonel motioned for Sacket to proceed with his story.

Sacket began by telling of his last flight with the Louise E. Ann, his bail out of the ill fated aircraft, and his capture by the Germans. He described his first meeting with Colonel Hibner and then the second one where he was told of a plan that the Commander had for an early surrender of his total command in exchange for the repatriation of all of the Allied prisoners that were being held at Stallage Luft #31.

Sacket described in detail the meetings he and Lieutenant Colonel Howard and Squadron Commander Owens had with Colonel Hibner and about how he and Sergeant Esser had been chosen to make contact with the American military.

". . . and that is why we were wearing medic uniforms and our transportation was the ambulance that got us through the German lines. Sergeant Esser did a remarkable job speaking with German guards. I am sure that you realize that he is fluent in English. I have encouraged him to answer any questions you may have for him and since he is a German he may have some very valuable ideas to share with you."

"There is one thing I should tell all of you," said Sacket. "There is a way to make contact with the prison camp and the people in charge there. There is a large field to the south within the prison grounds. We were told that it would be easy to parachute your instructions in by dropping them in a large white circle that the prisoners have been busy preparing. I think that Sergeant Esser should be allowed to speak to all of you, he may have some information that I have missed."

The General put his hand forward in a welcoming gesture. "Is there something that you would like to tell us, Sergeant Esser? Please feel free to come forward so that we can all hear you clearly."

Esser stood and walked to the front of the room. He had a shy way about him. He was tall with pleasant features, blond hair, blue eyes, and mannerisms that showed he was used to authority.

"I think all of you should know that you will have no resistance when you penetrate the lines. Colonel Hibner and his men will be waiting to be taken into custody. As far as the German defenses between here and the prisons location, they are very thin and without backup support. On our drive here we saw only two tanks and very few vehicles of any kind at their front. The German troops are confused and disorganized. We would never have made it across their lines if they felt any sense of unification in their leadership. I am sure they feel victory is close for the Western Allied Nations and they are feeling a sense of defeat. I see a map on the wall there and I can give you an exact location of the prison that may help you with rescue plans for the prisoners at Stallage Luft #31."

Esser walked to the map and with a marker he drew a circle around the area of the prison. He turned and, with a gesture of respect and a slight salute, he left the front of the room.

An anxious Sacket jumped up. "Please, can we get started on this rescue mission? There are good men who have been in that prison far too long and they are waiting for their freedom. Some of the men were sick and they are so close to being rescued, it would be a terrible thing if they were to die just as they are about to be released."

Sacket collapsed into his chair. He was wet with perspiration and tears of relief streamed down his face. He put his head in his hands to cover his uncontrolled emotion.

Esser stood up and said, "There is one more thing that

you should all know. There is an element of danger here and extreme caution should be taken. The morning we left, Colonel Hibner told us that two of his guards had been shot and killed because they were ready to leave the prison grounds and relay information about this plan to the German authorities. That would have meant total destruction and death to all at Stallage Luft #31. Any plan of action must be done as quickly as possible so that the prison and its grounds can be secured and the safety of all there assured. Sergeant Sacket and I would be glad to go back the same way we came, if you think it would be in the best interest of the people back there."

"Thank you, Sergeant Esser, for your comments. We will proceed immediately but cautiously with a plan for the release of all the prisoners and the capture of all German personnel at Stallage Luft #31. I personally think that an airborne drop of army troops and equipment on the prison, and a direct high speed armed attack across the gap between the prison and our present location would succeed. It just might help to end this war a few days sooner too," commented the General.

"I want to further commend both of you, Sergeants Sacket and Esser, for the valiant effort you have put forth to bring freedom to so many men. You have done this without concern for your own lives. We will keep you informed about the progress of this mission and you will hear when it is completed," said the General.

TWENTY

The injured German Soldier, Herman, was still in pain and would be for several days. He now occupied the room that had been Mickey's since his capture some eight months ago.

Mickey had gone into his room to get some of the few possessions that were his and found Frau Miller and Inga there with Herr Graef who said, "I think it would be best for this injured soldier if one of you nurses stayed here in this room with Herman, at least until morning, so that he can have care during the night if he needs it. Would you mind making a bed in the other room, Reber?"

Frau Miller said, "I will stay with young Herman tonight. He will have all the care he needs."

With gratitude in his eyes, the injured soldier said, "Ich bin dankbar, Frau Miller. Du sind gutig," and the tired young man closed his eyes and slept.

Mickey had no real choice, but stated, "Yes, I will be glad to do that. It is nice by the fireplace and I won't mind."

Mickey left the room that had been a place of rest and contemplation, and this would be the first time since his capture that there would not be a lock on his door at night.

Inga followed him and took hold of his hand. For a moment they stood outside Mickey's room, which seemed to have been turned into a recovery room.

"Put on your warm coat. I want to talk to you alone, outside," said Mickey.

"Everyone is in there with Herman and the other young people are doing chores in the storage area, come with me while I get my coat."

She led him to the partitioned section of the big room

that was her sleeping quarters. There was just enough room for her bed on one wall and another bed just across from Inga's. She shared this small space with Frau Miller. Between the cots was a small night stand and in one corner of this tiny room was a roughly made cabinet where Inga and Frau Miller kept their few personal belongings. On one side of the little table there was a picture of a young girl and four other people standing together, all holding hands. A small silver crucifix hung on the partitioned wall at the head of her bed.

Inga picked up the picture and explained, "This is the last picture I have of my family. It was taken ten years ago. I was fourteen and I lived in a very nice home in Frankfurt with my father and mother, and my two brothers."

They were alone and Mickey had been hungry for the feel of Inga's warm body and he had missed the fragrance of her skin. He took advantage of this moment of privacy and pulled her to him. He held her tightly while kissing her on the forehead and cheeks. He teased the inside of her ear with his tongue, then kissed her on the lips ever so softly.

With a fierce urgency, she returned his kiss, turned her head and whispered, "Don't move and don't say anything, just hold me close. It feels so wonderful."

There was a light cough that caused them to separate in embarrassment. They had tried to be so careful around all the other members of this group of people and now Frau Miller had unintentionally found them together.

"Inga needed her coat. We were going outside for some fresh air," stated an ill-at-ease Mickey.

"I understand your feelings," stated Frau Miller. "I'll be staying in with Herman tonight so that I can keep a close watch over him. My bed will be empty," she stated with a knowing smile. "Just be discreet and come in here, Sergeant Reber, after everyone else is asleep."

She turned and said, "Take your short walk outside, Inga, and then we had better prepare an early supper." She left to go to the kitchen.

"There is something that has been bothering me, Inga, and I really must talk with you about it. Please come outside with me for some air."

"I'll put my coat on and meet you in just a few minutes," answered Inga.

Mickey put an old coat on that hung by the door for anyone to use when it was cold and they needed to go outside. He had been thinking for some time about the possibility of there being a child from the relationship that he was having with Inga. Was this really fair to her when there was a chance that he would not see her again for a very long time? He was torn between his desire for this woman and the possibility of the hardship it might bring to her if this did happen. What would she do in a situation like that?

The door opened and Inga was there. They walked a little distance from the building so that they could have some privacy.

"Inga, what would you do if you found that you were pregnant? I am so concerned for you and I really fear what might happen since it may be months until I can contact you."

Inga had thought of the same thing some months ago and now that the war was coming to a close she had even considered not telling Mickey if she found that she was going to have a child.

"Mickey, I love you with all my heart and having your child is something that I have thought about, and yes we both know that there could be consequences from the relationship we have had. I don't know what to say. We have so little time left to be together and I am not willing to give up one second of any time that we can share. I will always cherish the times we have been together. I know that one day you will return to me and if at that time there should be a child we will be parents and we will eventually marry and have other children."

"How would you handle being pregnant here? It would be such a burden for you, things are difficult enough here without that happening," anguished Mickey.

"It is a chance I am willing to take, and I would get through it somehow if it should happen, Mickey. Just keep me in your thoughts and get back to me as soon as you possibly can. Who knows, I may have a real surprise waiting for you. I promise you that there will never be anyone else in my life but you, so if there should be a child it will be yours and carry your name."

"I have been thinking, I want to stay in the military, Inga, and I will ask for duty in this theater in the Army of Occupation. I can get back to you sooner that way and I really think I could help the people here. You know, some of my ancestors came from Germany. You would be comfortable here too and in a few years we could travel to the United States. What do you think of my plan, Inga?"

"If that is really what you want, Mickey, it would be wonderful and I love you all the more for having suggested it. Now, I had better go inside and help Frau Miller with dinner. She has so much to do with the extra work she is doing for Herman." She kissed him lightly and turned and walked toward the main building, leaving Mickey to think about their discussion.

He turned toward the door just in time to see Inga wave to him as she closed it behind her. He would be with her tonight, and excitement cursed throughout his body. They would think of nothing but their own pleasure when they were together tonight, he thought.

A light dinner was served. The food was always very much the same, but somehow there was always some little variation that kept the meals interesting. The girls all helped to wash the dishes and clean up the kitchen.

Everyone wanted to sit by the fire and sing some songs. Then some of the children wanted to play a game having to do with geography. They loved it and each one of them raced to answer questions that Inga and Mickey would ask them in turn. Frau Miller had fed Herman and he seemed much improved tonight. Maybe he would be well enough to get out of bed tomorrow.

It was soon time for bed and Mickey placed a blanket in front of the well banked fire and put a sweater down to use as a pillow.

Inga was in charge since Frau Miller was in with Herman. "It is time for all of you to be in bed," and she assisted those who needed her to help them get ready for the land of nod. She assured those who were worried about the days ahead and tucked little Willie into his cot and said, "Good night little one, rest well." Then she blew out the light that hung in the center of his room.

Herr Graef retired to his quarters for the night and Frau Miller put on her heavy night dress and entered the room where Herman slept and closed the door. Inga went to her small partitioned space and Mickey was left to his first night of freedom in eight months.

The large room was warm and the glow of the fire had softened from the bright blaze and the crackling sound of a first set kindle to one of soft flickers that threw shadows across the large room. It was almost midnight and everything was quiet except for an occasional sound from the wood in the fireplace that cracked and threw embers against a fire screen on the hearth.

Mickey got up and left his pallet and with bare feet he quietly walked across the dimly lit room and entered the small partitioned area that belonged to Inga and Frau Miller. Inga lay under a coverlet and seemed to be asleep. He tried to make as little noise as possible and removed his shirt and pants and pulled down the blanket from around Inga to reveal her nude body. She smiled up at him and she put up her open arms to welcome him into her bed.

There was little room on her cot, but for these two who were so much in love, it made their closeness all the more wonderful.

"We must be quiet, Mickey, so that we don't wake anyone and you must leave before daylight," she whispered.

They shared an ecstatic night of love, one they would remember for many months to come.

Morning came too early and Mickey roused himself from the bed he had made by the fire and was dressed and ready for the day before any of the others were up. He left the room to wash and when he returned Frau Miller was coming out of Herman's room. She looked at Mickey with a smile on her face.

"Herman is very much improved this morning. He will

feel even better after he has eaten something."

Inga was preparing the morning meal as the others were setting the table.

They all sat down to eat. It was a wonderful time of day when there was shared conversation between this mixed group of children, young adults, and their seniors.

Herr Graef stated with a happy smile on his face, "I can tell that this is going to be a very good day."

Before breakfast was over there were sounds of aircraft in the sky. They could be heard clearly there in the big room. Inga told some of the girls to clear the table and to care for the younger children while she and Herr Graef and Mickey went outside to see what was going on.

The three put on heavy outer wear and opened their door to the disquieting sounds of aircraft in the sky. The snow had been heavy and there was not traffic on the ground, but there were flights of fighter planes sweeping down through their valley.

There was not a cloud in the clear blue sky and the sun was shining brightly. In the distance, to the west, a formation of transport aircraft could be seen dropping what appeared to be men and equipment.

"This is it, today we will meet the Western Allies," stated Herr Graef. "Inga, you and Sergeant Reber stay here. I must get everyone else and see them safely into the bunkers until we know that no harm will come to them."

Before he could leave, two men on skis approached up their road from the highway below. They stopped when they saw Herr Graef, Inga, and Mickey. Graef could see that they were suffering from fatigue and the cold and they were showing signs of fear and concern.

"It's all over," stated one of the men in German.

"Your flight from the Western Allies is useless. Stay here where you have protection and shelter and have something warm to eat and drink. Come with me to one of our buildings," replied Graef in German.

The two young men smiled and one said, "Thank you. All our comrades to the west are surrendering, all we want to do now is live!"

"How far away are the Western Allies, are they moving in this direction?" asked Herr Graef of the two German soldiers.

Pointing in the direction they had just come from, one of the young men stated, "They are just a few kilometers down the road and they are Americans. There are a lot of them and they are driving jeeps," came their answer in German.

The two young men removed their skis and followed Herr Graef through the door to the main central building.

They stood in front of the large fireplace and rubbed their hands. "We are glad you were kind enough to bring us here. We will follow your orders and help in any way we can."

Herr Graef quickly explained who he was and what the purpose of this small community was.

"If you will wait here, one of the children will get you something hot to drink. Frau Miller, just as soon as these men have something warm to drink please get everyone else, including Herman, to the bunkers and stay there until I come for you. I must return to the other two outside. We are waiting for the Americans to arrive," directed Herr Graef.

Herr Graef went back to where he had left Inga and Mickey and asked if they had seen any new developments.

Mickey stated, "We saw two large formations of transport planes fly over. The first had dropped men and equipment farther east and up the valley towards the heartland of Germany. There was an even larger sequence of transports that crossed over the hills to the south of this valley and they appeared to have already dropped their loads of cargo and men. The cargo doors were still open and some of the planes were trailing the long lanyards that open the parachutes for the cargo ejected from the airplane."

"The time has come for all of our fears to be calmed," stated Graef. "Those two young men told me about the Americans arriving by parachute and they have taken charge of the massive surrender of the German army in this part of our country. I believe Germany is ready to stop fighting and may surrender this very day, but only in this area for now. The die hard SS will not let the people of the central part of our country give up yet. Inga, Frau Miller and the other women have all gone to the bunkers. They have taken Herman with them. There will be a decision made after the Americans reach us about what will be done with all who live here, Sergeant Reber, Herman and our new guests. Inga, I want you to go with the other women for now. Please hurry.

"Sergeant Reber, when the Americans arrive, it will be safer for all concerned if you are the first one to make contact with them. I will be right here to help you," stated Graef.

Farther down the road to the west, a small convoy that consisted of two jeeps and a weapons carrier crossed over the rise of the valley and headed in the direction of Herr Graef's small community. The warm sun had started to melt the snow on the road and the ditches were filling with running water.

Mickey looked up into the sky to see a formation of B-17s. He had a sudden rush of emotion as he recalled the crew of his fallen aircraft, the Louise E. Ann.

"I wonder if any of them are alive? Is it possible that I will ever see any of them again?"

When the vehicles on the road clearly became American, Staff Sergeant Mickey Reber walked out into the middle of the road and held up both of his hands and started waving to attract the attention of the Americans in the convoy.

The second and third vehicles came to a stop approximately one hundred yards away, while the lead jeep with a 50 caliber machine gun on a turret, manned by a soldier standing directly behind the weapon and who had his gun pointed straight at him, stopped within ten feet of him.

Mickey was dressed in his worn and patched Air Force flight suit and still held his hands in an upraised position. "I am an American and all those who are within the grounds of this farm community and those here are friendly. There will be no resistance from anyone."

The soldier behind the machine gun yelled back, "Who is the man behind you?"

"He is Herr Graef, a General in the German army. I have been his prisoner here for nine months."

There were three men in the jeep. The driver stayed in his position and the third soldier jumped out of the vehicle and ordered Herr Graef to put his hands in the air.

"I am Staff Sergeant Mickey Reber, AF 31272281, US Army Air Corp. I was captured after I bailed out of my Aircraft, a B-17, and landed on the ground, by General Graef. I have been treated well. I have been held here at this camp for orphaned German children since early 1944. There are some thirty women and children, one injured German soldier who Herr Graef rescued from the cold and snow and two other German military who arrived here just about two hours ago. This gentleman is the leader of this community. If you want me to, I will show you around the area and help you in any way I can."

An officer from one of the other vehicles came forward. "This is a strange story Sergeant Reber. Stand by for a few minutes while I interrogate this man."

The officer, a Lieutenant, walked over to Graef and spoke to him in German.

Graef stated, "I speak fluent English sir and I am no threat to you whatsoever. I offer any assistance I can give your cause."

"You may put your hands down, General, but for now hold them at your sides and don't move quickly," ordered the Lieutenant.

The Lieutenant ordered one of his men, "Take charge of this man. He will ride into the grounds in your jeep."

Graef was led to and seated in the second vehicle.

Walking back to where Mickey stood, the Lieutenant shook his head and stated, "This is really strange, but from what you have stated it seems to be on the up and up. Get in the jeep, Sergeant, and we will go up and check out the area."

There were eight Americans in this group. Each of their three vehicles had a trailer in tow that was loaded with what appeared to be cans of fuel, boxes of ammunition, and other weapons. They had a few blankets and other supplies, probably food rations and water.

Mickey climbed in the back seat of the first vehicle and remarked, "Thank God this is almost over."

"Reber, give my sergeant directions on how to get to the place the German calls the 'main building,'" stated the Officer.

"OK, sir. Follow the road to the right. It's just a few hundred yards beyond those trees."

The convoy arrived at the main building. Reber got out and walked back to the weapons carrier. He saluted the Lieutenant and asked the officer, "Do you want to hear about the women and the young people that are hidden in the underground bunkers of that hill nearby? This building is their living quarters and for now they are all over there." He pointed his fingers in the direction of the hill.

"Just a minute Reber, before we can go any farther I am going to talk to my command center and get some instructions on just how to handle everything here, including you," stated the Lieutenant.

He picked up the microphone to the radio that was installed in his vehicle and called in his identification signal to a center somewhere in this area. Within seconds the voice of the receiving person stated, "Go ahead, blue fox nine! Read you loud and clear."

The Lieutenant described their location. He stated that there was a captured American airman there and that he would get back to them with his military ID and his Air Force organization within an hour. He explained that he would need to know what he was to do with the airman and stated that he was going to inspect this location for a future command center. He asked if there were any instructions from headquarters for him.

"Call back within the hour and be sure the area is secured."

"Roger and out! Sergeant Reber, I want you to take me and my men on a tour of these grounds and all the buildings. I want the elder German to come along too," directed the Lieutenant. "Three of you stay here and keep a watch on the surrounding area. All the rest of you follow us on this inspection and have your weapons drawn. Don't fire unless we are threatened. We have been told there are children and women here too. Herr Graef, do you have any weapons on the premises?" questioned the Lieutenant.

"In the bottom drawer of my desk in my office there are three Luger Automatics. One of the guns is my own and the other two belong to the two German officers that arrived here this morning. I insisted that they turn over any weapons they had and they complied," replied Graef.

"Let's start with your office, Herr Graef. According to the rules of war it is my duty to take possession of all fire arms. I will do that when we reach your office. Do you understand?"

"Yes, of course, I will give them all to you," stated Herr Graef.

The group of American soldiers, led by Mickey and Graef, entered the small building that was both an office and sleeping quarters for Herr Graef. They checked out the two closets and a small sort of bathing area where Graef dressed each day.

"We have no running water or electricity here. All our water must be carried in from our reservoir," stated Graef.

The Lieutenant opened the bottom drawer of a desk that was in the room and found the three weapons. He looked relieved and his concern seemed to lessen because he had been told the truth by the German General. He took the three guns and handed them over to one of his men.

"Now lets take a look at those out buildings over there. You lead the way, Sergeant Reber," directed the Lieutenant.

The cluster of men went into the two storage areas. They found stored potatoes and cabbage in vats, dried vegetable tops that had been prepared for the few animals and other food stuffs that had been stored against the cold and snow.

"Things look in order here," stated the Lieutenant.

The other small building held farm tools and supplies, and one end of it was completely empty.

"This is where we will stay tonight. You can drive the jeeps and trailers up to this area when we have finished our tour," directed the Lieutenant.

"Yes sir," came an immediate answer from one of his men.

"Now let's take a look at the grounds. You lead the way, Sergeant Reber."

Mickey walked them through the fields and showed them the reservoir that held the water supply. He was not ready to tell them that he had helped build it and put together a generator to help power it. They all walked to the upper edge of the fields where there was a long view of the valley.

"Really nice up here," commented the Lieutenant.

"Looks like a grave site here, Lieutenant," said one of the soldiers.

"What happened here, Reber?" questioned the Lieutenant.

"It was a fighter attack that came down the valley. One of the girls was hit when the planes strafed the area," replied Mickey.

The Lieutenant shook his head slightly. "Sad," was all he said.

"Lieutenant," called Herr Graef. "Can I have one or more of your men accompany me to the bunker where the children are? I want to have them return to the main building."

"Sergeant Reber, is there any reason that I should not grant that request?" The Lieutenant looked Mickey straight in the eyes.

"No sir," came Mickey's reply. "It is perfectly safe and I will be responsible—with my life, if it were necessary."

"OK, two of you men go along and escort the General and the children back to that main building. We will be there in a few minutes."

As the rest of the party walked toward the main building the Lieutenant said, "You have had quiet an experience here over these last months, Sergeant Reber. You look as though you're in good health and like you have been treated well."

"Yes sir, I have. I have learned that we can really get along with very little if we really try. These people here have worked very hard to support those that live here and the crops that were grown were sent further into Germany for those that were in need there too."

"Were you reported as having been captured?" asked the Lieutenant.

"I was told by Herr Graef that the US Government had been notified and I had no reason to doubt him. He was firm in the beginning, but later he was more friendly. I was asked to work here with these people and at night I have been in a locked room," replied Mickey.

As they looked down toward the main building they saw the children come from the bunkers where they had been hidden. They were all in an orderly row marching toward the main house. Behind them were two women helping Herman, then came two other men. There was an American soldier following all of them. Herr Graef was in the lead guiding his children to safety.

"That old gentleman is very protective of those kids, isn't he, Reber?"

"Yes sir" said Mickey firmly.

"Let's have a look through that main building and then I will get my men settled in for the night, and I have to report back to my contact," said the Lieutenant.

The inspection team entered the main building and they were greeted by the young people that lived there. Inga was standing at the side of the young people and she said, "Now children," and in unison they all said, "you are welcome here and we are glad that you came." They all sat down on the floor.

"Who is that pretty blond German woman, Reber? She is a knock out!"

Mickey said, "Her name is Inga and she and Frau Miller take care of all these kids." He did not elaborate further.

It was obvious to the Lieutenant that things were in order here and secured.

"We will have to find out what needs to be done here. I need to know how to handle those three German soldiers. I am almost certain they will have to be taken as prisoners. I feel that you should prepare yourself to leave here with us, Reber. You should start by eating with us tonight and you can sleep with us out there tonight too. Now I must get outside and make my report. I have lots of information to turn in. I'll get back to you soon, Herr Graef. For now carry on as usual. You and the women remain in charge of these kids. Please let them know that they are safe and will not be harmed."

It was only noon when he called his command post

located several miles away. He was able to give his officer in charge what he considered to be good news.

"No losses, no big problems, except we have three German military men here, and a German General who is in charge of this encampment and thirty children and a couple of women who are caring for these kids. I have Sergeant Mickey Reber that I told you about and I have told him he will need to leave here with us. If I have done the right thing, let me know where we are to take him. Roger and out!"

The Lieutenant got his answer within a few minutes. He was told that a team of specialists with all the information would arrive tomorrow. Herr Graef's future would be determined by them too.

Inga, Frau Miller, and Herr Graef offered to fix food for the Americans tonight, but they were thanked and told that they were self sufficient and had everything they needed.

"Sergeant Reber will stay with us now too," they were told.

Inga felt queasy and knew that she could not approach or talk to Mickey now or before he had to leave. She had to trust that he would return to her one day.

Mickey realized that for now the relationship he had with Inga was over. He could say nothing to her, not even good-bye. How was he going to get along without her, he loved her so much. He thought about how perfect these past few months had been, how understanding she had been. They had not even had one argument or misunderstanding. He would not ever find someone so perfect for him. He recalled the conversation they had about the possibility of there being a child, and something had bothered him ever since. She had said, "There will be no one else in my life and if I should have a child it will carry your name." Did Inga know something then that she had not told him?

TWENTY-ONE

Captain Wilson had been given time to catch his breath from the long run up the hill with Stan and he was still amazed at having found these two American Air Corp. Officers at the location of this small German air field where he had been able to belly in his P-38, after it had been hit by enemy fire while he had been flying a mission this afternoon. It was almost as if fate had stepped in to help save the lives of these two misplaced men. Now he had to hope that he could also get out of this unexpected predicament.

Wilson stood up and stretched before he started to investigate the surrounding interior of the building that Stan had brought him into. There were two other rooms, across from one another, and their doors had been left wide open. He had one of the flashlights that Brad had put on the counter for his use and he was checking around in the room that was clearly a small arsenal. In all his experience, he had not seen so many weapons and so much ammunition in any one place.

He heard a sound.

"I'm in here," he called out.

"Did you ever see such an assortment of weapons in one place?" asked Stan.

"God damned, there are enough explosives here to blow this whole place off the face of the map," agreed Wilson. "I would sure like to have one of these Lugers. All the troops think they are really something."

"Go ahead and take one. I don't see how one less can make a difference here, and you can make a good story out of it when you tell your grandkids how you got it. Let's go out in the other room. I have a lot of things that I need to tell you," stated Stan.

"Bet you do at that," said Captain Wilson and the two men left the room and closed the door behind them, on the German arsenal of destruction.

Stan spent the next hour explaining about the last flight of the Louise E. Ann and their bail out over German soil, and of their strategy for evading capture and what they had done to survive until now.

"We decided to come up here on the hill. We really do have a bird's eye view of the air and the valley from this position, and by watching what's been going on for the last week or so we could see that the war is winding down. We sure as hell have enough stuff to defend ourselves with and we have been watching the German troops dwindle down to almost nothing. We figured we could tell when the Western Allied forces were going to come through. We have white flags and a megaphone to use if we saw friendly troops, and there are machine guns set up on both sides of the hill if it should have been the enemy. Amazing what we have been able to hear from up here. The acoustics of the valley are something else.

"Anyway, we have been lucky here. We have had the food and water we needed, sure could have used a good old hamburger and fries sometimes. We are sick of the beans and fish and some of the other not so great stuff we found. Guess I really shouldn't complain, better than nothing. I can't say much for the facilities. Can't wait for a good hot shower or bath and a john. Something other than trees or bushes would be great, but all in all we have had what it takes to make it, Captain, and for that we are grateful. I think I can speak for Brad too.

"I've had some survival training in my day, but Brad was really green at first. He's shaped up really well and I think we have a budding Air Force pilot on our hands. He had a little training and was the copilot on our B-17, but he has been watching all you jocks flying up and down this valley and he is really anxious to get back and go to flight school. He watched Goebbels' pilot land down there where your P-38 is and that really got him going. He is young and just maybe he will do something really great one of these days. As for me, I'm going back to school and finish. I want a law degree. I want to be a criminal lawyer."

"You two have really had quite a time of it here and I have an idea about something that might speed up things. Let's go down to my plane and check out the radio and see if it is still operative. Might be best if we wait for an hour or so until it is a little darker. If the radio is OK, I can tell them where we are and maybe get an answer in the next three or four hours."

"Great idea," said Stan enthusiastically. "Come on Captain, I want to show you around the rest of this fort and check with Brad before we go down to your plane."

The two men went outside and found Brad watching intently to the southwest with his binoculars.

"What's going on over there Brad?" asked Stan.

"It looks like the Allied Forces are given them hell, lots of Artillery fire going in and some planes have been dropping bombs. Maybe this friggin war will be over with soon and we can all get back to the real world and start living again," said Brad hopefully.

Stan began showing Wilson around the outside of the main building. He took him to the shed that held the external power generator and told how they had sabotaged its engine and its supply of fuel.

"See, the Krauts left you a nice supply of coal," said Wilson.

"Yeah, that has really been great. At least we have been warm. You can see that our clothes are not in the best shape. We used blankets to make ponchos and since they were white I figured we wouldn't have been seen against the snow," said Stan.

"Yeah, I got it figured out that Goebbels used this place to control the German population. He sent out his voice propaganda over these radio waves." Stan motioned to the radio antenna that hovered over the building.

"It looks clear down there around my old bird. I'd like to go down to it before it gets any darker. We don't want to waste her battery power by putting on any lights," said

Captain Wilson.

"OK Captain, you and I will go down to your airplane while Brad stays up here and covers us with the machine gun."

Stan called Brad who was still watching the progress of the war, "Brad, come on over here and cover us while we go down to the airstrip."

"OK, be right there," came Brad's reply.

"See that little hanger just beyond your airplane, Captain? That is the only structure here that we have not gone into or near, and for some reason my better judgment tells me that we need to avoid it. I woke up one night thinking that this whole place could be rigged with explosives, can't imagine the Germans would be so stupid as to leave all this stuff here if it were not for a reason. Anyhow, let's not push our luck for now, just don't go near it!" said Stan with directive concern.

"All right, Lieutenant, we'll do it your way," agreed the Captain.

Brad walked over to where Stan and Wilson were standing. "I'll keep a close watch," he said assuredly. "Don't fire at anything unless you see us running. I'll shout 'Germans' if there is danger. You should be able to hear me OK. We will be just long enough to accomplish our mission. Take charge Brad!"

It was fifteen minutes later when Farnsworth and Wilson arrived at the site of the bellied in P-38. The Captain climbed up on the wing and crawled into the cockpit.

"Stay there on the ground and keep watch," came his instructions to Stan.

Darkness was almost on the valley as Captain Wilson turned on the battery power switch, to his great relief the indicator light burned red, showing energy. He turned on his head set and throat mike and selected the radio guard channel. It took ten seconds for the radio to come alive and make the sound of an operating communication system.

Pressing the throat mike against his neck, he called, "Big Dog Leader this is Fox Trot Tango Three, do you read me? If affirmative, come in and give me an answer!"

It took one more transmission and the familiar voice of one of his squadron buddies came in loud and clear. "Roger, we read, where the hell are you?"

Wilson took a deep breath and replied, "Thank god. I am down in a small valley seven miles northeast of the target we shot up today. I am safe and here with a couple of Air Force troops who have been evading the enemy for a long time. It is nearly dark and we are on top of a hill, in back of the park and to the left of the lake. Tell the rescue troops it would be best to come after us during the daylight hours. We will give the American surrender signal when we are sure of the designated rescue teams. Over!"

"Roger Fox Trot Tango Three, we will get the ball rolling ASAP! Hope to see you tomorrow. Big Dog and out!"

Wilson gave Stan a 'thumbs up' signal. He left the radio on for thirty seconds.

"Got to be sure they haven't anything more to tell me. I got through to them and I am sure they will take immediate action," he told himself.

He turned the radio and main power switch off and climbed out of the cockpit and onto the wing and in one jump was on the ground.

"It worked! I got hold of Fox Trot Tango Three and he knows I'm here with you and the Lieutenant. I'll try again tomorrow at sun up if we don't get some fast action."

The two men jogged the distance up hill and found Brad waiting for them.

"Put the machine gun away, Brad. We may need it later and it should be in place," directed Stan.

Brad followed instructions and came into the building.

"I don't know if either of you is ready for some chow or not. I opened a couple of cans of our gourmet stuff. You can imagine it's steak and what ever you like. I'm too excited to eat anything," said Brad.

It took a couple of hours to eat. There was a lot to discuss about the last months, and Wilson was telling them about being hit by German fire that afternoon when all three men stopped short in their conversation and turned their attention toward the door that was slightly ajar and listened.

"I'll be damned if that doesn't sound like jeep engines out there," said Stan.

They all raced out the door and to the edge of the hilltop. Looking down into the darkening park below them, they again heard the sounds of engines. They could just barely see lights as they flickered past the trees below.

In the next instant came a C-47. It passed over the lower end of the park and two objects were jettisoned from its open cargo door. The masses were suspended from parachutes and suddenly ignited.

"Those are the new million candle power flares that we heard of early last year," shouted Stan.

"God damned to hell, I never thought I'd ever be so glad to see a Gooney Bird. Did you guys ever see anything so fantastic in all your lives?" Brad said with real admiration in his voice.

Before the first set of flares could reach the ground and burn out, the C-47 made a sharp turn to the right to make another pass over its target area. Within one minute the airplane had started its second run on the surrounding area, this time the plane appeared to be higher and there were four flares and at least a dozen other objects dropped from the plane.

Stan rushed into the stone building and came out with a box of green flares. "Help me light some of these and let's wave them around and get the attention of those troops down there!"

Brad grabbed one of the flares and without asking, Stan shouted through his cupped hands. "We are up here on the hill, we are Americans!"

There was an immediate answer from the floor of the valley. "Stay where you are. We will be up there soon. We know who you are. Is this area down here secure?"

"Yes sir, so far as we know," said Stan.

As the three men on the hill watched the action below and as the last group of flares extinguished themselves, more and more flash lights could be seen amongst the trees below them. What an amazing sight. Each one of those little lights represented an American GI.

The lights began to ascend the hill and soon a voice shouted out, "I am Major Harold Nickson, Third Battalion, U.S. Army Rangers. Is there a Captain Wilson up there with you?"

"Yes sir, that is his P-38 down there on the landing strip," informed Brad.

"Glad that you survived your mission, Captain. We got word that you were here when you radioed in several hours ago. Looks like that bird of yours has had it. We may have to destroy it before we leave here."

The Major finally came into plain view, with some of his men behind him. He was a tall and well built Negro, and exuded authority. "Sergeant, give me the microphone," he ordered of the radio man at his side who was carrying a large radio pack on his back.

"Ranger One to Blue Leader One, come in! Do you read me?"

"Affirmative, Ranger One. What is your position?" came a voice from the radio.

"We have arrived and the mission has been accomplished. The area seems to be secure. I have ordered some of my men to stay below and check the field. Some are up here with me. I will get back to you after I have had a chance to inspect this area further and make a decision on how we are to handle these Air Force troops. Get me information about their destination ASAP. Ranger One out."

The Major stated, "We have some vehicles down below. Is there a road of some sort up here? I want to get a truck and jeep to this position if we can."

"There is a road that comes up the back side of this hill. Now that the snow has melted it will be easier for a four wheeled truck to follow the road. It's just north of the park boundary, just off the highway to the left there is a gate. It's very hard to see because there are a lot of trees and bushes," informed Stan.

The Major turned to one of his men and said, "Did you hear the Lieutenant? Send someone down below and give them the word. We don't need to do anything tonight, but we sure as hell want to get moving in the morning, early!"

"OK Major, I will take care of it and if we have to put wings on one of those trucks it will be up here at dawn!" said the efficient Sergeant.

"Come on Major, let me show you around these buildings. I have things to show you that I am sure you and our government will be interested in," directed Stan.

"There are three rooms in this main building. One is full of radio equipment, one is a veritable arsenal, and the other is full of filing cabinets and maps. We have a couple of lantern type flash lights. We have been using them sparingly. I really don't know how long they will last, but take them and they will make viewing all of these rooms much easier," suggested Stan.

"Thanks Lieutenant, I will take two of my men and go over the areas you have told me about and then we will take a look outside," stated the Major.

"Wonder how they will handle all this," questioned Wilson.

"I really don't care so long as we can get out of here within the next day or two," spoke Stan.

"Do you think the Major can get word to our families, Stan? I guess we were reported missing and nine months is a long time to wonder if someone is alive or dead," remarked Brad.

"God damned son of a bitch, we have got to get all those files to headquarters. Sergeant Johnson, really work on getting those trucks up here as early as possible so we can get all this stuff out of here and on the road," ordered the Major. "You may have really stumbled onto a find here Lieutenant Farnsworth, and you too, Lieutenant Freestone. What's in those out buildings and that hanger down by the air strip?" asked the Major.

"More radio equipment and the antennas for them are out under those trees in the rear. We sabotaged all of it just before Goebbels came in and flew out of here a couple of weeks ago. We didn't want to try and use any of this, as it might have alerted the Germans. Down there in those cabins in the valley are a lot of very expensive paintings," said Stan.

"Yeah, and in cabin number seven there is a hand carved

box that I am very interested in. We don't know what is in it, but if the military wouldn't mind I would like to take it home as a souvenir," commented Brad.

"There is one other thing, Major, and it is about that hanger. It is the only building we did not investigate and somehow I just had the feeling it was better to leave it alone. We have really had very little happen here that we could have considered hazardous. We had one unavoidable death of a German, self defense sort of thing that I'm not afraid to admit. War is war. All in all we have been damned fortunate, warm but hungry," informed Stan.

"Don't worry about things here, Lieutenant. We will get it all together as soon as possible and move it out. If you want that box ,Lieutenant Freestone, get it tomorrow and if it doesn't have something of real importance in it I think it would be OK for you to keep it," assured the Major.

"Now, I have to get back outside to my radio and see if they have information for me about your getting out of here. As soon as I know what's going to take place I'll let you know. In the mean time carry on. It's warm enough in here and I'll have one of my men bring you in some good old K-rations. Bet it will be as good as anything you have had in a while. By the way, your families have or will soon receive word about your whereabouts. It's been a long time for them," stated the Major.

TWENTY-TWO

"I know this has been a very long day for you two men, but we have to get those men out of that prison as soon as possible. Now that the weather has started to improve I think we should get started with a plan to get Operation Rescue under way immediately. We will have a company of paratroopers dropped on the target area of the prison itself early tomorrow," said the Colonel who was in charge of the logistic part of the rescue program.

He walked to the map and said, "Most of the area between us and the prison has been won by the Western Allies and we should have no problem getting two battalions of troops through that area by early morning. They will be ready to act as soon as we get word that our paratroopers are on the ground and the area is secured. We will have transportation ready to get the prisoners out and we will be ready to take the Germans into custody. An armored back up will be following right on their heels. By that time an area of at least twenty-five miles that surrounds the prison will be in Allied hands and the war will be that much closer to an all out Allied victory.

"The offer that you two Sergeants have made to lead a party back to the prison was appreciated and considered, but we will need both of you to answer a lot of detailed questions tomorrow, back at Division Headquarters. You have both done well and you deserve the gratitude of everyone concerned.

"Our capture of Stallage Luft #31 will start in a few hours and there is still much detail work to be done. Sergeants Sacket and Esser, tomorrow you will be transported to our

Division Headquarters in Reims, France."

The Colonel turned to Staff Sergeant Kirk Sanders who had first taken custody of Sacket and Esser and said, "Because of your interest in handling these two men so well, I am asking you to be their driver and escort tomorrow. Your platoon leader, Lieutenant DePaul will accompany you and he will be in charge of your party. You had all better get some sleep because I want you on the road by 0800 tomorrow morning. Sergeant Sacket, you will be told about the success of this mission in due time. Good luck to both of you."

Sergeant Esser stood up, "Sir, may I thank all of you for your kind treatment. I have heard stories of how Americans are with prisoners of war, but one never really knows until it has been experienced. Thank you for allowing me to be a part of this rescue mission and one day I hope to go to the United States for an extended visit."

"Thank you Sergeant Esser and good luck to you," said the Colonel.

The next morning, as planned, a company of Paratroopers was flown over and dropped onto the target area of Stallage Luft #31. The sun had just started to light up the eastern sky when the billowing chutes came into the view of the Allied prisoners who were waiting to be liberated. All the troopers in the rescue party landed safely and were enthusiastically cheered by the men who had held a constant vigil since Sacket and Esser had driven out of the main gate. The German officers and the guard personnel were assembled out in front of the headquarters and mess hall buildings.

There had been no resistance to the airborne landing, and as promised by Colonel Hibner, not one weapon of any sort had been fired. There seemed to be complete cooperation on the part of the Germans at this prison. The paratroopers had fallen into a defensive formation and were surprised to see so many of the prisoners on the field waiting to greet them. There were shouts of welcome and expressions of happiness and gratitude displayed for these men, who had risked their lives on a mission to save so many here in this German hell hole.

Colonel Howard and Squadron Leader Owens were the

first to walk out to meet the newly arrived company of paratroopers. A young Captain rose from a hastily dug gun position. He waved his hands at the approaching officers and started to run toward them. As they met, there was much excitement and confused talking. Attempts were made at a welcoming salute.

A young paratrooper was the first to take control of this almost frantic group, "Gentlemen, I am Captain Harold Miller, are we secure here sir?"

Just then, three P-47 Thunderbolts passed above the open field of the prison. Their thunderous fly over drowned out any attempt at conversation. They were gone as quickly as they had come and Colonel Howard shouted his answer to the young paratrooper, "Yes, so far so good Captain! All the German Officials of this prison are out in front of Prison Headquarters and they are waiting for your men to take them into custody."

Sergeant, take a team of men and assemble all of the Germans in the center of this open field. Have them sit down in one place. They are to remain at ease until the rest of the division arrives," directed Captain Miller authoritatively.

Within minutes the sound of rumbling vehicles could be heard and then they drove into view, one after another. They were moving along the outside of the prison's barbed wire borders. Then American soldiers were cutting away the wire and the sounds of posts being crushed by armored vehicles could be heard. It all happened so fast and the prisoners were waving their arms and shouting greetings to men of their own forces.

Klein and a lot of the officers and enlisted men had assembled around an American Army Colonel who was standing in a jeep. He had dispatched several sergeants from his organization into the group of repatriated prisoners to take their names and serial numbers, and now it seemed that some order was taking place amongst these excited and happy men. They began to form into small platoons.

A tank battalion had rumbled onto the prison grounds and had taken strategic positions on both ends of the captured area. Within several hours of the arrival of the paratroops, the whole prison site had been occupied and had been organized by the American military. The British prisoners were represented by Squadron Leader Commander Owens and they were happy and knew that they would all be going home now too.

"Attention," ordered the Army Colonel, "I have just received word that an area of fifty miles surrounding this prison has now been won by the Western Allies and the L-5 spotter planes above us gives us an all clear. You are all free men!" confirmed the Colonel. "You're all going home!"

Sounds of marching came from behind and silence came over the yard as all the German personnel, herded by American soldiers were led to waiting trucks to be transported to a POW holding area in France. It was obvious that these Germans were not war weary soldiers. They were fat and happy to be facing an end to this war.

Shouts could be heard and the pent up anger from the months of captivity and inhumane treatment burst from the men. "Better than you deserve, you sons of bitches, and we hope they kick your ass, you mother fuckers!"

Then it was over, finally it was over, and an end had come to all the unbearable days in this hell hole.

Early that same morning Technical Sergeant Sacket and German Master Sergeant Esser had risen from a good yet restless night's sleep. They had showered and dressed, had eaten some breakfast, and had time to return to their assigned tent and sleeping bag to prepare for the trip to Reims.

"Before we go I want you to know that I really hope we have a chance to meet again. Who knows what fate has in store for us," said Esser.

"Yeah, me too. There was a time when I thought I'd kill you if I ever got the chance, but things did turn around, didn't they?" answered Sacket. "We did somethings really great in these last few days that are going to make a lot of people in the world happy. We sort of took a chance with our lives, but someone bigger than us got us through it," said Sacket.

"I have done some things in my lifetime that now I have had time to think about it, and I'm really sorry for. Guess it was just the way I was brought up. Life was really cheap and meaningless and that made it easy to be cruel," Esser said as he looked down at his hands.

"Can't worry about that now, got to look forward to good things ahead," advised Sacket. "Anyhow, guess we had better say good-bye here." He reached for Esser and found his hand and took hold. With a firm grip he said, "I have a feeling that something really great is ahead for you. I really mean that."

"You too," said Esser, and he gave Sacket a firm pat on the back, picked up his POW uniform cap, and left the room.

Sacket followed him out the door.

Sergeant Kirk Sanders was waiting for them outside and showed them the jeep they would be traveling in. "You guys can call me Kirk. I think that DePaul will want to sit up front and he usually brings a big bag with him. Neither of you have anything, so if you ride in the back, you can sit on either side of it. Here he comes now. Good morning Lieutenant."

"I'm Lieutenant DePaul, I heard about you two last night. Good show. From what I heard this morning things moved right along and your friends will be out of there before long. OK if I sit in front, Sanders?"

"Yes sir, just put your bag on the floor in back."

It took about ten minutes for the jeep to get through the bombed streets.

"Heard this morning that the area fifteen miles ahead has been taken by our forces, so our trip should be a good one. It's auf wiedersehen to this cotton picking place," said DePaul, showing his dislike for the surrounding German area.

After driving through the war torn country side and destroyed towns for more than an hour Sanders said, "The French border is just up ahead. I will sure be glad to be leaving Germany behind! How about you, Esser?" he asked, talking over his shoulder. "At least you're leaving here alive. I've seen so many dead Germans that it makes you wonder who's left."

Looking straight ahead Esser replied, "I'm glad to be alive, but I am looking forward to a new life and maybe a new country, God willing!"

"If things work out the way I hope they will we will be reassigned. We've been on steady combat duty since D-Day. Now you Sacket, you will get the Air Force treatment and that is probably going to be a lot of R and R, and you might even get sent home on leave or into another theater of operation. Esser, because of the way you cooperated with us, you stand this smelling like a rose. The both of you are probably going to have to go through some heavy interrogation for a few days," said DePaul, like he was the voice of experience.

"Hey are either of you married?" asked Sanders.

"I'm not," said Sacket.

"Neither am I," added Esser. "Why?"

"Be careful when you go out after we get into France. I think every one of those French women is looking for an American GI to marry or shack up with. There is lots of VD around, so better keep your pants on. That's going to be rough for you when you have been out of circulation for such a long time. You're long over due some of Uncle Sam's money too. Better put it away. Just watch out," warned Sanders.

On the way to Reims, Sanders pointed out the towns and places that his platoon had fought its way through on the way into Germany.

"My best friend Chuck Dorn was killed going into this little town of BarLeduc. A sniper got him. He was a Corporal when he died. He just got word the day before that he was going to get promoted. His wife had just had a kid too. Really sad."

When they entered Reims the traffic was heavy. They saw there were even a few civilian cars on the road. They stopped at an Army post to ask directions to Army Headquarters and an M.P. gave Sanders a recently printed map and explained how to get there. "Watch out for these Frenchies. They're all in the black market and the whores all got VD. Things are really rough around here!" He gave a salute and stepped back from the jeep.

Guess Sanders really knows what he is talking about, thought Sacket to himself.

Sanders followed the directions he had been given and soon he was pulling up in front of a building. It was old, but still looked very important. There was an archway with a drive way under it that led into a courtyard.

A guard with lots of decorations on his chest, who wore the stripes of a buck sergeant, stepped out of his booth and said, "May I help you, sir?"

Lieutenant DePaul replied in a loud, forceful voice, "We have been ordered to appear here on a very important matter and we need a place to park. Give us directions, Sergeant!"

"May I have a copy of your orders, sir?" asked the guard.

The guard moved back into his station with the set of orders he had received from DePaul and got on a two way communication system. He read the orders to someone in charge. A response came, but it was not audible.

"Yes sir, where shall I have them park their vehicle?"

There was another unheard reply.

"Yes sir!"

The guard came out of his booth and walked to the Lieutenant's side of the jeep. "Our Commander, General Ellis wants to have you men directed to his office ASAP. Park your jeep anywhere you wish. I will have someone escort you and help you with any baggage you have. If you want me to, leave the jeep where it is and I will park it for you," stated the guard.

"Good idea, Sergeant. Come on Sacket and Esser, and you too Sanders. Let's get up there."

The four men were out of the jeep. Before they could turn around, a Second Lieutenant appeared and gave a snappy salute to Lieutenant DePaul. "Let me assist you with your bags Lieutenant and I will ask that you all follow me."

The four men picked up what bags the Second Lieutenant could not manage and followed him across the courtyard and up the stairway to the second floor. He opened the door with a name boldly painted on it, "General Matthew Ellis, Commander," and Sacket, Esser, Sanders, and Lieutenant

DePaul followed the assisting Lieutenant into the outer office of the General.

A sharp looking WAC was at a desk. She looked up and said, "We have been expecting you four." Then she stood and opened the inner office door.

"Lieutenant DePaul and his party to see you, sir!" She beckoned all of them to follow her into the General's office.

As Sacket passed the WAC on entering the office he got a whiff of a slight fragrance. Wow, this girl really has class, and what a body, he thought to himself.

The General sat behind a huge desk piled high with papers and maps. There was a telephone at his elbow, a coat rack nearby held his Officer's Garrison hat, an overcoat, and an umbrella. The General had gray hair and wore glasses. His uniform collar was open at the throat. He had a pleasant expression on his face and he had smile lines at the corner of his eyes.

With a smile on his face he said, "It will probably please all of you to know that the mission named 'Operation Rescue' has been a complete success and all of our men have been accounted for. Just within the hour I received a call from the front and they gave me the latest news. There has been a complete collapse of the German defenses in that area. The German officials and personnel who ran the prison have all been taken into custody. I have also received news of some other Americans who have been found and of one who has been repatriated. In a day or two they will be coming here to this headquarters for processing.

"Now all of you can be seated. Barbara, get these men some coffee or soft drinks, and if you want to smoke gentlemen, please do," spoke the General.

"When you have had time to relax for a few minutes we will talk some more. I have an errand to run, so please excuse me for a time," said the General, who rose from his desk to leave the room. He was very tall with broad shoulders. He reached for his Garrison cap and left the room.

Staff Sergeant Barbara Hatfield returned to the room with a Corporal who had a tray of drinks and a Thermos of coffee. "I hope that I have brought refreshments that will please you," she said.

Sacket looked at her. She was young, trim and blond he thought, and yes she would be very pleasing. He looked at her hands. They were smooth and white, just the sort of hands he would love to have caress his head and back, and when it got down to it, she could go farther if she wanted to, he thought to himself.

"Sergeant Sacket," he heard from a distance, "would you like coffee or a soft drink?"

Sacket shook his head so that he could return to reality, "Coke would be fine, Sergeant," he said.

It had been thirty minutes and the door opened and the General came back waving papers in his hands. "Hope you have had time to refresh yourselves and rest a bit. We have captured hundreds of German prisoners in the last week or so and they will be sent to a camp somewhere here in France. Sergeant Esser, for now I want you to remain here with Lieutenant DePaul and Sergeant Sacket. You too can remain, Sergeant Sanders. I understand there may be another assignment for you. You will be informed in a day or two.

"Back to you Sacket and Sergeant Esser. Our intelligence people will have many questions to ask of you both. I want to spend a few hours with the both of you. I am sure that you have some interesting facts that may be helpful to the cause of the United States Military Forces."

I'll be damned, thought Sacket, that Sanders is one sharp son of a bitch, bet he has really been around!

"Sergeant Hatfield, I want these men to have comfortable quarters. I am sure they are tired and they need to eat and bathe and sleep. Please arrange that for them. Now you may retire for the rest of the day and I will see you in the morning following breakfast, about 0830 in this office. Good day, gentlemen. Enjoy this evening," said the General pleasantly.

"Begging your pardon, sir, I have already taken care of rooms for these men and I will escort them there myself.

"Come on along, all of you. Somehow I think a great big hamburger and some fries would taste really good to you right now. I'll show you the way to the cafeteria, and then I'll give you the keys to your quarters. May I be excused for the evening General?"

"Of course Sergeant Hatfield, I'll see you as usual, at 0730 sharp in the morning," stated the General.

TWENTY-THREE

Lieutenant Marvin Goldstein of the United States Infantry called Mickey over to the building where they had spent the night and asked him, "I need for you to write down some information for me. You know, the same old stuff, your name, rank, and serial number and the name of your organization in England and the Commander of that station. I am going to call in everything I can come up with about you and this retreat for women and children and Herr Graef to Headquarters as soon as I have it completed. We are going to try and get you back to the Air Force tomorrow.

"You know Sergeant Reber, you have been in a really strange situation, to say the least. The big brass will have some very heavy questions to ask you when you get back. I would advise you to get your belongings together and say your good-byes. You have been here a long time, and I am sure that there are a few of these Germans that mean more to you than others," insinuated the Lieutenant.

Mickey had already been asked questions by some of the other infantry men. "Hey Reber, have you ever heard the rule about fraternization with German civilians?" Another had said, "You're no longer their prisoner, so you had better stay away from all of them, and that means that good looking blond too!"

Mickey fought back an angry reply and said, "I understand, but I want all of you to know how glad I am to at last have been found and rescued. It has been nearly ten months of captivity for me here and I am looking forward to being back with my own people."

He had spent last night in the custody of the soldiers of

the American Infantry. They provided him with a sleeping bag and a C-ration for dinner. Mickey spent the rest of the night thinking about Inga. He reassured himself with the thought that she would understand what was happening and that for a time he would have to be away from her. He had to see Herr Graef one more time, but somehow he just could not bring himself to see Inga again. He knew how strong her feelings were for him and another good-bye would be too difficult for the both of them.

When morning came, Mickey got up and looked out the door. It was a beautiful day with a cloudless sky. Most of the snow in the valley had melted and the only sign of the war now came from the east. There were two American guards outside by the truck.

Really not necessary, thought Mickey, but I guess the Lieutenant is used to high security. If I were in his position I might feel the same way.

The Lieutenant had finished lacing his boots and announced, "As soon as the prisoners are picked up and the civilian check up Squads are here, we will be leaving. Sergeant Reber, I will turn you over to them."

The platoon NCO asked, "What's the big rush, sir?"

Lieutenant Goldstein shouted back at the Sergeant, "I got news last night that the enemy is in full retreat and they want us to push them hard towards Frankfort. We have to be very careful because the SS has placed snipers all along the way. Let's get this show on the road so that we can go home before the Fourth of July! Get all this gear loaded up. I have to go to the main building for a few minutes."

"Yes sir! We will be loaded and ready to go when you return," answered the NCO.

Goldstein entered the office of Herr Graef and found him sitting at his desk. "I need to speak with you for a few minutes General," stated the Lieutenant.

"Here are some notices for you. You must read them and obey what is written. These rules are enforceable by the Army of Occupation. In a few minutes I will be relieved of my duty here and my men and I will move on with the Allied Forces and into the final stages of this war, with what should result in complete victory over the military forces of your country."

"I am aware that you speak fluent German, Lieutenant, so for now I would like to talk to you in the language of my own people. Since 1942 I have been in charge of this farm for orphaned children. The women here came to assist me with this project. We have raised food crops yearly for the German people who needed our help, and yes we sent food to our military. We are all noncombatants and we look forward, soon, to a day of peace. I want you to know that I have not always agreed with my top German officials and so for now I wish you complete success in the victory you pursue.

"Everything that has taken place here has been my responsibility. The capture and detention of Sergeant Reber was my decision. Through force, he was used as a farm laborer and was threatened with far worse punishment, even death if he should try to escape. His work here on the farm will leave a lasting impression on everyone here and we all have much a better understanding of the nature of America and her people. Please let his superiors know that everyone here thanks him and respects him for saving some of our lives. He has given our children hope for the future and for that we are grateful too."

Outside came the sound of vehicle engines on the road and they brought Herr Graef and Lieutenant Goldstein to their feet.

"Almost time to go, General, but before we leave I want to say thank you for your cooperation. Your explanation of your operation here and of Sergeant Reber's conduct while he was being held as your prisoner has been very helpful. You are to be commended for your part in the care of these women and children." Out of respect for the German General the Lieutenant saluted and turned and left the office.

Mickey was just a few steps away from Herr Graef's office when he saw the Lieutenant leave. He knew he had little time and took the steps two at a time. He knocked on the door and heard the familiar voice of the elderly gentleman. "Come in, the door is open."

Mickey stepped in and said, "I just had to say good-bye

to someone. I can't see Inga again. It would be too difficult for her. Please let her know that I saw you. I am sure it is no secret to you about how we feel about each other. Just tell her I love her and that I'll communicate with her as soon as I can." Mickey reached out and grasped Graef's hand. "Thank you, sir, for all your kindness. I meant what I said, I really do hope that we can see each other again. Good-bye sir."

"Wait Sergeant Reber, Inga gave me something to give to you." He opened the drawer of his desk and handed Mickey a small package. "She said to tell you to wear it and think of her. Good-bye Sergeant Reber, and may God bless you, and everyone of us will miss you."

The newly arrived American forces consisted of two jeeps and a truck. There were two officers, three sergeants, and one corporal. Lieutenant Goldstein took the officers on a quick tour of the grounds and its structures and then returned to the building they had spent the night in. It had been turned into a command control center. A Sergeant with a note pad joined them. There was a discussion between the officers in charge. Reber stood at the edge of the group and never spoke a word.

Finally, a captain who seemed to be running the show motioned to Reber to come over to the table. "Pull up a chair and sit down, Sergeant. I'm Captain Joseph Tilton and I have some papers that I need to have you fill out. If you have any questions, I'm here to help you. The sooner we get done here the faster we can get you back to your Air Force command. I will drive you back to your processing center today. If you have any belongings, get them as soon as you're finished here and put them in my jeep."

"Thank you, Captain, but I really don't have anything, just the clothes on my back. I sure could use a coat or field jacket," said Mickey.

"I can take care of that, Sergeant, I have one in my vehicle, so finish those forms and we're on our way!"

Mickey quickly read the questionnaire in front of him and filled in the necessary answers. There was nothing complicated about it and within minutes he was finished. He stood up and looked all around the area. There was not any one he recognized and none of his past captors was watching him.

He walked to the jeep and the Captain handed him a field jacket. "Put it on, Sergeant, and get into the jeep. I'll be right back."

While he had a moment to himself he reached into his pocket and took out the small package from Inga. He opened it to find her silver crucifix on a silver chain, the one that had been hanging over her bed.

"Oh God, what will I ever do without you Inga?" he asked.

They had not married legally, but through their acts of intimacy he felt morally bound to this woman he had grown so close to over these last months. Fate had brought them together and surely his life would take the necessary turns to bring him back to her. Somehow, he recalled a wedding that he had attended some years ago and the words, "What God hath joined together let no man put asunder," and in this instance he considered fate, God.

Mickey looked around one more time. He saw American GIs in the familiar buildings, not the people he had lived so closely with for these long months, and Inga was no where to be seen.

Quickly Mickey put the silver chain around his neck and made sure that it was under his clothing. He felt the coolness of the cross against his skin. "I'll wear this always, Inga, and I promise you that I will return to you one day. You will be my wife."

Just then the Lieutenant got into the jeep and started the engine. Mickey took hold of his arm and said, "Nobody will ever understand what has happened here, sir. I only hope that these people will all be safe and that they will have a good future life."

"You don't have to explain anything to me, Sarge. In this job I have, I've seen it all, from sadness to joy. Most all the German people are victims of the Nazis," said the Lieutenant.

After breakfast that morning, Inga put on her coat and told Frau Miller she would be away from the main building for several hours. She quietly left the compound, and when she was sure that no one would notice her, she worked her way to the fields and from there, ran the distance to the top of the hill. She had a view of everything below and could see the American vehicles and soldiers. She was sure that she saw Mickey get into one of the cars. She watched, with tears in her eyes and a prayer in her heart. "Please God, protect this man I love, bring him back to me soon."

She had such an ache in her breast and now the tears were blinding her eyes. As she wiped them away, she saw the car leave the grounds of the farm and drive to the road. She watched it go until it was out of sight. She sat on the old tree where she and Mickey had spent so much time and held the ring he had made for her. "I love you, Mickey Reber. There will never be another man in my life for so long as I live. Good-bye for now, my love."

The jeep drove down the road to the main thoroughfare that passed through the middle of the valley. Mickey could see the fields and the small reservoir that he and Inga had built. It was full of water now. The neat rows that had been planted with potatoes, onions, and other vegetables were now bare of any growth. It had been a good growing season and the harvest had been a complete success. There would be many away from this farm that would share the benefit of their efforts.

The vehicle passed the old barn and the pasture where he had been captured. He put his head down between his hands and cried.

Finally the road joined the main highway, a sign pointing to the west read, "Saarbrücken - 60 kilometers."

The Captain reached over and put his hand on Mickey's shoulder. "You have been through a lot here, haven't you

Sergeant?"

"Yeah, when I first landed in that pasture back there I wondered if I would ever get out of here alive. I did and I will be OK now. Just a case of nerves, Captain," said Mickey.

"If we don't have any problems, we should be in France in about an hour, and then it's on to Reims for some good chow!" commented the Captain.

"You're going to spend sometime at the Headquarters Unit. It's a joint operation between the Army and the Air Force and they are taking care of all repatriated fly boys. They will give you the VIP treatment. You really don't look like you have been starving, but they will treat you really well. According to my boss, we are starting to find more and more American POW's," informed the Captain.

"That's good news, Captain. I sure hope some of my crew members are there. I think that there were at least four of us who bailed out of our airplane and made it to the ground," said Mickey with anticipation in his voice.

"Our outfit has a list of all missing airmen and you were one of them. When I called in this morning they said the Army liberated a whole POW camp of American and British fly boys not too far from where you were. We will be bringing them back by the truck load in a day or so and most of them will be taken to a special camp on the outskirts of Reims. You and a few others must be special cases because we're taking you to the headquarters building in downtown Reims," said the Captain.

They completed the trip without incidence and crossed the border into France. At about 11:30 the Captain passed through the archway at Headquarters and was stopped by a guard.

"Give him the set of orders I gave you this morning, Sergeant Reber," instructed the Captain.

The guard hastily read the paper and spoke quietly into his two way "squawk box" on the wall inside his station.

An answer came back immediately. "Send him over here to us, ASAP!"

The Captain circled the court yard to its far side. "See that set of double doors?" he said, pointing in the direction of the building. "Go upstairs to the door marked Headquarters, Intelligence. Good luck, I hope things work out all right for you," the Captain gave Reber a reassuring touch on the arm as he got out of the jeep.

Mickey did as the Captain had instructed him. He pushed open the door marked Headquarters and found himself facing a very pretty WAC Staff Sergeant. The large room was nearly empty.

"Let me have your orders Sergeant and I'll see how I can help you."

Reber handed her his papers and she began to read them.

There was a smile on her face. "I'm Staff Sergeant Barbara Hatfield. You're in the right place, but everyone except myself has gone down to the mess hall. I doubt that you have eaten, so why don't you and I go down there now. I'll be glad to show you where it is, never can tell who may be down there!"

Barbara stepped out from behind her counter and took Reber by the arm and led him out of the office and down the stairs to the ground floor. She hurriedly led him through a hallway toward an open door with a sign saying, "MESS HALL." The aroma of typical American food was in the air and as they entered the large chamber Mickey saw men seated at tables who were busy feeding themselves with large portions of meat and potatoes. Each table had its own supply of condiments with napkins. There was a large counter with huge coffee makers and soda dispensers. These were things Mickey had been used to, but he had not seen them in the months of his captivity.

"Come on over here, Sergeant," said the WAC and she headed for a table where two men were busy eating. She pushed Reber toward one of the men with his back to them and in a loud voice said, "Hey Sacket, here's one of your buddies!"

Sacket dropped a fork full of food and knocked over his chair as he rose from the table. "Well I'll be a son of a bitch!"

Mickey reached for his friend and they clenched each other with hugs of friendship while Barbara and the German POW, Esser, looked on with real pleasure at this reunion.

Reber was trembling and said, "Are there any of the others

here?"

Before Sacket could answer, Staff Sergeant Hatfield said, "Two more, maybe, tomorrow."

"We've got to get caught up with these past months, but let me introduce you to these people. This is Sergeant Esser, and you have already met Sergeant Hatfield," said Sacket.

"Barbara to you Sergeant," said the WAC. "I don't know what you want to eat Sergeant Reber, but I will be glad to get it for you," offered Barbara.

"The biggest hamburger you can find will do nicely," answered Mickey, "and a chocolate shake too, please."

"Hey, Mickey, we made it, we made it. God damn it, we made it!" Sacket kept repeating.

"It will be great to see Farnsworth and Fuzz again too, all this time I have prayed that some of the others survived too, and you know I've never been very big on religion," said Reber.

"You look pretty good, Mickey, but you can't say the same thing about me. I know that I've lost a lot of weight and I am really tired. We have a lot to talk about. I've always said, U.S. Gunners were too mean to die!" stated Sacket.

Esser had just been sitting back and watching these two good friends. Seeing them reunited after their long separation was a touching sight to observe.

Sacket pointed to Esser and said, "This man has been a true friend and he saved a lot of us from death."

Esser stood up. He was wearing the fatigues with the large letter P on the front and back and said, "It's an honor to be an American POW, but one day I hope to be an American citizen and maybe a soldier too."

"I have got to go now, all of you have a great night and I'll see you at 0800 hours in the morning," said Sergeant Hatfield.

TWENTY-FOUR

It was early the next morning and the day promised to be an exciting one. Captain Wilson, Stan, and Brad were anxious to get things moving and they were all ready to get back to their respective home squadrons.

"Let's eat one of these C-Rations that they left us last night and by that time someone should be up here to load those cabinets into trucks," said Stan.

"Hey Captain, do you want to come along outside with me? I can show you the best trees to use for your morning's morning. We don't have any running water up here, but we do have some water in cans that we brought up from the lake and it's OK to wash up in," Brad said helpfully.

"Sure, that would be great, Brad. I was wondering how we were going to take care of that. I'm about to bust a gut, let's get going."

Brad led the way and the Captain followed him out the side door.

All the rest of the officers and enlisted men had spent the night down in the park area in the building where Brad and Stan had first located. Stan knew this was probably going to be his last day up there on the hill, so he began to gather some things that he wanted to take with him. He got a Luger and a rifle and ammunition for both. We just might need this on the trip back, thought Stan. He looked around the big room. There really isn't anything here that I need. I just want to get the hell out of this place, and the sooner the better. Be so great to be back on home turf again. When those two get back we have got to go down the hill and see what progress they have made, contemplated Stan.

"Here we are, both fresh as a new born baby's ass," said Brad as they came back from their outdoor privy and cold water bucket bath. "Next," he said as he gestured with a flourish of his arms.

"OK. I get the hint," said Stan, and he headed for the door.

"Got anything you want to take with you, Brad?" asked Captain Wilson. "I have a feeling we are all going to be out of here very soon now."

"I just want to get back down to that cabin and pick up that carved box. The Lieutenant said he thought it would be OK if I took it. I already have a Luger and some ammunition, and other than that, there is not one thing here that I can't do without. How about you, Captain?"

"Got my plane down there, but it looks like that is one old bird that's going to end her career right here. The Colonel said she might have to be destroyed before we leave today."

Just then Stan returned and said, "Let's all of us get down below and see what's going on."

"You two go on. I'm going to stop by that cabin and pick up that box I want. I'll meet you at the big building. I won't be but a few minutes behind you," said Brad.

Captain Wilson and Stan took off at a slight run, the sun was warm today, the air was invigorating, and they were both excited with the idea that they would be leaving today and would soon be returning to their bases.

Brad got to Cabin #7. He had the key to the door in his pocket. He entered and found the box he had left there. He opened the inside shutter so that he would have some brighter light and sat down at the table that was next to the window. He placed the intricately carved box on the table and turned it around and around, then turned it up side down to look at the bottom of it. The box was very well made, smooth on all sides, except for the top. He judged the box to be about six by four inches and at least three inches deep.

As he turned it he saw one corner that looked slightly different. He pushed and pulled at it with his fingers and to his amazement it slid open. There was a small slot with a key inside. The box had not rattled when he shook it because the slot fit the key perfectly.

"Wonder what we have here," mused Brad. Only one way to find out. I'll open it."

He put the key in the lock and opened the box. It was lined with velvet and there was a small, heavy dark blue pouch laying inside. Brad carefully picked up the bag and underneath it there was a small card with the words "Zu E. Mit Mein Liebe Und Befriedigen, H."

"What the hell is this?" said Brad.

He undid the top of the bag and poured the contents into his hand. A beautiful necklace and earrings slid out.

"Wow, these could be priceless if they are really diamonds, sapphires, and rubies. What a find, but now what do I do?" he asked himself. "The Captain said I could keep it, but he didn't know what was in it. Should I leave it here or take it with me?"

Brad had a strong sense of conscience and it bothered him to no end when he thought he had done something wrong.

"I'll just stick this box in with some things I have and wrap it up. If someone asks me, I'll tell them, if not, I might just as well keep it."

He replaced the jewelry in its velvet bag, put it back in the box and locked it. He put the key in its own compartment and replaced the hidden cover. The box was small enough that it could fit in his worn flight suit pocket. It was a little bulky, but he patted it with his hand and left the cabin.

"I'm not going to lock this place," he decided, but he did close the door behind him.

When Brad got to the main building he found everyone inside.

"Come on in Lieutenant Freestone, this is Colonel Wesley Dallas and you met Major Nickson last night. We have been talking about getting some trucks up that back road so that we can load all those filing cabinets that contain all those cards with the names and history information about those hundreds of thousands of German people, there probably are other nationalities there too. They could be very important."

"I'll go up with you," said the Colonel.

"Be sure that we have at least ten men to come along and help with the job at hand," ordered Major Nickson.

The Sergeant broke into the conversation. "These two officers that are here with us now are probably hungry and they are really in need of something to wear. They have been evading capture by the Germans for more than nine months now. I am sure they can show us how to get on top of that hill."

"As soon as we get our trucks and men up there, get them fed and clothed," agreed the Colonel.

"Food is the least of our concerns, Colonel, but we both could sure use some socks and shorts. The ones we have been wearing have seen better days. We had a couple of C-rations this morning and that will do for now. Let's get going with this project so that we can all get out of here," said Stan.

Stan climbed up into the front seat of the lead truck and sat beside the Colonel. "Just down the road to the left there is a gate hidden by trees and bushes. There it is Sergeant, turn in here," directed Stan.

"I'll jump down and open the gate for you. Might be a good idea if we leave it open to expedite our exit. Is that OK, Colonel?"

"Good idea Lieutenant," said the Colonel.

The two four wheel drive trucks ground their way through the mud and water and then up the steep back road to the hidden German radio station. Everyone else, except the drivers of the other vehicles, had walked up the hill and Major Nickson was coming out of the concrete building to meet the truck convoy and its passengers.

Colonel Dallas looked around and said, "So this is the place where that dirty, son of a bitch Goebbels did a lot of his dirty work."

"Yes sir, and those two fly boys actually saw him leave here! Come on in and take a look at what we have. I think this collection of names and the information on these cards may be just what the Allies are looking for."

The Colonel and the Major spent an hour or so talking to Farnsworth and Freestone about how they had managed to find the park with its cottages and the incredible art collections, and how the two of them had managed to get into this main building with all its records and weapons.

"That must have been a real sight to see Goebbels fly out of here," stated Major Nickson.

"Major, get on your radio and tell them I am bringing these two officers and Captain Wilson back with me this afternoon, and tell them to expect a big surprise too!"

"Sir, can I interrupt for a minute. I have something that is of concern to me," said Stan.

"Go ahead, Lieutenant, what is it?" questioned the Colonel.

"There is only one structure that we have not been in since our arrival and it is that hanger down there on the air strip. We have been down there when Captain Wilson landed his P-38. The day that Goebbels flew out of here I saw his driver go over to the building for just a second and then when he returned to his car he left as soon as Goebbels' plane flew out. Something, intuition if you want to call it, has told me to leave well enough alone. There are all these weapons and records here. There is enough ammo to blow this whole place off the map," said Stan with concern in his voice.

"Never mind, Lieutenant. Major Nickson will stay here and he will be in charge. He will go ahead and check out the whole area here. I am going to come back and I will stay in touch with him until I return. My main concern now is to get you, Captain, Wilson and Lieutenant Freestone, and all these records back to headquarters. I'll need a driver that knows his way around this country and a radio in the jeep that we will be traveling in. Take care of our regiment, Nickson, and I'll return as soon as possible," ordered the Colonel.

The four officers and a driver took one of the jeeps and drove down the back road to the main thoroughfare. As they approached the road, the Colonel looked to his right.

"Would you look at all those burned out vehicles, and there is nothing left of those big guns. What in hell happened here, Farnsworth?"

"There was a convoy of Germans that came through here

some months back and our bombers made run after run on
it. They really tore them to shreds, and it's still an ugly mess!"
exclaimed Stan. "A couple of other German convoys came
through after this happened and they did not even bother to
take the dead away. Most of the bodies were burned so badly
from the napalm and explosives that there really was not
much left anyway, not a good sight to have seen," said Stan.

"It's amazing how you two managed to stay alive through
all this," commented the impressed Colonel.

The jeep turned left and headed west with its passengers.
The Colonel turned on the radio and tuned in the
headquarters station. He held the mike close to his mouth
and started his transmission. "Headquarters, this is Red Bird,
how do you read me?"

"I read you loud and clear, go ahead," came the response.

"I want to speak directly with General Ellis. Put me
through to his office ASAP!" spoke the Colonel.

There were some moments of static on the radio and
then a loud, demanding voice came on. "Who in the hell is
this, identify yourself!"

"Sir, this is Lieutenant Colonel Wesley Dallas. I hope
you will excuse the improper radio transmission. I am
returning from Sector G-15 with some objects coded as N-
113. I also have the officers responsible for the discovery
and identification. We should be arriving at your
headquarters before 1300."

Again there was static and the transmission light cut
out and then again burned red, "Dallas, I want you to pull in
and park your cargo at the boarder guard station. Don't even
try and explain what's going on to anyone. A protective
convoy will be there to escort you and the rest of your party
to my office. Do you understand? Just follow your escort."

"Yes sir, I will follow your orders," replied the Colonel.

Stan, Brad, and Wilson, who were seated in the back seat
of the jeep, had watched the Colonel's neck turn red from
tension, and then, like a switch, it had turned white and
there had been beads of sweat forming while the radio
transmission was in progress.

"Shit, did I ever screw up. There go my birds!" spoke the

chagrined Colonel.

The jeep had been on the road for no more than thirty minutes when all of a sudden the earth shook. There were red flashes in the sky and from a distance bombs could be heard exploding. Back to the east the sky was a scarlet red.

"What in the hell was that?" questioned the Colonel. "Stop the jeep."

He got out and faced the east. All one could hear were loud explosions and, in the distance, there were still flashes of red high in the sky. It looked like fireworks. Again, the ground beneath the jeep trembled and as they all watched to the east, flames shot high into the sky.

"Jesus Christ," screamed Stan. "I know what that is. I'd bet my life that someone opened that hanger door. If my suspicions are right the whole place had been booby trapped and that park and everything in it has gone up in smoke. Good thing we got all those records out because there won't be anything left back there, Colonel. Your plane is gone too, Wilson. Good thing you decided to come along with us. God help those poor bastards that stayed behind. Are we going to send help back to them, Colonel?" asked Stan.

The Colonel was still awed by what may have happened. "Yes Lieutenant. Those are our men back there and we must get help to them," he picked up the radio again and began his transmission, "This is Red Bird. Come in. This is an emergency."

The radio sputtered with its usual noise, then came a reply, "Read you Red Bird, go ahead."

"There are signs that explosives have been set off at our last position and we have troops that remained there. They will need help! Send medics and at least three ambulances ASAP!" said the Colonel with authority.

"Read you sir. They will be on their way. Best you come on in and let them take care of things there, over and out."

It would take an hour for help to come from the border and another two hours for this convoy to get into Reims. When everyone realized what must have happened they were all full of concern for those that had been left behind them.

"I just had a gut feeling that somehow that place was

going to be destroyed," said Stan.

Brad looked at Stan with utter amazement in his eyes. "Do you realize how damned fortunate we are to be here, after all those months prowling around that place, getting into all those cabins and buildings and now this! If I never believed in fate, I sure do now. Someone up there is sure looking after us, that's for sure," said Brad pointing his finger skyward.

"Driver proceed to the border station," said the Colonel.

When they arrived, there were four military policemen who stood in the middle of the road. They lowered the heavy gateway lined with flashing red lights. A guard appeared on both sides of the jeep and one went to each truck.

At the roadside, there were four ambulances and a jeep with several medics waiting to proceed.

"I had these vehicles wait for your arrival, sir, so that you could give them directions."

"Thank you, Sergeant. I only hope they will find some of those men alive and be able to help them when they get there. It's about thirty-five miles straight back the way we came. God only knows what they will find on their arrival. A Major Nickson was left in charge and I intended to return to that position, not later than tomorrow, but, now of course, we will wait to hear from you. Please notify headquarters when the rescue party comes back through here and let me know what casualties were sustained. There is a road on the left, just this side of the park area, and they should be able to get up on top of that hill that way. Have them check out a large building about two hundred yards off the highway, some of the men may have been in there. Tell them good luck and we hope that they find our men," said the Colonel.

"I'll pass your instructions on to the medics and drivers sir, and I am sure they will do all they can to help those men back there. I'll return in just a few minutes sir, soon as I have spoken to the drivers of the rescue vehicles," said the sergeant in charge.

One by one the ambulances drove through the check point and to the east. Everyone watched until they were out of sight.

"Back to the business at hand, Colonel. I will have to request identification from your party," said the master sergeant in charge.

He took all the papers to the guard house and within a few minutes he returned. "Everything is in order, sir. You and your party may proceed. There are two armored vehicles just ahead and General Ellis has asked that they escort you to headquarters."

The Sergeant stepped back and gave a sharp salute to the Colonel and his party as it proceeded past him. One of the armored cars pulled in front of the Colonel's jeep and the other moved back behind the rear truck.

Just as the convoy was ready to leave, a Military Police jeep with a fifty caliber gun mounted on the rear and a gunner standing behind it at the ready pulled to the lead position.

Brad whispered to Stan, "Hell, they sure aren't fooling around with this are they?"

As Colonel Dallas looked around, he slowly shook his head and said, "I should have thought of all this preparation!"

As the convoy left the guard station, two motor cycles pulled up ahead and became the forward out riders. Because the patrol cleared highway for the one hundred and thirty kilometers between the border and Reims, it took the convoy about two hours to arrive at the Army Headquarters courtyard gate.

A space directly in front of General Ellis's office had been cleared to make room for them. There were two fork lifts with operators standing by. The General, dressed in his combat fatigues with a belted forty-five on his hip, stood on the steps. The rest of his staff stood on the walk way in front of him. The photographer was already taking pictures from every possible angle.

A second Lieutenant ran up to the side of Colonel Dallas's jeep. "All of you, get out and approach the General and salute him now! Driver, you stay in the vehicle."

"Someone's going to get some publicity out of this," commented Stan as he climbed out of the jeep.

Brad and Wilson and Colonel Dallas were right behind him. They all formed a line, came to attention, and saluted the General, and the photographer continued taking his pictures:

The General came forward and shook hands with each of the officers, according to their rank, and when he had finished he faced Brad and Stan and Wilson. "What a remarkable experience you three have had. We will have time to discuss it at length when you come to my office."

He turned his attention to Colonel Dallas. "I want you to accompany these materials, and our intelligence people who are here, to the secured place that I have selected for their safe keeping. Intelligence will take care of the processing. When you have received a receipt for all these items, come up to my office and we will talk further."

At that moment the General turned toward the building and looked up to the second floor and gestured to the two faces that were looking out of the window of his office.

Both Farnsworth and Freestone looked up to a welcome sight.

"Hey Fuzz, Hey Magellon, where in the hell have you been?"

Tears of joy and surprise were streaming down the faces of the four crew members of the ill fated, old B-17, the Louise E. Ann.

General Ellis brought the group to attention after this emotional convocation. He stood at attention and saluted the three young officers. "Let's all go upstairs and you can see your old crew members."

As they filed up the stairs and into the headquarters office, all the personnel stood and applauded in appreciation of this very special moment. Reber and Sacket rushed forward to give welcoming hugs and words to their friends.

"God damn, it's great to see you two again," said Mickey, who was visibly shaken.

"Yeah, me too, we got a lot of history to catch up with," said Sacket as he stood between his two friends, his arms around their shoulders.

It had been months since either Stan or Brad had even thought of a woman, and when Staff Sergeant Barbara Hatfield greeted them inside the office, it was an added

pleasure. Both men looked really rugged with their worn
out clothes, long hair, and sunburned faces that had not been
properly shaved in a long time. Captain Wilson was certainly
in need of clean clothes and a shower, but he had only been
in a distressed state for a couple of days. Still, he needed a
shave too.

Stan felt a jolt of emotion that had been subdued for
months when the very pretty WAC offered him her
assistance.

"Here are seats for all of you." She gestured to the five
comfortable looking chairs in front of the General's desk.
"I'm sure that you are all thirsty after your long trip and I
have arranged for some hot coffee and cold drinks to be
brought up, and there will also be a tray of sandwiches," she
said, as she caught Stan's eye.

"That would be great." Stan was sure he was blushing
under his growth of beard.

Barbara turned her attention to Captain Wilson. "Your
squadron has been notified of your whereabouts, Captain,
and as soon as we hear from them we will help you return to
your duty station."

"Thank you, Sergeant. I am glad to have been a part of all
this, but I know that I must get back to work as soon as
possible. I appreciate your help," replied the Captain, with
an admiring glance at the pretty young woman.

The General sat back in his big leather desk chair and
really seemed to be enjoying the activity that was going on
in his office and he went along with it for some minutes.
The refreshments came and everyone had some food and
drink, enough to get them through until dinner time.

"Gentlemen, may I have your attention," spoke Sergeant
Hatfield. Her voice was feminine but strong and in her
position as Aide to the General, she had to be efficient. "Each
of you has been successful at survival in your own individual
situations, and it has been nothing short of miraculous. Both
the Army and the Air Force will be asking you for information
so that, in the future, your experiences may be of help to
others who may face similar circumstances, and your
answers may very well help to upgrade survival and training

manuals in the years to come. There will be other department officers who will want to speak with you about subjects that are of importance to their operations. The General has a few questions of his own and then the five of you can retire to your assigned quarters for a time of sharing." Barbara turned and gestured to General Ellis. "Will you proceed now, sir?"

"Thank you, Sergeant Hatfield. Lieutenant Farnsworth, tell us briefly about your organization and describe what the last assigned mission was for your aircraft. Tell us about the others in your crew and what you think may have happened to them.

Stan stood and described the last flight of the Louise E. Ann in detail. He told what he knew of the other members of his crew. "We were all very close, sir. It is a tragedy that they can't be here today with us. They should be honored and we will miss each one of them."

It was plain to see that the General was impressed with his knowledge of his fellow crew members and the aircraft they had flown in. "You speak proudly and positively of the officers and enlisted men you flew with and of your organization, and I want to commend you for your positive attitude."

The General asked questions of all the others. "Remarkable move you and Sergeant Esser made, Sergeant Sacket. There are a lot of American and British airmen who will be forever grateful to you both."

Then the General turned to Sergeant Reber. "It must have been a real experience for you being forced to live in a situation like that with the German enemy for such a long period of time Sergeant."

"Yes sir, I was fortunate and saw the good side of the German people and in some ways it was rewarding," commented Mickey.

The General turned to Lieutenant Freestone. "You and Lieutenant Farnsworth have made the task of dealing with those who will be accused of unspeakable crimes against innocent people much easier."

With a turn of his head, the General looked at Captain Wilson. "Lucky for you that these two airmen were in that

location when you had your forced landing, not easy to set
an aircraft down on enemy territory is it?"

"It is a disconcerting experience, sir. I had seen that
particular small air strip while flying missions over it on
several occasions, but I never thought that I might have to
use it."

Just then there was a knock at the door and Sergeant
Hatfield quietly opened it. "Colonel Dallas is here sir, and
he has some important information for you that concerns
some of these airmen."

"Come in Colonel, we have been waiting for you. What
news do you have for us?" asked the General.

"I'm not sure if you were informed that we suspected
explosives had gone off at the location where we rescued
Lieutenants Farnsworth and Freestone and Captain Wilson.
We saw evidence of such activity about an hour after we left
that position and I asked that medics be sent to assist the
men who were left there as a surveillance team. It has been
confirmed that the park was indeed a huge mine field and as
Lieutenant Farnsworth suspected it was probably activated
by someone opening the door to the building near the airstrip
Lieutenant Farnsworth had identified as being a hangar. I
am sorry to say that everything in, near, or around the area
was demolished. There were no survivors from my group of
men. We were fortunate to have retrieved the records now
in our possession as we are sure now that the German
officials never intended for them to be out of their hands.
The deaths of these fine men seem doubly tragic when we
are so close to the end of this war. I will personally write
messages to each concerned family, sir."

The room had suddenly become very quiet. Everyone
was saddened at hearing of the deaths of the Americans that
had rescued Brad and Stan, and Captain Wilson.

"We are all sorry to hear your news, Colonel. If there is
anything that I can do to assist you with your notification to
the next of kin to those men who were lost, please let me
hear from you," said the General.

"Thank you sir, and now if I may be excused I must
proceed with my official duty to the families of my men.

Good afternoon and good luck to each of you here." The Colonel gave a sharp salute and turned and left the room. The General shook his head. "Very sad news indeed, but now we must go on. I must inform you four men that there will be complete physicals for all of you and we will have that information for you later today. I expect they will begin tomorrow. Sergeant Hatfield will find out the time of your appointments. Following that and in the next day or so you will be given a list of officers who will want to speak with each of you individually. I have a personal interest in each of you and I will join you on some of your sessions. For now I must attend to some important business away from my office. I'll see all of you sometime in the morning."

"Take over here, Sergeant Hatfield, and tell these men anything else that they should be informed of," directed the General.

"Just one or two more things, sir. Tomorrow morning, after breakfast, our personnel and finance people will get with each of you and bring your payroll to date. I understand too that there are some promotions and awards for each of you. You will each have a significant amount of money and if you like our finance officer can advise you about its safe keeping. We have notified your families that you're safe, but I can arrange to have any personal messages sent to those special people in your lives."

Barbara looked around the room to see which of the four might want to take advantage of her offer.

"I will write something tonight, if it's all right Sergeant," said Brad.

"Is it all right for us to give it to you in the morning?" asked Sacket.

"Yes, of course, Sergeant. We will get it off as soon as I hear from you," said Barbara.

"I will have something to send too," offered Reber.

Sergeant Hatfield looked directly at Stan. There seemed to be sparks in the air. "Is there anyone special for you, Lieutenant?" she asked.

"Just my immediate family," said Stan with a smile, as he made eye contact with this pretty woman.

"I am going to turn you over to Lieutenant Gerald Peterson. He will assist you for the rest of your stay here. He will have all the information about your meetings and your physicals, and he will help you with the various locations of the officers you are to visit. Tonight he will go to the messing facility with you and direct you to your quarters. Have a good night gentlemen, and I will see you in the morning," said Barbara as her eyes scanned the room. Finding Stan last, she shyly lowered her head and smiled.

TWENTY-FIVE

Lieutenant Peterson gathered his four wards in the hall way and spoke as he led them. "I have been instructed to take you to our medical facility. You will all start your physicals with some blood work and x-rays today and then complete your examinations with the doctors in the morning. You should be finished by late tomorrow afternoon, and then there will be quarters ready for you here at this facility."

Peterson led his charges into a four bed ward. "The shower and bathroom are through that door," he said, as he gestured with his hand to the far end of the room. "You will find everything you need in the way of personal items in the drawers of your night tables. Just wear the hospital pajamas, robes and slippers through tomorrow and after your physicals we will get you into some new clothes. It is getting late, so I suggest that you all have a quick shower and get rid of those clothes you're all wearing. As soon as you are ready, go down and report to the lab for your tests. Have an early dinner at the cafeteria down the hall and get some rest so that you will be ready for the doctors in the morning. You should all be done by late afternoon and then we will get you into your quarters for the remainder of your stay with us. If you should need me, my extension number is on the pad by the telephone. I will see you early in the morning, shall we say, 0800 hours."

The Lieutenant had been very thorough with his instructions. "Got to go for now, enjoy the rest of the day," and he left the room.

"God, a hot shower really sounds great," said Sacket.

"I'll race you to it." Farnsworth closed the door and the

clothes began to fly to a pile in the center of the floor.

Brad was one of the last to undress. I have got to do something with this box I took. I don't want to answer any questions about it now, he thought to himself. He chose a bed and put the box in the night stand drawer. He would put it with some of his other things later.

There was singing and splashing and personal comments made in the shower.

"Hey Mickey, I thought you were the one who was not religious. What is that silver crucifix you're wearing?" asked Farnsworth.

"It's too long a story for now. We have got to get a move on," came his reply.

These four men were a real picture in their hospital garb. With clean shaven faces and fresh from their showers they proceeded to the lab where they were taken in turn for all the necessary tests. When they had finished they headed for the cafeteria and had hamburgers and fries and shakes, something they had all missed for these long months.

They went back to their room and tried to carry on conversations, but the events of the past days had worn them all out and it seemed that all they wanted was a good night's sleep.

"We can get all caught up with each other in the next day or two," said Stan, as he clicked off the lights.

In just a matter of seconds there were sounds of deep breathing coming from each bed. Stan swore he heard one of them whisper, "Inga," and then everything was still.

A knock came at the door and Stan awoke with a start. It was 7:30 and they had all slept soundly through the night.

"Hey, you guys, wake up. We are due for our physicals in thirty minutes," shouted Stan.

Lieutenant Peterson stuck his head in the door. "You all have about fifteen minutes to use the head. You're going to go in what you're wearing so get moving. I'll wait in the hallway for you."

Stan had jumped up and was in the bathroom and Brad followed him, then came Reber who splashed some cold water on his face and ran a comb through his long hair.

"This has got to go sometime today," he commented.

Sacket was right behind him and in the allotted time they had all put on robes and slippers and were in the hall where Lieutenant Peterson stood waiting for them.

"Guess you all had a good night's rest. That's just what you needed and the doctors will be pleased to see you in such a relaxed condition."

Just as they entered the corridor where the doctors had their offices, Sergeant Hatfield appeared walking toward them. She was a brunette and her thick, short cropped hair was combed back into soft waves and into a duck 'tail at the back of her neck. She had flawless skin and green eyes and a figure that complemented her uniform. Even with the plain military issue shoes she wore, she had very shapely legs.

As she got to where the four new arrivals were standing she said, "You all look rested and refreshed. I know that you have to spend most of the day here, but maybe we will see each other later this afternoon."

She glanced at each man. "What a difference to see you all clean shaven. There is a barber shop here too," she said as she looked at Stan with obvious interest. "Got to go, see you all later." She strode off, with a very appealing feminine, yet sedulous walk.

"Hey Stan, what's going on between you two? It's like bolts of lightening go off when you're around each other. Did you know her before this?" asked Reber.

"Met her the same time you three did," said Stan feeling a wonderment at the attraction he had for this young woman. "She is really something, isn't she?"

The four survivors of the Louise E. Ann spent the rest of the day with the doctors. Sacket was the one who needed the most medical attention. He was a very thin one hundred and forty-nine pounds, with his ribs and cheekbones showing.

"You need lots of food and rest. Eat what you like. It might be difficult for you to eat rich foods for a while. Take it easy and your digestion will get used to your eating normally again. Your x-rays and blood work are all normal. Other than being thin, I find nothing really physically wrong, you're one very lucky young man!"

Sergeant Reber was the next to be analyzed by one of the
Army physicians. "You're slightly underweight, but you seem
to be in good health. I see your right arm shows signs of a
past injury. How did that happen?"

Reber explained that he had been hurt during the attack
by the three German Folkwolf fighters on the day the Louise
E. Ann was shot down. "Our Bombardier, Bottom Ball Turret
Gunner and Waist Gunner were killed in that attack too.
Our Pilot and Tail Gunner went down with our aircraft."

Mickey's emotions were very close to the surface and he
put his head down for a moment to regain his composure.

"The rest of us were lucky because we were able to bail
out. I managed to stay in good health after my capture
because of the kind treatment given to me by the Germans
who took me as their prisoner. I would like to explain all
this to someone who evaluates the plus side of the German
people," said Mickey with a quiver in his voice.

"I think it is important that you talk to someone about
these penned up feelings of yours, Sergeant. I am going to
recommend that you speak to a psychiatrist for a session or
two and then we can start to work on your reassignment.
That is in your plans for the future isn't it?" asked the doctor.

"Yes sir, I would like to get back to Germany with the
Army of Occupation, if they will allow me to do so,"
answered Mickey.

The doctor looked Mickey squarely in the face when he
spoke. "Somehow, I have the feeling that there is someone
that you want to get back to. Am I right, Reber?" queried the
doctor.

"Yes, but I am afraid to speak about it for fear that I will
get that person in serious trouble, sir," confided Mickey. "You
need have no fear here, Sergeant, as I am a doctor and
anything I hear from you is privileged information. You will
get a chance to tell your story to the right people after you
leave here and I hope that things work out for you when
you're reassigned. You will be awarded the Purple Heart for
the wound you sustained from the enemy. For now, get lots
of rest and try and clear your mind of things that are troubling

you," suggested the doctor.

In the next office Stan was being given the once over by Doctor Wesley Engh, who was a Captain in the Army medical services.

"Blood pressure is good, chest sounds OK. You're a little underweight, but time will take care of that. Have you got any other complaints, Lieutenant?" questioned the Captain.

Stan looked down at his feet from where he was sitting on the examination table. "Yes sir, it's my feet. They hurt sometimes and itch like the devil!"

"Lay back on the table and let's have a look at them, Farnsworth," ordered the doctor.

"How long did you wear the same boots and socks?"

Stan shook his head. "There were times when Brad and I didn't take our boots off for weeks at a time. We were on the move constantly for a while and the weather was really cold. We didn't have a change of socks until just recently. We tried to wash the ones we had, but there were times when it was impossible to take care of the clothes we had. Bathing and toilet facilities were a constant concern for us. We slept indoors when we finally got to a location that allowed it, but there was no indoor plumbing."

The doctor put on some surgical gloves and proceeded to go over Stan's feet.

"Somewhere you suffered some frost bite and then that went into common athletes foot, but this is now a little more serious. I would say that it is lupus vulgaris. In layman's terms, you have tuberculosis of the skin on your feet."

Stan took a deep breath and there was concern in his voice when he spoke. "Am I going to be OK, Doc?"

"There is treatment for this condition, and starting today you will come in here twice a day and soak your feet in a solution that we have for this sort of thing. I don't want you wearing anything on your feet but clean white socks and slippers. The socks should be changed twice daily. It will take about ten days and there should be improvement. The itching should be all gone in two or three days. Back to something else you spoke of, have you got any digestive or constipation problems?"

"Yeah, a little I guess. I am hoping that will improve when we get back to eating normally," answered Stan.

"You're right," answered the Captain. "I will give you something to take for a few days. You can stop taking it when you feel that things are regular again. OK Lieutenant, go on down the hall and get started with your foot treatment and I'll see you again in a few days. It would be a good idea for you to stay off your feet and drink lots of liquids. In about two weeks you should be able to make a trip to Paris for some R and R. When you get down there I want you to go by the main hospital. I have you set up for an eye examination. It may be nothing important, so don't worry about it."

"Thanks Doc, it is sure good to be back in good hands. I already feel better just knowing that I'm still in pretty good condition." Stan dressed and left the office.

Brad was seated in a chair in the hallway waiting his turn to see the doctor.

"What's the good word Stan?" he asked.

"I've got some good news and some bad news. What do you want to hear first?" said Stan with a grimace on his face.

"Give me the bad news first," came Brad's reply.

"I've got something called lupus vulgaris, and the good news is that I'd bet you have it too," said Stan.

"What in the hell is that, sounds terminal whatever it is," said Brad with a half grin on his face.

"Go on in and the Doc will give you all the info on our problem," directed Stan.

Just then the doctor stuck his head out the door. "Lieutenant Freestone, please come on in. Just take off your robe and P.J. top and let's take a look at you."

Doctor Engh did all the usual examinations and gave Brad his blood work and x-ray reports. "It all looks good, so far. Now let's check out your feet. You're the officer who was with Lieutenant Farnsworth, right?"

"Yes sir, I am, are we going to be OK?" asked Brad questioningly.

"I gather you heard about your foot problem," stated the doctor.

"I heard about something. I'm not sure that it had to do

with my feet."

When the doctor had finished checking Brad's feet he looked up and smiled. "You and your fellow officer have both suffered nearly identical problems and you will need the same treatment. You are both slightly underweight, but as I told Farnsworth, that will take care of itself. I would guess by the time you leave here you both will have gained back all the loss. I have duplicated instructions for you. They are the same as for Farnsworth. You should both have your eyes checked while you're on R and R in Paris," directed the doctor.

"Young man, you have been through a very exciting, yet traumatic experience. Both you and your senior officer are fortunate to have survived it. I am sure that your being together helped you both through it. You and the three others from your organization will be interrogated by our intelligence and logistical people for the next few days. Return here for your treatments or any other problem that may arise. I understand that you want to sign on for another tour of duty with the Air Corps, is that correct?"

"Yes sir, that is true and I can't wait to get started!" spoke Brad enthusiastically.

"That sounds good, Lieutenant. Somehow I feel we may be hearing some good things about you in the future. That's going to be all for now. I have an appointment down the hall. I'll see you soon," and the doctor left the examination room.

Brad looked down at his feet and grimaced. He put on his socks, finished dressing, and went out into the hall where all his friends were waiting for him except Stan.

"Stan has gone on to the treatment room ahead of you, Brad, so you go on and we will wait for you both in the bar on the third floor. You're all going to wear your hospital uniforms until further orders so the both of you come on up when you're done," directed Lieutenant Peterson.

Brad found Stan in a treatment room full of metal cabinets with all sorts of surgical tools encased in secured glass doors. There were many male medics and some nurses going in and out of sectioned off tables where patients were being given what medical attention they needed. Stan was seated in a corner away from the heavy traffic area of the room and had his feet in a deep tub of some sort of solution.

"Come on over here, Brad. We have been expecting you," Stan pointed his hand at a medic who was coming their way with another tub. "That one is for you Brad, have a seat here with me. You can believe me or not, but my feet already feel better and they have only been in this stuff for about fifteen minutes," said Stan.

"Here you go, Lieutenant. Take off your socks and let's get started with your treatment for those feet of yours. In about forty-five minutes I will bring you each a towel so that you can dry your feet thoroughly and a supply of clean white socks and a plastic bag for each of you. When you change the socks the prescribed times per day, put the old socks in the bag and return them to us here. We will give you new ones for old when you come in for treatment," instructed the orderly.

"Thanks, we will do what you want us to. We are really anxious to get rid of this stuff and I already feel it working," said Stan.

Brad sat down and put his feet into the almost hot liquid. "That does feel good," he said as he leaned back and began to relax in his chair.

They talked some about what they would do while they were on R and R in Paris and about how good it was to see Sacket and Reber again.

"Stan, I've got a problem and I need some advice on how to handle it. The day we left Germany I went to that cabin and picked up the box I told you about. I had time to examine it and got it opened. I know what's in it. There is a really beautiful necklace and a pair of earrings and if I am right the gems are real. Do you think I should turn it over to the authorities?"

"Hell no, Brad. Put it with some of your personal things and forget about it. If the place had not gone up in smoke it might be different. Just think of all those pictures and God only knows what else were destroyed. Everyone takes home war souvenirs. Don't think you're the only one to have done it."

"Thanks Stan, that is sort of what I thought you might say. I won't say anything to anyone. You won't either will you?" asked Brad.

"God damned it Brad, just forget about it and relax," admonished Stan.

The treatment time passed and the medic came loaded with the supplies he had promised. "Dry those feet good and we will see you back here in the morning," he directed.

"Hey Brad, before we go upstairs I want to find that barber shop the Sergeant told us about. This long hair of mine is about to drive me nuts. How about you? I'd bet you would look better without bangs," teased Stan.

"Yeah, you're right, Stan. Let's go get these heads of ours back to looking like we belong to the military," said Brad.

"We have an hour before the dining room opens and your doctors said it would be alright for you to have a couple of beers before meals," said Lieutenant Peterson as he led Reber and Sacket up the stairs to the third floor.

They entered a large room at the end of the hall. It had large windows that looked out over the center of town. Sacket went over to look out at the town. How great it is to be free again, he thought to himself.

Lieutenant Peterson, followed by Reber, came up behind Sacket. "Let's take this table. It has six chairs and you can enjoy the view," suggested the Lieutenant.

"That's the Reims Cathedral at the end of the street, it is amazing that it has received so little damage during this war, hardly any to speak of," informed Peterson.

"There are lots of bars and restaurants down there and the streets are full of soldiers and women," commented Sacket.

"And most of the women are full of VD," stated Peterson. "Got to be really careful, you would all be wise to keep your pants on!"

"Looking down there it seems hard to believe that there's a war going on. Last fall my outfit came through here and we killed us a bunch of Germans. I guess I'm lucky to have gotten through it and somehow I wound up here with this job. I lost a lot of good friends out there in the country and in and around this town," reminisced Peterson. "Fate seemed to have stepped in because both the Americans and the Germans left this part of the municipality alone," continued Peterson.

A Frenchman, who was the bartender, came over to the table and offered to take an order for drinks.

"By the way Roger, I understand that you have just received some canned American Beer. What kind is it?" asked the Lieutenant.

Before the drink orders could be given there were voices at the far end of the room. "Wait for us before you order," it was Brad and Stan with new hair cuts.

"Do we know you two?" asked Sacket.

"You look so different without that long hair. The beards were a real shock but this is almost too much!" spoke Sacket.

"Come on you guys, sit down here and join us. Roger was just about to tell us what kind of beer he had. Go on Roger, the gangs all here and we are all ears, what have you got!" said Peterson.

Roger spoke with a flourish. "We now have Acme, Lucky Lager, and Pearly Beer. They just arrived within the last three days. What's your pleasure, gentlemen?" he asked with his order pad in his hand.

Everyone ordered Lucky Lager until Roger got to Lieutenant Farnsworth.

"Since we are in France, I want a glass of your best red wine."

"Where is everybody? This place is so quiet," spoke Reber, directing his question at Peterson.

"This bar is only for the officers and men that work here at headquarters, and of course, for those such as yourself, and in your situation that would include you, Sergeants Sacket and Reber," answered Peterson.

Roger brought the cans of Lucky Lager to the beer

drinkers and then with a flourish placed a large glass of red wine in front of Farnsworth. "You have chosen wisely Monsieur, this is a very fine bordeaux. There are still a few bottles of this excellent wine that the German's did not get!"

"There's always got to be someone different in every crowd," said Sacket who turned his head to face Lieutenant Peterson. "I'm pretty sure that you hear about what's going on around here. Tell me, where is my German friend, Esser?"

"He has been transferred to a special unit that interrogates German prisoners. You will see him again when our intelligence people talk with you about your association with him. Believe me, he is being treated very well, you don't need to be concerned about him," replied Peterson.

"At five o'clock, many others will appear here so don't be surprised by some of the characters you may meet. General Ellis may even show up. He is a fine officer and I am sure that he likes all of you. The fact that you're here and not over at the normal repatriation center tells me that your activities before your arrival here have had an affect on the war and its eventual outcome. There have been others ahead of you and there will be more to come that the General and the high Command will want to look at very closely."

Peterson continued, "I am one of those that was studied and because of their observation of me I have been given a position here at Headquarters so that I will be available for more of their interrogation, if it should be needed. General Ellis is very knowledgeable and he runs the show here."

"Hey Peterson, it is getting late. Are you sure it is OK if we remain here wearing our hospital clothes?" asked Sacket.

"If you look around the room you will see others. Some of these men would live here if the inquisitive head shrinkers would let them," came the Lieutenant's answer.

Several of the incoming men stopped at the table and made friendly remarks to Peterson and his four new proteges. One said, "Don't recuperate too soon. It won't get any better than this place."

Some of these men were swathed in bandages and some were using crutches or canes. There were even a few using walkers and there were two in wheelchairs.

Peterson said as they were finishing their second round of drinks, "Let's head for the mess hall, don't want to overdo this tonight. Don't forget your robes or slippers, some of the men do."

The mess hall was typically military, lots of tables and chairs with the food being served cafeteria style. Large urns of hot coffee stood nearby. There were trays of desserts and iced milk cartons and pitchers of iced tea. Lots of hot food trays rested behind glass covered counters with personnel to serve a varied selection of meats and vegetables, mashed potatoes and gravy.

"This sure beats the food and service in that hell hole I just came from," commented Sacket as he took some butter and hot bread to add to his dinner tray.

They all ate well, but the quantity and richness of the foods served were overwhelming for each of these four men, "I let my eyes overload my stomach. I just can't finish what I took," said Brad.

"That's all right, don't worry about it," said Peterson. "They have places for all the extra food to go."

Stan looked at the Lieutenant and said, "Guess you're right. There are probably lots of very hungry souls outside these gates who will take whatever they can, any way they can get it."

"Well gentlemen, if you're finished, I have a surprise for you. Since you're all doing so well I got word today that you would be moved into your assigned quarters tonight. When ever you're ready we can move in that direction," said Peterson as he looked at the pleased faces around the table.

Sacket was the first to respond. He jumped up from his chair. "Come on you guys, lets go see these new digs. I'll bet there is a nice warm bed and another hot shower just waiting for me to get into them, I can't wait."

"Yeah, I agree with you, let's go," said Farnsworth, who gave Sacket a gentle push in the back.

Brad and Mickey got up and followed their friends, while Peterson led the way to their new quarters.

They all walked through the long hallways and finally came to a door marked #321.

"This is it," and Peterson as he unlocked the door and pushed it open. As they walked into the room they were all pleasantly surprised to see that they would be rooming together for the remainder of their stay.

"This is really great, we all get to sleep in the same room. As I remember Farnsworth, you snore and you, Reber, talk in your sleep, but that's all right. We can put up with that for a few nights," said Sacket.

"I can think of a few things that you do too that I can do without," said Brad.

"OK, Fuzz, you know that I was only kidding. It is great and it will give us time to catch up with each other," said Sacket.

Peterson stood for a few minutes listening to these four men torment each other and finally said, "If you need anything, give me a call. My room number and extension are on that pad by the phone. I'll come by at 0700 in the morning and your busy day will start after breakfast, about 0830. Don't forget your appointments in the treatment room." He pointed his hand at Brad and Stan.

"No way," said Stan, "we have got to get rid of this shit. I think I'm on the mend already," and Brad shook his head in concurrence.

The room was huge and accommodated four large single beds with clean sheets, warm blankets, and two pillows. A night stand was beside each bed equipped with a night lamp. There was a comfortable chair for each occupant. There were two bathrooms fully equipped with showers and tubs.

"God damned, all the comforts of home, and I get this bed," said Sacket as he jumped and landed on the bed of his choice.

"Where are the things we had in the other room," questioned Brad as he began to look around the room.

"They are all in the closet," said Peterson as he raised his hand. "Good night, see you in the morning," and he left the room.

Brad went to the closet and, sure enough, there were small bags with each of their names on them. He found his and felt for the small box he had worried so much about. It was there. Tomorrow he would make it more secure and he promised himself he would not think or be concerned about it any longer.

Sacket was the first one in bed and was sound asleep before any of the others were ready to get in bed.

"He really seems worn out, guess he needs lots of rest to get over the environment he came from," said Brad.

They had spent the day inside and had not realized that it was cold outside. Farnsworth went to the window and opened it slightly. It had begun to snow outside and he changed his mind and closed the window against the cold air. "Thank God for His favors, we four made it, and we're all here, safe and warm."

TWENTY-SIX

Early the next morning Stan awoke ahead of the others in his room. He realized that he had been dreaming. *What the hell is going on with me*, he thought to himself. *I can't get this girl out of my mind! I know that it has been a long time since I had any sort of a relationship with a woman, but this is so strong. I have never experienced anything like it before. It's like a magnet pulling me towards her and I can't stop!*

Stan took a deep breath and realized that he was sweating and somewhere deep within himself he felt strong sexual desire building up and it was overwhelming him. *God damned, I have to get hold of myself right now!* He jumped up out of bed, headed for the shower, turned on the cold water, and forced himself to get in under the spray. He pulled the shower curtain closed after him.

"Shit, I'm freezing to death," he said under his breath as he shivered from the icy cold water.

"There, I feel under control now," and he turned the warm water until it became hot.

He let the water play on his shoulders and back. He lathered himself with soap and rinsed off, still luxuriating with the feeling of warm water. This was something that he had really missed while he had been in Germany. He turned off the water, grabbed a towel and rubbed himself dry. He left his feet till last. They looked and felt one hundred percent better. He wrapped the towel around himself and looked in the mirror.

"Time for a shave and with this new hair cut I will really look pretty good."

Stan was not egotistical, but he was self assured, with
an outgoing personality. He was good looking in a rugged
sort of way. "I'm going to make one hell of a great lawyer,"
he said as he spoke to his reflection in the mirror, "and I'm
going to have a little talk with Sergeant Hatfield today," he
said under his breath.

He finished in the bathroom and came out into the
sleeping area. "Hey, all of you had better get with it! Peterson
will be here before we know it, wake up, get in gear, rise and
shine!" He pulled blankets from the beds of Reber and Sacket.

Just then there was a knock at the door and Stan heard a
cart rumbling outside in the hallway. He opened the door
and to his surprise it was not Peterson, but Sergeant Hatfield.

"Well, what a surprise this is!" she said as she observed
Stan with only a towel wrapped around his waist. "It looks
like I'm just in time," she said as she pointed to the cart near
her. "I thought you would like to have something else to
wear besides those pajamas and robes. I brought all of you
some fatigues. I think you will find everything else you will
need for the day."

She could not take her eyes off of Stan, nor could he take
his from her.

"Thanks Sergeant. I was just thinking about you, I wonder
if it would be possible for you to come down and sit with me
while I take the treatment for my feet this morning? I will
arrange to go anytime you can spare about forty-five minutes.
I'm having a hard time asking you to do this, it's been so
long since I had a good looking female to talk to. Oh hell,
I'm making a mess out of this," stammered Stan.

"I understand Lieutenant, how about 0900 in the
dispensary. I'll bring each of us a cup of coffee and we can
talk. Mind if I tell you that you really look great with your
hair cut and that towel is very stylish. See you in a couple of
hours." She turned and walked down the hallway, while Stan
just stood in the doorway and watched her leave.

Stan closed the door and walked back into the room with
a smile on his face.

"Where in the hell have you been dressed like that?" asked
Sacket.

"Sergeant Hatfield brought all of this," said Stan as he pushed the small cart in ahead of himself.

"Would you look at all of this, clean undies and everything," said Brad in a joking manner. "Bet she got an eyeful of you with your towel, huh, Stan?" he added.

"Come on, knock it off, and by the way Freestone, I'm going alone for my treatment. She is going to come and sit with me for the forty-five minutes, so you arrange to go at any other time than 0900, got it!"

"Yes sir, Lieutenant," said Brad with a grin on his face.

They were all showered and dressed when Peterson showed up at the door of Room #321.

"I see someone brought you some other clothes this morning. I thought of it, but kind of had a feeling that some kind person would take pity on the four of you."

"Yeah, and they really feel great too," said Brad trying to take the edge off for Stan.

"Let's get up to the mess hall and have some breakfast so that you can all keep you appointments for the morning. I saw that you're scheduled for your treatment at 0900 Farnsworth, and you're at 1000 Freestone. Sacket, they want you in Intelligence at 0830 and some one wants to see you in room 223 for an hour at 1000 Reber. After that I am sure the person in charge will direct each of you to your next appointment. There are going to be some very busy days ahead for all of you."

The mess hall was full of soldiers and officers from Headquarters. Some of those who had been in the bar last night, who had been in various stages of recuperation from wounds and injuries that they had received in battle, were also present.

The foursome from room #321 and Lieutenant Peterson had eaten breakfast and they were just finishing a last cup of coffee when Farnsworth looked at his wrist watch and said, "It's that time, I've got to go. I have an appointment in fifteen minutes. We all have busy schedules today, so I'll see you all later." He got up from the table and started to leave.

"Don't get lost on the way to soak your feet," taunted Brad.

Stan turned around. "Don't you worry about it, son. I
know my way around," and he continued on towards the
door and was gone.

"I've got to go too," said Brad. They want me downstairs
for something before I go to my treatment at 10:00. I'll see
you all later."

"You all know where you're supposed to be this morning.
Sergeants Reber and Sacket, you have about thirty minutes
before you're due and I have some business to take care of,
so I'm going to leave you for now. I'll check back with you
sometime later this morning to make sure things are going
all right for all of you," said Peterson as he picked up some
papers in front of him and left.

"I'm glad that we have some time to talk alone," said
Sacket. "I've noticed how quiet you have been, Mickey.
You're just not yourself. Is everything all right for you? We
have been friends for a long time and I have never known
you to be so withdrawn."

"I do have a lot on my mind, Sacket, and I think you
might understand. Can I talk to you in confidence?"

"Hell yes, Mickey. What's going on, maybe I can help,"
replied Sacket.

"It goes back to my capture and a German girl that I met.
At first I was her prisoner and then one thing led to another
and as time passed we really got serious about each other.
She has become very important to me and I am in love with
her, and I'm worried about her. I promised that I would
contact her as soon as I could, but God only knows when
that will be. I can't get her off my mind and I really miss her.
We have plans to be married. The crucifix I'm wearing
belonged to her. Remember, you asked me about it day before
yesterday? She might be pregnant and I'm worried about that
too."

"God damned Mickey, I guess you really do have a
problem! Have you talked to anyone about this?" asked
Sacket.

"Just the doctor and somehow he guessed that there was
someone I was anxious to get back to. I think that is what
this appointment that I have this morning is all about. I sure

hope someone can help me. I don't want to get her in trouble and I want the authorities to know that this is just not another case of fraternization. It is serious between us and I want to get back to Germany with the Army of Occupation when this war is over. I think that would be best for Inga and at a later time we can make arrangements to get her into the United States. I have learned a lot about the German people Sacket, and I think I could be of real service to their country and the U.S. on duty there," said Mickey.

"I know what you mean, Mickey. I want to help Esser some how too," replied Sacket.

"I am worried about my career too. I really want to stay in the military. I hope this won't ruin my chances," said Mickey.

Stan found Sergeant Hatfield waiting for him. "You're a little early, Lieutenant. Here, I brought you a cup of coffee and here comes the medic with a pan full of solution for your feet."

"Here you go, Lieutenant. Get those feet in here and I'll get back in forty-five minutes. This might be a little warm for starts, but it will cool down."

"Thanks Corporal, it will be just fine. The feet are feeling better all the time," said Stan in an appreciative tone of voice.

"Come on Sergeant, sit here beside me so we can talk a little. I really don't know where to start," said Stan.

"Maybe I can help you, Lieutenant. From the moment I first laid eyes on you I felt a real attraction for you; and I don't want to seem presumptuous, but I think you feel the same way about me," said Barbara.

"You're right on, Sergeant. I can't get you out of my mind. I even woke up thinking about you this morning," said Stan.

"Strange you should say that, Stan, because I thought about you not only this morning but all last night too. I hope you won't mind my calling you Stan. I have all your records you know," said Barbara as she looked at the coffee cup in her hands.

"I really don't know what we can do about this Barbara. I don't know if you know it or not, but I am soon going to return to the States and I am going to ask for a discharge. I want to go back and get my degree in law. I am already half way finished, so it won't take too long for me to accomplish my goal. I know that you have a tour of duty to finish and when you come home maybe we can see each other," said Stan.

"How odd that one meets the very person they could share the rest of their life with in a situation like this. Yes, I do have to finish here and then I will go home to California. I will give you my address and I hope with all my heart that I will hear from you sometime in the future. I am not married or engaged, and I have never met anyone who I have been so physically attracted to ever before in my life. I think I could honestly say that I am in love with you right this very minute, and I have never said that to anyone in my life before," said Barbara with a serious tone in her voice.

"I feel the same way about you," said Stan. "We have so little time here because I am scheduled to leave in a week or so and for now the military seems to have lots of plans for me before I finish up. I don't think it would be fair for us to have some sort of a wild relationship and maybe wind up with some undesirable consequences, but I won't promise you that I won't flirt like hell with you and maybe even catch you unawares with a kiss sometime when you least expect it. You should know too, that I am not or have I ever been seriously involved with any other woman," confided Stan.

"I don't know what religion you are Stan, but I am a Catholic and I am determined not to have sex until I am married, but there is nothing wrong with a kiss or holding hands sometime. If things are meant to work out for us, fate got us this far and I am sure that somewhere in the future we will get together again. Well, it is almost that time and the both of us have a lot to do today. Just maybe I'll see you in some dark hallway sometime today or tonight." And Barbara got up and gave a startled Lieutenant a kiss on the forehead before she turned and left the room.

The day had been a long one for the occupants of room #321 and they were all tired. They decided that after dinner they would return to their room and relax and talk a bit.

Peterson had been with them for the evening meal. "You have all been here for the better part of a week now and the General thinks that you don't need to be supervised any longer. He told me to tell you that if you should need any assistance to let his office know and they will send someone over to help you, probably me. I have enjoyed helping you and today I got a list of the things that will be required for all of you for this next week. I have copies to give to you now before I go." Peterson stood and handed out copies of next week's appointments to his wards.

"Thanks for your help, Lieutenant. I am sure that I speak for all of us here. You have made our return from our rather grim situations much easier and we want you to know that we appreciate it," said Farnsworth.

"I am sure that you will all be well enough to go out on the town one of these nights. I have to caution you to be careful. There are still a few German sympathizers out there who would not hesitate to take an American scalp," cautioned Peterson.

"We would all like to have you go out with us, sort of our way of saying thank you for helping us. Can we give you a call one night soon?" asked Sacket.

"That would be great, and I will look forward to hearing from you. I have some things that I need to do, so I will say good evening." Peterson got up and after shaking hands with everyone was gone.

The next week was busy and flew by. There were never ending meetings and interrogations.

Farnsworth and Freestone spent lots of time at the dispensary for their appointments.

Reber finished his counseling and talked openly about what had happened while he was in captivity. It had been determined that he would not be reprimanded for what might have been fraternization with a German and that what he had experienced might well be used to the advantage of the American Military Forces, following the wars end.

Sacket was on the mend both emotionally and physically from his imprisonment in Stallage Luft #31. He had been interviewed, with Esser, and was satisfied that the German was being well treated and that he might even have a place in the American government rebuilding his own country when the war was finally over. In reality, it would take Sacket years to get over the cruelty, death, and suffering he had seen. He would always remember the cold, the bed of wood he had slept on, and the filth that all the men had been forced to endure. He would forever remember the cross in the yard the men had been led to as a form of punishment. He shuddered even now as he thought of seeing his fellow prisoners' thin bodies whipped by the guards when they had been unable to perform some task that had been required of them. He could take heart in the knowledge that he had helped to release those men from their suffering. He wondered what had happened to his friend Klein. That man had kept him from going out of his mind. He hoped that he had found his family and that he was at last happy and at home again.

During this next week Sergeant Hatfield continued to be of concern to Lieutenant Farnsworth and keeping his word, he made every effort to catch her off guard in the evening in a hallway or outdoors where there was a little privacy. They had held hands and kissed passionately and wondered how in the world they would let each other go their own ways.

"Our day will come," Barbara had said as Stan held her in his arms one evening.

Mickey continued to dream of his love for Inga. Time was passing and he was desperate to see her again. What was going on in Germany? Somehow he felt sure that he was to be a father and he wanted in the worst way to help this girl who had become such an important part of his life.

At the end of the week, Stan and Brad were given a clean bill of health and they were finished with the doctors.

"What a relief to be rid of that damn stuff," Brad had said, and Stan had wholeheartedly agreed with him.

"I've got some spare time now, Stan, and I'm going to go down to Headquarters and see if they can give me some information about airplanes. I really want to get started as soon as I can. I'm ready to get back to work," Brad told Stan with enthusiasm and passion.

"I think you're going to fall in love with some damned airplane and marry it one of these days," baited Stan.

It was a Friday night and they had returned to their room following dinner. Farnsworth put the key in the door and went into the darkened room. He reached for the light switch.

"Hey would you look at this! What are all these packages doing in here?"

There was one on each bed.

"It looks like Christmas," said Brad.

"Let's open them right now," said Sacket as he yanked open the box on his bed.

"It's all our stuff from the Squadron. My dress uniform and flying gear are here and there is even some civilian stuff, this is great. Tomorrow I'm going to get back into these duds. We each have our squadron cap too," he said as he paraded across the room to a mirror to check out his reflection.

"Hey, here are some large envelopes, one for each of us," said Mickey as he roamed around the room giving them to their respective owners.

Stan was the first to open the official looking envelope. "Well, there goes Paris. I can't speak French anyhow. We are all going back to England."

"What the hell, I'd rather be with my old Squadron buddies anyway," said Brad with excitement in his voice.

"Will you look at the date on these orders," directed Sacket. "We have only got five more days here. What say we get a hold of Peterson and go out on the town tomorrow night?"

"Maybe we should wait until Tuesday to do that. It looks like the General has plans for us on Monday. He wants us all in his office at 1000 hours and we go down in the afternoon to collect all our back pay. If we wait, we can take Peterson out in style," said Brad.

"Good thinking, Fuzz," said Sacket. "Tuesday it is!"

TWENTY-SEVEN

Saturday and Sunday gave the rallying foursome time to get reacquainted with their personal belongings and also some time to tell each other about their experiences of the past months. There had been a phone call for Stan and he had been noncommittal when he had said he would be away for an hour or so. They all knew that he had seen Sergeant Hatfield some during these past days and they all suspected that this was the reason he was going now, but why not let him enjoy himself.

Brad put his hand up to quiet any remarks that might come from the others in the room. "See you when you get back, Stan. We will wait for you to go to dinner," said Brad.

Stan went down the hall and out a door that led to a small courtyard in the rear of their building. "There you are," he said, as he saw Barbara sitting on a little bench at the end of the walk.

"I heard that you all got your orders today and I wanted to be sure you had my address so that you could call me when I got home," she said.

"I have thought about that, Barbara, maybe it would be best if I wait to hear from you. I don't want to cause any problems with your family."

Stan reached into his pocket and pulled out a piece of paper. "Here is my address and phone number. If I'm away when you call just leave a message and I promise to call you just as soon as I can."

"That sounds good Stan, I am going to hate seeing you leave here in a few days." She put her hand to her eyes to wipe a tear away.

"Don't cry, sweetheart, the time will go by quickly and before you know it we will be back together," said Stan reassuringly.

"I just don't know how to deal with these feelings of mine. I have never been serious about anyone before and now that I have found you, I have to say good-bye," she said sadly.

They stood up and moved into the shadows of the building. Stan put his hand under her chin and turned her head up so that he could see her eyes. "You have the most beautiful eyes. I will never forget their color, green as emeralds."

He moved his fingers up to her face and traced it down to her mouth and then he kissed her, softly at first and then with such passion that it surprised even him.

"I had better go inside now. I've got three suspicious characters up there in my room and I don't want to give them any reason to wonder what is going on with us. Remember, we still have a few days to see each other before I'm off to England. This war has got to end soon and then you will go back to the States, just as soon as we can we will see each other."

Barbara reached into her coat pocket and gave Stan a piece of paper. "You can write to me here if you want to. I'll be waiting to hear from you, Stan."

"I'll see all of you in the General's office in the morning," said Barbara.

"Do you have any idea what he wants us up there for?" asked Stan.

"Yes, but it is sort of a surprise and I don't want to spoil it for you. It's something good, so don't worry about it," she answered.

They kissed again and said good night. Stan walked her to the door and they each went back to their quarters.

"Anyone ready for dinner?" asked Stan as he entered his room.

They were all up early Monday morning, each wondering why the General wanted to see them. "I have a feeling that we should all wear our dress uniforms today," stated Reber.

"Yeah, I think you're right. The last time we were up

there we all looked pretty rough. He won't know us with hair cuts and clean shaven faces," stated Sacket.

They had breakfast, talked some and stalled over a cup of coffee until 0930 hrs. Better get our butts in gear and arrive a little ahead of time," stated Stan.

When they entered the office of General Ellis they were all spit and polish, looking every bit like sharp, proud United States Army Air Corp men.

Sergeant Hatfield and Lieutenant Peterson greeted them. "What a difference a dress uniform makes. You all look really wonderful. Have a seat for a few minutes until the General is ready to receive you."

"This is going to be a very special day for each of you," said Peterson as he came to greet his men.

Just then another officer, a full Colonel from the United States 8th Army Air Corp, entered the door of the office.

"Good morning, Colonel Scott. It's a pleasure to see you again," said Sergeant Hatfield in greeting. "I want you to meet Lieutenants Farnsworth and Freestone and Sergeants Sacket and Reber."

"It's a pleasure gentlemen. I have heard lots of good things about each of you."

The door to the General's office opened and he came into the outer room to greet all those present.

"I have introduced everyone General and when you're ready we can proceed," informed Barbara.

"That's fine Sergeant Hatfield. Good to see you here Colonel Scott. Now, if you gentlemen will come into my office we will get started," directed General Ellis.

Chairs for everyone had been arranged in a half circle in front of the desk.

"You have all been summoned here today to receive your promotions. Colonel Scott has flown in from England to assist me with the presentation. I have been informed that each of you will be given medals of commendation and one of you will receive the Purple Heart. These will be given to you by your Squadron Commander in England. Memorandums have been prepared and will be a matter of record in your personal files. This is a special privilege for me, gentlemen. As I call your name will you please come forward and remain standing until we have completed all the formalities."

Colonel Scott walked to the front of the room and put some small boxes on the desk and then he stood at attention at the General's side.

"First Lieutenant Stanley Farnsworth please come forward. I am honored to promote you to the rank of Captain in the United States Army Air Corp." The Colonel took a small box from the desk. "I am pleased to award these to you Captain Farnsworth. I understand that you have requested a discharge and that you plan to return very soon to the United States. I wish that there was some way we could change your mind. We need men of your caliber in the military."

"Thank you sir. When I finish school and get my law degree, I just might reconsider my decision."

"Second Lieutenant Bradley Freestone, please step forward. I have the honor of promoting you to the rank of First Lieutenant in the United States Army Air Corp." Colonel Scott reached for another box with silver bars in it. "It is with pleasure that I am able to award these to you Lieutenant Freestone. I have been told that you're interested in continuing your career and want to fly again."

"Yes sir, just as soon as possible," said Brad.

"We just might have some good news for you when you return to your base in England," stated the Colonel with a smile on his face.

"Technical Sergeant Tony Sacket, please stand and come forward. It is my privilege to promote you to the rank of Master Sergeant in the United States Army Air Corp. You have gone above and beyond the call of duty with your outstanding achievement at Stallage Luft #31. The men you helped free will be forever grateful to you. It gives me great honor to present these stripes to you." Colonel Scott handed Sacket his earned chevrons.

"Sergeant Michel Reber, please step forward. I am honored to promote you to the rank of Technical Sergeant in the United States Army Air Corp." Colonel Scott reached for the last packet from the desk. "It is a pleasure to award you these, Sergeant. You have earned them. It is my understanding that you also wish to continue in the service of our country."

"Yes sir, I look forward to a long career in the military," stated Mickey proudly.

"I understand that there is some good news waiting for you at your home station that I am almost certain you will be very happy with."

"Well gentlemen, that concludes this morning's activities. I have been told that you have all received your orders and that you will be leaving France very soon now, is that true?"

"Yes sir, we thank you for this special occasion," said Stan, speaking for his friends and himself.

"One more thing please," said the General. "Barbara, there should be a photographer in the outer room, please have him come in so that we can get pictures of these proceedings. Be sure and have a copy made for each of these men and Colonel Scott, and I will want one too. Best to have a couple of extras so that if we need one for any reason they will be available."

The photographer came in and with lights gleaming from the flash bulbs, he took several shots of the returning heros and their superior officers.

"Lieutenant Peterson is going to take you all down to the finance office and he will help and advise you. If you don't mind some fatherly advice I would recommend that you put most of your money in a soldier's deposit account. It will be safe there and is always accessible for you," advised the General.

"There is one more thing that the four of you should be aware of. Your time is short here and if I were you I would be prepared to leave within a few hours notice."

The newly promoted men saluted the General and Colonel Scott and thanked them for making their promotion presentation so memorable.

"Your families just might be surprised one of these mornings when they see your pictures in their local papers." Colonel Scott and I have some business to take care of now, you are free to leave," said General Ellis.

Lieutenant Peterson followed them as they left the office so that he could assist them in the Finance Office.

"Put most of your money in a soldier's deposit account, it will be safe and always accessible to you. To carry a large sum of money in your pocket around here can get you killed!"

"God damn it, I never dreamed I would ever have this much money at one time. I'm going to invest some of it toward my retirement," said Brad. "Can't call you Fuzz any more Brad, we will be calling you 'Old Mr. Gotrocks' one of these days," commented Sacket.

"Come on Reber, let's you and I go on down to the BX and get these stripes sewn on. All these other two have to do is pin those bars on," said Sacket.

"We will go with you because we all need to buy a B-4 bag to haul all our stuff back to England in," said Brad.

They all walked around the BX looking for things they needed. Sacket and Reber found the tailor shop and took off their uniform jackets so their stripes could be stitched on. They had to wait, but not for long. It only took about twenty minutes.

Stan spotted a silver I.D. bracelet. It was pretty and feminine, he looked around and seeing that he was alone he got the attention of the clerk. "Will you wrap that bracelet up for me? I'm really in a hurry," he asked.

The woman made the transaction and was back at the counter with it. "Here you are, Captain. You can have this engraved here if you want to."

"Thanks, but I won't have time to do that now," he answered. He paid the clerk and put the small package in his pocket.

"Hey Stan, I found the B-4 bags over there. They all look the same to me," informed Brad.

"Let's go look over the stationary while we are waiting for Sacket and Reber," suggested Stan.

They walked around and picked up a few other things.

"This V-mail really does not impress me very much, how about you Brad?" asked Stan.

"The only thing good about it is that it's free, sure isn't very personal," came Brad's reply.

Mickey and Sacket came into view from around the corner.

"Those new stripes really look sharp," said Brad.

"Let's each get a B-4 bag and get out of here. From what the General said it sounds like we had better be ready to go anytime now," said Mickey.

They all chose and purchased the same piece of luggage and headed back to their room to spend some time packing and writing to people back home.

"Do you think all our families have the news that we are alive?" asked Mickey.

"Yes, and I would not be surprised to have letters waiting for us when we get back to England," said Stan.

"Guess we can mail these at the BX tomorrow. My Mom and Dad will really be anxious to hear from me," said Brad.

They got to the dinner line and filled up their trays with the foods of their choice. As the days had passed each of them had been able to eat more and the medication the doctor had given to Stan and Brad was no longer needed. They sat at a table together and ate quietly. They all liked to have coffee following their meals.

"This really tastes good, don't know when I have enjoyed just resting after a meal as I have here," said Stan as he sat back in his chair and relaxed.

"You know, there is something I just thought of," said Brad in a surprised tone of voice. "I just realized that none of us has been smoking. The last cigarette I even tried to smoke was the day we bailed out and Stan chewed my ass out because I tried to use my lighter. How about the rest of you?"

"I smoked one in the office of that German son of a bitch," said Sacket. "I really have not missed smoking and I don't think I will start again," said Stan.

"I sure as hell didn't have a chance to smoke while I was in Germany and I agree with Stan," said Mickey.

"Well, will you look at the four of you. You're sure a different bunch of soldiers from the first day you arrived here."

Stan turned his head as he recognized the familiar voice. "Come on you guys, move over so that Sergeant Hatfield can join us for coffee."

"I had an idea, but this is the first chance I have had to speak to any of you about it and if I don't do it now it may be too late. I wondered if you would like to go and see the Cathedral in the morning? You really should not leave France without visiting it. I might be able to go with you in the morning, it only takes a few minutes to walk there," said Barbara.

"Thanks for suggesting it Sergeant Hatfield. It is a place with a lot of history and you're right, we should not leave without at least seeing it," said Brad.

"Yeah, that would be great," said Stan.

"How about it, Sacket and Reber?"

"Good idea and we are free in the morning," said Mickey.

"Fine, I'll meet all of you in front of Headquarters at 0930 in the morning. Thanks for the coffee, I have to go now, I've got some reports that the General wants on his desk in the morning and then I should be free for a couple of hours," she said as she stood and left the mess hall.

"Our time is short here, so I think I'll go back to the room and get the rest of my things together and I have some more letters I want to write, besides we will have a full day tomorrow. We go sightseeing in the morning and then we promised to take Peterson out on the town at night and then I bet my life that we will be leaving on Wednesday or Thursday," said Brad.

"Brad is right, guess we should all go upstairs and be sure we got all our stuff together, everyone agree?" asked Stan.

"Let's go," said Sacket and they pushed back their chairs and filed out of the mess hall, all following one another.

They had all packed up everything except their personal items and the clothes they would wear today and on the trip back to England. They ate a quick breakfast and went to the front of Headquarters where they were to meet Barbara. It was ten minutes past the time she had promised to meet them. Stan looked up to see her running out of Headquarters.

"I'm sorry, but something has come up. I can't go with you. Just go ahead and walk. It is only about twenty minutes and it is really worth seeing. I'll see you sometime later today,

I really have to go now," and she turned and ran back into
the building.

The four walked the distance to the Cathedral. The closer
they got to it, the larger it appeared. It was really a spectacular
sight to see. The exterior glowed pinkish white in the sun. It
had huge pillars up the front and tower like spirals above
that. It seemed to be at least fifteen or more stories high. Its
exterior was very ornate, with three very large stained glass
windows placed high across the face of the structure. There
was another enormous and very colorful window sited dead
center and high above the first set of windows. There were
four sets of huge red doors that were high and heavy situated
under the windows that were very outstanding. When they
all went to the interior they were astounded by its size. The
center aisle seemed to go for miles down to the alter that
could barely be seen in the distance. Huge stained glass
windows of bright colors that threw lights across the
sanctuary when the sun shone had been placed high on the
walls and were spaced the full length of this immense
cathedral. Against the walls were all sorts of very large,
statues of lifelike figures. There were little anti rooms with
smaller alters at the rear of the sanctuary, and there were
hundreds of small candles burning at the bases of shrines in
each of these rooms.

Three aisles went from the back of the church to the
very front with hand carved pews going down the full length
of this immense French church. None of these men were of
the Catholic faith and did not understand the religion, nor
did they know how to be respectful in its atmosphere.

"Let's just sit here for a few minutes, I don't want to go
down those cobbled stone floors any further, my boots make
too much noise," whispered Sacket.

"Yeah, let's just thank God we are alive and be on our
way," said Brad quietly.

On their walk back to town Mickey said, "Now that I
have been in there, I'll have to read more about it when I
can. With all the damage here from the war, it is really
amazing that it made it through without being destroyed."

"Even the German's fear God!" said Sacket. "Besides, from

what I have read about it, there was a lot of damage during World War I and they were able to restore it.

TWENTY-EIGHT

After their sightseeing tour, everyone decided that they should go back to Headquarters, have some lunch, check and see if there was any word on their departure, then call Peterson and take him out on the town for a couple of hours that night.

"I'll go up and see Barbara and see what I can find out," said Stan.

"We will all wait for you in the mess hall, come on up as soon as you can," advised Brad.

Stan was always eager to see this girl who had completely charmed him. He walked into the building and up the two flights of stairs to the General's office and opened the door.

Just as he was going in, Barbara came out of his inner office. "Hello there," said Stan in a flirtatious tone of voice.

"Hello yourself, handsome. Did you and your friends see the Cathedral?" she asked.

"Yes, we did, and you were right. It is really something special and everyone who comes to Reims should see it. We are all going up for some lunch, can you come along?" inquired Stan.

"Not now, I have so much work to catch up on, I'll be here until late tonight," she said.

"He really keeps you hopping. He is a very nice man, but it seems to me that he is a little demanding. Are you all right with that, Barbara?"

"Yes, he is good to me and I really don't think I'll be here long after the war is over, so why fight city hall at this point. Besides, I have so much to do that it keeps me really busy and I don't have much time to think about things or get myself into trouble," she said as she looked Stan in the eyes and smiled.

"Is there any word on our flight back to England yet? Those three friends of mine are so anxious to go that it's not even funny."

"What about you Stan, are you wanting to go too?" she asked.

"It's a means to an end, the sooner I get going the faster I go home and hopefully this war will come to an end and then you will be home and we can do something about our futures," he said.

"Well, I can't give them the news they would like to hear but I wouldn't be surprised to have something come in later tonight or in the morning. I'll try and see you for lunch tomorrow and maybe we will know something then," she replied.

"Would you do me a great big favor, honey, and call Peterson and ask him to meet us in the mess hall as soon as he can. We will wait for him there. By the way, I have something for you," he reached into his uniform pocket and pulled out the tissue wrapped bracelet he had purchased.

"What is it, Stan?"

"Just something I got for you yesterday. Here, open it."

She tore off the paper and sighed as she saw the pretty piece of jewelry. "I love it Stan and we are allowed to wear something like this. It was thoughtful, thank you. It will remind me of you."

"I wish I had time to have it engraved for you. Just know that I will be thinking of you." He grabbed her and gave her a kiss and a big hug.

"I had better get out of here before I get caught making eyes at the General's secretary." He turned and left the office, leaving Barbara with feelings of sadness.

When or will I ever see him again? Guess only time will tell, she thought to herself.

He went on up to the mess hall and found that everyone was there except Peterson. "I asked Barbara to call him, he will show up sometime soon. I guess while we wait for him I'll go get a sandwich, something tells me that we should all

have something in our stomachs before we go out tonight."
He left and got a roast beef and cheese on white bread and
returned to the table.

"Did Sergeant Hatfield have any word on our flight, Stan?"
asked Brad in anticipation.

"No, not yet," came the answer, "but she seemed to think
it would be any time now."

The door to the mess hall opened and Lieutenant
Peterson came in, looking around, he found the foursome in
the uncrowded room and he made his way to their table.

"We had better go because there is something coming in
that I have to be here for, I will only have three hours before
I have to be back at Headquarters," he said without sitting
down.

"Let's go," said Brad. They all got up and followed
Peterson out the door.

The five men walked in the direction of the Cathedral
and turned the corner after a few blocks. They were all
looking at the shops; a bakery had wonderful odors coming
from it. There were lots of soldiers and women walking
together and some children were on the paths. Within a few
blocks everything changed and it was one bar after another
with lots of GIs standing out front of them just looking in.
At less than a block down this street there came the sound
of a big American style band.

Reber turned to the others and said, "Listen to that, it
sure does sound good! Let's go in and see what's going on."

The band was playing "In The Mood" and there was a
sign over the door saying "Noir Aigle."

In the doorway there were five scantily dressed French
girls. There were three very slim women and two who were
heavier. The tight bodices of their dresses allowed their full
bosoms to crest above their tight fitting bandeau type under
garments. Below their very short skirts, showed shapely legs
that wore black net stockings and they all had various colored
high heeled pumps on their feet. They were all heavily made
up, and the three who were blond had their hair piled high
on top of their heads. The two brunettes had long hair that
fell loosely to their shoulders. They were all very seductive

females who were ready to do anything to please the men they were with. At tables throughout this cabaret there were soldiers who where becoming very intoxicated, not only on alcohol but with the intimacies that these ladies of the night could offer them.

The four newcomers looked first at the girls and then at Peterson, asking for approval. "What do you think, Lieutenant?"

When he nodded his head to the affirmative, Brad said, "The first drinks are on me," and he started forward, going toward one of the blond girls who was beckoning her finger at him. Brad followed the girl who ushered him to a table near the band stand. The rest of the heavily perfumed girls were dragging their prizes along to the same table. More chairs were being moved across the dance floor to the place that had been selected for them.

The table would have normally seated four people, with five chairs it was crowded. The girls had crawled on to the laps of their new patrons.

"These women know who will spend the most money. I've been here before," said Peterson.

The interior of this cabaret was dimly lit and seductive. Some noise prevailed, but one could talk and be heard. The smell of perfume in the air was overpowering. Cigarette smoke was thick and seemed to float like clouds toward the ceiling.

The band began to play a new song called "Sentimental Journey" and the dance floor had started to fill with couples.

"OK, you guys," hesitated Farnsworth as he looked around at each of his friends, "when I say let's go, we go!"

"Take it easy, Captain, let your hair down and enjoy yourself a little," said Brad and all the others nodded in agreement.

"Yeah, I will, but just don't let yourselves get talked into something you might regret. We have all been through too much to mess up now," admonished Stan.

Just behind Stan there came the sound of a voice with a southern accent. "What can I get you gentlemen?"

Stan turned to see a good looking black man with a thick

head of curly white hair.

"This is my place, I am called the Black Eagle."

There was a long pause and finally Brad asked, "Please bring us some champagne," he circled the table with his hand, indicating that everyone was to be served.

The proprietor made a slight bow, followed by a salute to everyone at the table. The girls all laughed and the men gave quizzical looks to one another.

While they were waiting to be served, the girls were running their fingers through their patrons' hair and softly whispering sensual and sexual inferences in their ears. Mickey began to turn red in the face and pushed the girl sitting on his lap away. "You sit here and I'll get another chair!"

"Don't bother, there are others waiting at the door who will please me," and she walked away with her head held high.

The champagne was delivered by Aigle, who properly presented one of the bottles to Stan for his examination before it could be opened. With his approval, the cork was pulled with a flourish and it exploded to the ceiling. The other waiter assisted his employer and was pouring all the girls and men full glasses of the fizzing liquid. By the time everyone had been served the third bottle was less than half full.

"Better bring another round," said Brad.

Stan picked up one of the empty champagne bottles and read aloud from the label. "Epernay, the true gourmet's of the world say it is not real unless it comes from Epernay here in France."

Sacket had already found out the girl's name who was on his lap. "Come on Beverly, let's dance."

As soon as the two of them were on the floor, they were swept away by the throng of circling couples around them.

Finally Peterson and Freestone joined the happy moving throng and this left Stan and Mickey to carry on a conversation with the girl sitting with Stan, while the three of them finished a bottle of champagne.

"Don't you like to dance, Mickey?" asked Stan.

"Yes, but the right person is not here. Someday I'll dance

again but with her," insured Mickey.

"I understand, you and I should have a talk. I want to help you, but let's wait until we get to our base in England," said Stan understandingly.

"Thanks Captain," said Mickey, looking depressed and lonely.

The others returned to the table when the band recessed to have another drink. Farnsworth ordered another round of champagne and began a conversation with Aigle. "If you were in the first World War with the American Army, what made you want to stay here in France?"

"That, my dear young Captain, is too long a story to go into right now, but I will give you a short explanation. I met and married a French girl whose family likes me. Now she and I have a very large family of our own and we will live on here. As is said in America, we will live happily ever after."

Farnsworth reached out and shook Aigle's hand. "I'm going back to the States, but some day I would like to come back here and have a long talk with you."

Aigle replied, "That will be fine. Just don't wait too long, Captain."

After the fourth round of champagne had been consumed and its effects were being felt by everyone, Lieutenant Peterson said, "I think it would be best for all of us to return to Headquarters before dark. I have to be back soon anyway."

"I think you're right, Peterson. We don't need to have things get out of hand here."

Sacket and Brad came back to the table with their girls. "Let's have one more for the road," said Sacket thickly.

Captain Farnsworth stood and in an authoritative tone of voice said, "No, let's go. I'm going to tip this pretty girl that has been with me at least ten dollars. I hope the rest of you will do the same.

"I'm going on ahead of you, I have to be back in just half an hour and it will take some doing to corral these others," advised Peterson as he left the table and fought his way through the growing crowd and disappeared in the smoke filled room.

"Let's go home," said Stan as he pulled Sacket from the

hand hold his partner had on his arm."

Sorry, got to go now, maybe I'll see you tomorrow night sweetie," he said. "Come on Brad, the Captain says we have to go."

None of them were feeling any pain and Peterson had been right, it would take a lot of maneuvering to get these men back to Headquarters.

Stan and Mickey finally made it back to Headquarters with their inebriated friends. They had decided to go to the mess hall and have a hamburger and then they would all go back to their room and crash for the night.

"God damned Brad, are we ever going to be hung over in the morning!" said Sacket.

Brad and Sacket were arm-in-arm walking from one side of the hall to the other, and singing as they approached their room. Mickey and Stan were a little ahead of them.

"Hey, there is a note taped to the door. 'Tomorrow is the day, you leave at noon. The General wants you to come by his office and pick up pictures and some other papers to take with you. Flying gear is OK, get packed and be ready by 0900 in the morning.'" And the signature read, "Peterson."

"Well, this is it. Thank God we are all packed except for the stuff we will need for tomorrow. Better get a shower and go to bed and sleep off all this champagne we had," suggested Stan.

When the room was quiet and there were obvious sounds of sleep coming from the other beds, Stan was still awake. I wonder what the future holds for all of us in this room? Will I really see Barbara again, is she the woman I am destined to spend the rest of my life with? At this moment I can say that I love her, but our future is really uncertain. With these thoughts on his mind he closed his eyes and slept.

The bright morning sunshine flashed across the room from windows whose shades had not been closed last night. Stan awoke with a start and he suddenly remembered the note on their door last evening. It had said to be ready by 0900 and they would be leaving at noon. It was 7:30 now.

"Let's roll, we have two hours to clear out of here!" he shouted.

Reber came alive. "Thank God we had a lot of sleep last night, I think I will be OK after I have a shower and some coffee. Better get Brad up, Stan. He is dead to the world." Mickey was sitting on the edge of his bed.

"Let him sleep a little while longer. He is all packed and since we are in fatigues it won't take long to dress."

Stan had finished in the bathroom and came out to dress, "I want everyone to wear their squadron caps with your new insignia's on them, we left England in flying gear and that's what I would like to have all of us go back in," said Stan proudly.

"Hey, why didn't you wake me up?" said Brad sleepily.

"We are all done in the bathroom and we figured you needed a little more time to recover. Go ahead, it's all yours. We have got to have our bags ready to go, so don't take all day. Peterson will be here before we know it," advised Stan.

They were all dressed and packed. Brad gave his bag a little pat. He had almost forgotten the small box that was tucked down in the middle of the zipped pocket of his B-4 bag. Wonder what I'll do with that someday, he thought.

A knock came at the door. "That will be Peterson," said Stan as he admitted the Lieutenant to their room. "We are all ready to go. Should we take our bags downstairs with us?"

"Good idea, you can leave them at the gate while we go up to the General's office to say good-bye," answered Peterson.

With their bags properly tagged and stored they all returned upstairs to the Office of Headquarters. Barbara was just inside the door when they entered. She avoided eye contact with these men she had helped, especially Captain Farnsworth.

The General came out of his office. "Guess it's time to say good-bye to all of you. Barbara, give these men a copy of the pictures we took and there is an envelope for each of them that should be given to their Commander when they get to England." Barbara followed the General's instructions and gave each man the required materials.

The office door opened and a driver came in. "Sir, the bus you ordered is waiting outside to go to the Air Base."

"Take care and we will be waiting to hear good things about each of you," said the General as he reached out to shake hands with each of these men that had recuperated at this station in Reims.

"Good-bye sir, and thank you for all you have done for us, you too Sergeant Hatfield," they all turned and headed out the door.

At the last minute Stan turned. He could not help himself, he reached out for Barbara and gave her a farewell kiss. "I'll write soon. I'm sorry about our lunch date."

He looked at the General. "I'm sorry, sir. I hope that I have not stepped beyond the rules."

"Not at all," said the General, with a smile on his face.

In the courtyard everyone was waving good-bye to the departing foursome as they boarded the bus.

Lieutenant Peterson stood by the door as they got on. "Good luck to each of you, I hope everything works out OK."

"Thanks for all you did for us, Lieutenant. We really did appreciate it, hope we will see each other again sometime."

The door closed and their trip back to England had begun. It only took them fifteen minutes to get to the air base south of town. The driver pulled up in front of a large tent that had a sign reading "Base Operations" nailed to the wooden exterior door. A Gooney Bird was parked right in front with its cargo doors wide open.

"How about that? That Gooney Bird is our Squadron's shuttle aircraft. I've flown in that same old crate many times," said Stan.

"Yeah, we all have," Brad said nostalgically.

Stan went into Operations and came back out. "We are all cleared to go."

The crew chief of their transporting aircraft was there and was already throwing their bags into the cargo door entrance. Two other crew members appeared.

The one with the light Colonel insignia on his hat said, "Where in the hell have you guys been? I've been waiting nearly a year for you four to show up!"

Lieutenant Colonel Robert Bowman, the 390th Squadron Commander jumped down out of the aircraft and started shaking hands and hugging the four happy airmen.

"I hope all of you don't mind changing your plans about taking your leave in England rather than France. The whole outfit wanted you to come home to us. We have a big party planned for all of you. You're the first of any of our crew members to make it back. Bet you all have some wild stories to tell! I guess you know that each of you has bags of mail waiting for you. Enough of this small talk, come on everybody, inside, sit down, strap in and shut up, we're leaving!"

Five minutes to start engines, five minutes to taxi to the end of the runway, a two minute engine mag check, and they were headed down the runway and into the air, flying towards their destination in England.

The flight home was uneventful and when the old Gooney Bird landed, it bounced its way across the grass airfield to the familiar Base Operations building at APO 247. The engines were shut down and before the props could quit turning, the crew chief had opened the cargo doors.

Even though it was misting heavily, the men of the 390th Bomb Squadron had surged out of Base Operations and were all shouting greetings and waving enthusiastically to these men who had come home.

Colonel Bowman was the first one to stand in the cargo doorway and he yelled, "Here they are, the survivors of the Louise E. Ann."

The first Sergeant yelled out, "Everyone to the briefing room, the beers good and cold!"

"Attention," said the Colonel, as he raised his hand, "we received word this morning from 8th Air Force that our whole Bomb Wing will stand down for seventy-two hours. It looks like the war is about over."

There were loud shouts of jubilation from all the men of

the 390th Bomb Squadron.

"It won't be long until we can all go home."

Some even threw their hats in the air.

As the four surviving airmen got down from the old C-47 transport aircraft, the first Sergeant took over. "Haven't any of you people ever seen these VIP's before? Get out of the way and let them through!"

The officers had locked arms around Farnsworth and Freestone and were pushing them toward the familiar briefing room. Sacket and Reber had been bodily picked up and were being carried on the shoulders of their fellow enlisted men.

One of Reber's old buddies shouted out, "What some people won't do to get attention and a promotion!"

When everyone was inside the briefing room the Commander stepped up on the boards and asked for attention. "The first sergeant and I are asking all of you to remember that these men are not here to have a question and answer session, so take it easy on them for now. In the future you will all know their stories." As the Commander reached his hand out he said, "Captain Farnsworth, please join me up here," and he gave a friendly handshake and a salute to Stan that was cheered by all of the men present.

Stan put his hand up to get the attention of his comrades, "Please bring me a glass of beer."

A large mug filled to the brim was immediately given to him and he raised it high. "I want to drink a toast to our five crew members that lost their lives for a cause called freedom. Captain McCrea, Aircraft Commander; First Lieutenant Young, Bombardier; Staff Sergeant Barnes, Ball Turret Gunner; Staff Sergeant Moody, Right Waist Gunner; and Staff Sergeant Woods, Tail Gunner. These men and our memories of them should never be forgotten. Gentlemen we feel your presence and we drink a toast to each of you."

There was a reverent silence in the room and then each man drank from his glass.

"We will miss each of you and your memories will never be forgotten. At this time it is appropriate that we toast all the other airmen that have given their lives for this like cause."

And again the glasses were raised to honor those who had died.

The first Sergeant stood. "The men would like just a few words from these returning men, sir."

After a few moments of silent reflection Brad was the first to speak. "I thank God that this moment has finally come. This experience has made me all the more determined to continue my career in the service of my country."

Sacket stood and said, "Now that we have almost won this war against the hated enemy, I want all of you to know that there are some good Germans."

With that remark, Sacket could see questioning looks appear on the faces of these men who were his friends. Mickey stood and with a big smile on his face said, "I feel like my life has just begun, and now it's all ahead of me."

He could feel the warmth of the silver crucifix against his chest and he was sure he would get back to Inga someway, in the not too distant future.

Stan stood and spoke. "I'm going back to the States to get my degree in law. That won't take me very long, who knows, I may just come back and join up again," he raised his glass high. "I salute each and every one of you, in the name of Freedom."

Within a month the hostilities in Europe ended and the domination of a despised man was overthrown. The war in the Pacific would be over after the United States had used the most powerful weapon ever designed by mankind. It was victory through destruction, but what the consequences are to the perspective of the universe is yet unknown.

The future lives of the four men depicted in this story are just a trivial part of the big picture, and they would continue to reflect the ideas and opinions that were formulated by their experiences with the diverse actions they had witnessed.

The awesome, destructive power on humans and

habitations in the universe would temper their personal actions and ideas, both for good as well as evil.